a patch of cotton

For Brigetta
Blessings
Linda Dunlap Hulen
March 2, 2019

A Novel by

LINDA DUNLAP HULEN

ISBN: 978-0-9895978-2-1

Southern Heart
—PUBLISHING—

Acknowledgments

Thanks and appreciation to the Lake City Museum, Lake City, Arkansas, and its Curator, Brenda Hutcheson, and the board members, Sandra Nall, Martha Carter, Pat Ragsdale, Debbie Nunnally, Marie George, Stephanie Timms, Jerry Freeman, Gordon Freeman, and Danny Strickland. The support from this board and the people in my hometown is humbling. Thank you.

Thank you to my daughter, Kerri Hamm. She takes all my calls and listens to all my doubts. She is my encourager and one of my biggest fans. I love you.

Thank you to my husband, Howard. He listens to all my doubts in person! He is patient and supportive and has offered many suggestions which were very helpful. I love you.

Thank you to my granddaughter, Taylor Beth Owens, whose picture graces the book cover. I love you.

Thank you to Andy Huff for the beautiful book cover. I loved it from the first time I saw it!

Thank you to Jon Marken for your editing expertise and for being so amiable. Your editing and suggestions significantly improved the final product.

Thank you to Farmville Printing and Dan Dwyer for all your help in seeing this project completed so professionally.

DEDICATION

To all Christian parents who are struggling to raise children with Biblical instruction. A battle that at times may seem you are losing, when the world disagrees with you. All things are possible with God.

Love the Lord your God with all your heart, with all your soul, and with all your strength. These words that I am giving you today are to be in your heart. Repeat them to your children. Talk about them when you sit in your house and when you walk along the road, when you lie down and when you get up. Bind them as a sign on your hand and let them be a symbol on your forehead. Write them on the doorposts of your house and on your gates.

DEUTERONOMY 6:5–9

Message from the Author

Through all the years that I've been an avid reader, I often wondered if a writer knew everything about the book when it began, or if during the writing process the storyline took on a life of its own. I learned the story does evolve and change. Even though my first book, *Her Final Gift*, was based on a true story, parts were fiction, and as I wrote I was sometimes surprised at what the characters said or did.

A Patch of Cotton went through many twists and turns, and the final product didn't bear a lot of resemblance to the ideas I had when I began writing. It is important to me that the words I write have a message that will glorify God. I know that most people who read this book will do so because it is advertised as Christian fiction, but I hope it will end up in the hands of many unbelievers who don't have faith in God.

The society we live in today will not believe a character like Jake could be real. Or that he could have existed in the era of the 60's when the sexual revolution began. Even though every type of media in our world today promotes sexual freedom, and our young people especially are inundated with that message, it is possible to teach abstinence.

In the 60's and 70's, we didn't have every television show dripping with sexual innuendo and scenes in the movies that border on pornographic. But we also weren't told much about sex. Most of us learned from our friends who learned from their friends and, well, it was at best skewed information.

I grew up in a Christian home and went to church every time the doors were open. However, there were never sermons on God's design for sex—church just wasn't the place for that. So, not knowing can be just as detrimental as knowing too much. As a result of the promiscuous society of today, our churches have begun to teach what God says about sex, to help our young people make good and right choices. Hopefully, parents can be honest and forthright with their children and instill in them God's design for the physical aspect of marriage. It is one of the most beautiful gifts given to us.

So as you read this story, I hope you can believe that a young man like Jake could have the belief system that he does; that his relationship with God and His word that was instilled in him during his formative years carried him through the tough times in his life.

How can a young man keep his way pure?
By keeping Your word.
I have sought You with all my heart;
don't let me wander from Your commands.

PSALM 119:9–10

CHAPTER ONE

New York City
1971

THE WEATHER OUTSIDE this Christmas Eve morning was every kid's dream. Manhattan was blanketed in two feet of snow with drifts blown against the doors on the south side of the street as high as the door-knobs. The snow continued to fall as the gray light of dawn gave the scene an ethereal quality. The city was still sleeping, and the dense snow caused what few sounds there were to be muted and soft in this frigid winter wonderland.

Margaret Mae Roberts lay snug in her warm bed, unaware of the nor'easter that had unexpectedly descended on this city she'd called home for the past seven years. Even though she was twenty-six, she still had freckles sprinkled across her nose and silky blonde locks that had darkened only slightly since she was a toddler. Her long hair was splayed out across the pillow, and her dark lashes lay against her cheeks as she slept. The scar above her right eye had faded over the past few years and was only visible without makeup. The years had only added to her beauty, and most people who knew her wondered why this belle from the south was still single.

Maggie was dreaming. She stirred, moaning and restless as her dream took her back to the cotton fields in Arkansas where she'd lived until she could make her lifelong ambition a reality. The cotton sack was almost full, very heavy, and she was still half a field from the cotton trailer. Her slender sixteen-year-old body was weary after a long day of back-breaking work, and her fingers pierced by the cotton hulls were raw in places. She stared at her hands and wondered if she could bear the pain of practicing her piano.

Jake turned her toward him and took her hands in his. "Aw, Maggie, are your hands hurting?" He raised them to his lips and kissed each place where the tender skin was torn. With tears in her eyes, she managed a smile as they gazed at one another. She started to speak to him, but he vanished! A lingering haze, lying eerily over the rows of cotton, was all she could see. Her heartbeat quickened as she looked frantically around the field. Jake wasn't there. No one was. She was alone. Maggie cried out for him in her sleep and was instantly awake.

How many times in the past two years had she had this same dream? Not one thing in her dream was ever different— not their ages, not their clothes or where they were standing. They were always in the middle of Mr. Franceway's cotton patch.

It always took days for the memories to subside. She rolled over, closed her eyes and tried to go back to sleep. Maggie knew that wasn't going to happen, so she allowed her mind to drift back in time, just as she always did whenever this recurring dream interrupted her sleep. She smiled that she'd thought cotton patch instead of cotton field. That's what they called it back home, because that's what it was, a patch of cotton.

Knowing she should open her eyes to reality, she ignored the warning and let the vision of Jake take shape in her mind.

Jake had been her boyfriend and her best friend. In her dream he was always seventeen. He was wearing Levis and an old tee shirt, and the long-sleeved shirt he'd started the day with was now tied around his waist. Some kind of ball cap was always on his head, and as usual, the curls she loved were trailing out of the back of it, almost touching his shirt collar. When they rode in his car she couldn't resist reaching out and twirling those curls in her fingers as she absentmindedly stared out the window. Those lazy days were her happiest and most memorable, those "going nowhere in particular" rides through the country in his '57 Chevy.

Her dream was always about the fall of 1962 — the last time, thankfully, she would ever pick cotton to make money. Jake had been a senior and Maggie a junior at their local high school. As she lay in her bed allowing memories to wash over her, the desire to feel Jake's arms around her seemed all-consuming, and she tried to still her heartbeat. Her mind went from the memory of his arms around her to the memory of his lips on hers, and she could feel the tears gathering behind her closed eyes. She missed him, yearned for his touch, and as in the aftermath of all her other dreams, she found herself transported back in time.

Jake's Italian ancestors had blessed him with dark hair and brown eyes. His great-grandfather changed their last name from Martini to Martin when he came to America from his beloved country of origin. Jake was handsome, and in the beginning his good looks were the attraction for Maggie, until she began to know his soul. He had an old soul for someone only seventeen. Jake couldn't kill a bug. If he could scoop it up and take it back outside to free it, he would. He had a tender heart. And at that particular time, Jake's heart belonged to Maggie.

But her past was over and Jake was gone from her life, so Maggie chased the memories from her mind and opened her eyes to the present. Through her open bedroom door she could see her beautiful, ebony, baby grand piano. She had a love-hate relationship with her music. After her dream and the memories she'd just experienced, the feeling about her music at this moment was hate. Later, as always, the love for her piano and the music in her soul would surface, and the other love of her life, Jake, would be hidden away in the recesses of her mind.

It was 7:30 a.m. on December 24, 1971, and Maggie knew at any moment the phone would ring. She threw the covers back and sat up on the side of her bed. Stretching like a lazy cat, she found her warm, fuzzy slippers, slipped them onto her feet, and hurriedly put on her robe as she headed toward the kitchen to start the coffee.

Maggie had purchased this apartment almost two years ago on a whim. It had never occurred to her she would stay in New York City; she'd always planned to go home to Arkansas...someday. She'd fallen in love with the high ceilings and the large windows that offered her an impressive vista of the city, and before she knew it, it was hers. It had been expensive, very expensive. Her performances in the concert halls of New York and other great cities, here in America and abroad, had made her a wealthy young woman.

She opened the shutters over the kitchen window and was surprised at the scene outside. The city was definitely having a white Christmas. Her first thought was how beautiful it was, and then she realized the flight taking her home to Arkansas wasn't going to happen. Her phone began to ring as if her mom was watching and knew she was awake.

"Hi Mom, Merry Christmas Eve," Maggie said, knowing her voice still sounded heavy with sleep.

"Good morning, sweetie. Did I wake you?"

"No Mom, I've been up for at least five minutes. I've already started the coffee. Wish you were here to share a cup with me."

"Well, it won't be long before you'll be home and I'm so excited. Aunt Bridget and Uncle Mack will be here this afternoon. What time does the plane land?"

Maggie hesitated, knowing the news she was about to give her mom would ruin her Christmas. Her parents had owned a hardware store in Lake City, her small hometown. Maggie's dad had suffered a fatal heart attack. Her mom couldn't go back to the store—she said she saw him in every aisle and it was too painful—so she'd sold it. She also struggled to live without him in their home of thirty years. Much to Maggie's surprise and chagrin, her mom sold the house and built in a new subdivision on the outskirts of town. Since the funeral, Maggie had been home only once, to help her mom move into her new house. Now she had to tell her there would be no Christmas in Arkansas for Maggie this year.

"Mom, have you had the TV on this morning? Have you seen the news about the storm here in the northeast?" Maggie asked with a soft voice.

"No ... what storm?"

Maggie heard the apprehension in her mom's question. She wanted to be in the kitchen with her mom, to be cooking together like they'd always done on Christmas Eve. Not the kitchen in the new house, the kitchen in the house Maggie had grown up in. That house held all the memories of cold winter mornings where the love they'd shared could have warmed the room without the heat coming from the oven or the fireplace in the family room. Her mom could make the best biscuits and gravy of anyone in the whole state of Arkansas! Now some other family was having breakfast in her beloved home. Suddenly, Maggie felt the tears coming as she thought about her daddy, her house and all the other things that had become so different. How did this happen? She knew how. It had happened while she was away, building a career.

"Mom, we have two feet of snow on the ground and it's still coming down. There won't be any flights out today. I'm snowed in. I'm not sure I can even open my front door."

"Oh, Maggie, no—you're kidding, right?"

"No, Mom, I'm not. I haven't called Delta yet, though I can't imagine they could get a plane out in this storm. Maybe I can get out in a day or two, once the snow stops. I know you're disappointed. Aunt Bridget will be there and I know you two will have a great time together, right?"

Maggie noticed the pause before her mom answered her. She knew her mom was in the kitchen with her Christmas apron already on and pies ready to go into the oven. Annie Margaret, Maggie's mom, was a redhead with plenty of freckles of her own. Her family, the Shanahans, came from Ireland a century ago and settled in the South. Annie grew up in Arkansas where she met and married Oliver Roberts, Maggie's dad, whose ancestors arrived on these shores from England. So Maggie inherited her dad's blonde hair and fair skin, and from her mom she was blessed with a few freckles.

"Darn that northern weather! If you lived further south, you wouldn't be snowed in and could be in your old bed tonight. I've told you before you should move closer to home. Now look what's happened—you'll spend Christmas all alone in that big, cold city."

"Now Mom, you know anything could have happened regardless of where I live. We can open gifts and have Christmas when I get there. You'll have Aunt Bridget to help you in the kitchen, and you two sisters can cook and gossip to your heart's content," Maggie said, trying to sound happy and encouraging when what she really wanted to do was cry.

"Well, maybe so. I still think you should move closer to home. Life is short, Maggie. You're twenty-six and your biological clock is ticking, I can hear it all the way from New York City!"

"Mom! Please stop pressuring me about getting married and starting a family. I am totally aware of how old I am and the fact that I'm still single. I know that better than anyone." Maggie struggled to keep her voice from sounding as angry and exasperated as she felt. Her mom had casually mentioned, more than a few times, that most of the people Maggie had gone to school with had been married for years. More couples than Maggie cared to know about had already divorced and remarried. She was also well aware her daddy wouldn't be there to walk her down the aisle, and he would never know his grandchildren.

It seemed to Maggie that having grandchildren was all her mom and dad had ever talked about. She was their only child, and they'd put enormous pressure on her to give them grand-children. Now, Maggie thought, if she was blessed enough to ever have children they would never know their grandfather, and that made her sad. When she and her mom argued about this subject, it inevitably reminded her who was missing... her daddy, gone from her life.

"I'm sorry, I don't know how our conversations always turn to this subject and we wind up being upset," her mom said apologetically.

"I know how it happens! Now can we change the subject? I'll call you in the morning and wish you a Merry Christmas, and maybe by then I'll know when I can get a flight out."

"Oh, okay. I will miss you being here. I love you Maggie Mae," Annie said to her daughter as she fought the tears gathering in her eyes. This was the second Christmas without Oliver, and now Maggie wouldn't be here either. Sometimes life just didn't seem fair.

"I love you too, Mom. I'll call you in the morning. Try to enjoy Christmas, okay?

"I'll try."

Now Maggie was more homesick than she'd ever been, even more than when she'd first moved to the city, which seemed so long ago. Since her plans were to be in Arkansas, she'd not bothered to decorate. As she looked at her bare apartment, she felt as though everyone except her was celebrating Christmas.

Knowing her best friend Lizzie J. also thought she was coming home, Maggie knew she had to call and tell her too. Lizzie J. and Maggie had been best friends since kindergarten. Lizzie J. was petite; at least that's what she always told Maggie when Maggie said she was short. She was also striking with a combination of blue eyes, black hair and fair skin. Maggie and Lizzie J. were both beautiful, though as different as night and day.

It was still early, so Maggie decided to have her coffee and try to calm down before calling Lizzie J. As usual, the conversation with her mom left her feeling guilty about the choices she'd made since graduating from college and starting her musical career.

Maggie took her mug of steaming, cinnamon-laced coffee to the living room. She intentionally did not look at the piano and went to the window to draw back the draperies for a look at the snow-covered street. The parked cars were almost buried beneath the snow, and the Christmas lights left on the night before were flashing colored prisms on each one as if they had been placed there for decoration. Reaching for her warm chenille throw, Maggie backed up to her favorite chair and sat down while still staring out the window. As she wrapped the throw around her and snuggled into her comfy wingback, the scene outside her window suddenly changed to a memory of a long-ago Christmas in Arkansas.

CHAPTER TWO

Lake City, Arkansas
1961

IT WAS FRIDAY, December 22, 1961, and the stage in
the school auditorium was decorated for the annual
Christmas program. The Christmas tree gave off a
wonderful cedar aroma, stirring the kids to excitement as they anticipated their Christmas break. The room was
beginning to fill up, and the noise escalated until the principal,
Mr. Greagan, walked onto the stage and stared at the crowd.
His beady eyes, and the lights above him reflecting on his bald
head, caused a mood change in the room. A hush descended as
one by one they quieted under his glare.

Maggie and Lizzie J. had minor speaking parts and they
were excited, or at least Lizzie J. was. They waited backstage
with the rest of the cast as their drama teacher gave last-
minute instructions. Maggie was nervous. She'd agreed to play
Christmas music on the piano during the intermission. The
piano part was easy for Maggie, but speaking in front of the
whole school terrified her. Now she wondered how in the world
she'd let Lizzie J. talk her into this.

The first act went off without a hitch and when the curtain

closed, Maggie was left on stage alone. As the applause died down, she started to move toward the piano bench and saw the best-looking guy she'd ever seen. He was sitting in the second row on the same side as the piano, beside an older man. She assumed they were together; she'd never seen either of them before.

He was staring at her. Mesmerized, she felt she was moving in slow motion. He smiled at her as if to encourage her to begin. Maggie looked at the piano and then back to him, wondering how she would ever be able to play a note.

Maggie had begun piano lessons at age five, and it had been her passion ever since. She was gifted. She finally turned, sat down, rested her hands on the keys, took a deep breath and began. Her talent and hard work took over, and the melody of one of the new rock-and-roll Christmas songs brought the students to their feet. She finished with a beautiful rendition of "*Silent Night*." As usual, she got a standing ovation.

"Lizzie J., did you see the guy in the second row?" Maggie asked when she found her friend backstage, hoping she knew who he might be.

"What guy?"

"Some guy I've never seen before, and he was sitting beside a man, maybe his dad. I wonder who they are and what they're doing here."

"How do I know? Maybe he's here visiting someone and decided to come to the play. Why do you care?"

"He's the best-looking guy I've ever seen. You have to see him!"

When the play was over, Maggie walked back to her locker to get a couple of books to take home for the break. Even though there was no homework assignment, she wanted to read ahead in her history book and brush up on her algebra—the history book because she loved it, the algebra book because she didn't. Maggie wanted to keep her place in the Honor Society Club. Walking past the principal's office, she saw the new guy and the man he was with earlier having a conversation with Mr. Greagan. She was intrigued and even more curious about who they were and what they were doing here.

JACOB MATTHEW MARTIN and his dad, Sal Martin, were in Mr. Greagan's office to register Jake for school. He would begin classes with the other students when they returned after Christmas break. Mr. Martin was the new President of the local bank. Mrs. Martin had succumbed to cancer when Jake was twelve and his sister, Cara, seventeen. Cara recently married, and she and her husband moved into the family home in Marianna. Mr. Martin was happy to move to Lake City. The past few years had been difficult; he still seemed to see his late wife in every room of their house.

The job at the bank was the answer for the two of them to start a new life in a small town in the middle of a vibrant farming community. Jake was as happy as his dad to leave and start over. Only two hours away, it would be easy to see Cara whenever they wanted.

After Christmas break, Jake would begin his classes as a junior and turn seventeen in the spring. It had been hard to say goodbye to his friends, but as he watched the girl who played the piano walk by, he figured he might not miss them as much as he'd thought he would.

He was eager to know her name. Her slender frame, blonde hair and green eyes had captivated him from first sight. And after hearing her play the piano, he realized she was also talented.

Two weeks later when Jake walked into drama class, there she was. He signed up for that class after seeing her in the play. Drama had never been an interest of his until then.

During the past two weeks, Jake and his dad had been busy getting settled into a rental house. Every time he went to town for something, he hoped he would see her. Now, as he took the seat next to her, he realized she was more beautiful than he remembered. She had a sprinkling of freckles across her nose he hadn't seen from a distance, and he knew he would love every one of them.

"Hi, I'm Jake," he said to her.

Maggie was startled when she heard his voice. She turned to look at him, and her heart raced when she realized it was the guy she'd seen two weeks earlier during the Christmas program. She struggled to find her voice.

"Hi, I'm Maggie. Maggie Roberts."

"So, let me guess, your real name is Margaret?"

"Yes, and yours must be Jacob?"

"It is. Jacob Matthew Martin. No one has ever called me Jacob — it's always been Jake. I've told you my full name, now tell me yours."

"Margaret Mae Roberts, and I've always been called Maggie. Wonder why people name their kids and then call them something different?"

"Because they love us so much they need a special name. It's called terms of endearment."

At first, Maggie thought he was being sarcastic and then realized he was serious. It was her first glimpse into his soul.

"I never thought about it that way before — you're probably right. My mom and dad always say my name differently than anyone else," Maggie said.

"Yeah, when I was little my mom called me Jakey. As I got older she started calling me Jake, thank goodness."

"Does she ever slip up now and call you Jakey by mistake?" Maggie asked.

Jake hesitated and Maggie could sense something different about him. She realized her question had changed their light mood.

"No, she doesn't. My mom died when I was twelve. It's been four years since I heard her say my name," Jake replied softly.

Maggie was surprised by what he said and paused a few seconds before responding.

"Jake, I'm so sorry. I can't imagine losing either one of my parents. You were so young. Do you have brothers or sisters?"

"I have a sister, Cara. She married recently and lives with her husband Mark in our family home. She was seventeen when Mom died. It was a difficult time for her, especially when she started planning her wedding."

The teacher called the class to order, cutting short their conversation. Maggie couldn't concentrate. All she could think about was what Jake had told her. Her stomach was in knots; she'd never met anyone whose mom had died. She was surprised he'd given up such personal information so quickly.

When he looked the other direction, she stole a glance and realized he was even more handsome than she'd first thought. She loved his dark eyes, dark complexion, and the way his black hair curled up around his shirt collar. She'd not seen him come into the room, so judging by the way he sat in his chair, she guessed he was close to six feet tall. He was not skinny, just lanky. She did notice his hands were callused as if he used them for hard work. He had a beautiful smile and his teeth were very white against his dark skin. All she could think was *wow*!

Jake couldn't think straight, trying to focus on what the teacher was saying instead of Maggie. The scent of her perfume drew him, and he tried to look at her without her knowing. He wondered what she thought about what he shared about his mom. He didn't know why he'd told her—somehow he couldn't stop the words from spilling out. He was usually reluctant to talk about it. Most people either didn't know what to say, or they fell all over themselves saying how sorry they were for him. Either way was awkward, and he appreciated the simple way Maggie had said she was sorry.

When class was over, Maggie invited him to join her and some friends for a soda at the drugstore downtown after school. He gladly accepted. He didn't care about meeting her friends; he wanted to be with Maggie.

Jake had always been a confident guy, but going into the drugstore to meet Maggie's friends made him anxious. Of course, he'd never been in this situation before. He'd grown up with the friends that he left behind and had always felt accepted. This was definitely a new experience.

"Jake, over here." Maggie motioned him to a table where she sat with a couple he'd not seen before.

"Hi, thanks for inviting me."

"Jake, meet my best friend, Lizzie J. Raines, and her boyfriend, Andy Houston. This is Jake, short for Jacob Matthew Martin. Did I get it right?"

"Yes, Maggie, short for Margaret Mae Roberts, you did. Nice to meet you both," Jake said as he pulled up a chair and joined them at the table.

"I saw you in drama class today. I'm sorry I didn't have a chance to say hello. Where did you move from?" Lizzie J. asked.

Jake didn't remember seeing her in class, and he knew it was because he couldn't see past Maggie.

"Marianna, a town about two hours south of here. Ever heard of it?" Jake asked.

"Yes, never been there though. None of us have been much of anywhere, except here. All three of us were born right here in Lake City, and we've all been in school together since kindergarten," Lizzie J. replied.

"I know about friends like those. I was born in Marianna, and all the friends I left behind were born there, too. This place reminds me of my hometown; it's also in the middle of farming country," Jake said. He sounded melancholy and Maggie noticed it.

"Hey, you have new friends now. We'll do the best we can to keep you from feeling homesick, won't we?" Maggie encouraged as she looked from Lizzie J. to Andy for affirmation.

"Well, if Lizzie J. and Andy are going to be friends with me, I have to know their real names. How did you get the name Lizzie J.? The name Andy I understand," Jake teased.

"My name is Elizabeth Jane. I've always been called Lizzie J., and I never thought it was an odd name. Now that I think about it, I guess it is."

"Well, I didn't say your name was odd; however, I have definitely never heard it before. It makes you unique. So Andy, I'm guessing your name is Andrew?"

"Andrew Alexander Houston, Jr. Thankfully, I've always been called Andy and not Junior," Andy said with relief.

"Since we've been formally introduced, I can say I'm happy

none of us are called by our real names," Jake said, and they all laughed.

"What did you do for fun in Marianna?" Andy asked.

"I love farming, so most of my free time I worked. Sounds boring, huh?"

Everyone at the table laughed.

"What's so funny?" Jake asked.

"We had to drag Andy here this afternoon. His family has a farm and he loves being there more than anywhere. He only goes to school because it's required. Andy's favorite quote is, there's more to life than farming, but not much. I think you two will have a lot in common," Lizzie J. explained as she looked at Andy.

"Really? That's great. What kind of farm? Do you grow cotton?"

"We always have a cotton crop, and some years we also grow soybeans. Watermelons too. You'll see plenty of those when we have the Watermelon Festival. What kind of crops do they farm where you're from?" Andy asked.

"The same, except the watermelons. I'd love to see where you farm someday."

"My truck is parked outside; we can go as soon as we finish here," Andy said with excitement. A lot of the guys Andy was friends with couldn't wait to get out of school and join the army and see the world. Not Andy—he loved the farm and had no desire to do anything else with his life. Now, he would have a friend who obviously loved farming too.

"I'll need to stop by the bank and ask my dad. It'll only take a minute," Jake answered with as much excitement as Andy.

Lizzie J. looked at Maggie and rolled her eyes. She and Andy had liked each other since third grade and knew someday they would get married.

Andy was average looking with brown hair and brown eyes. He had a solid build and was strong from the work on his family's farm. He was confident about who he was and where he wanted to go in life, and once you knew him, his character somehow would convince you he was more handsome than he really was.

Andy's dream life was joining his dad in business on the family farm. And Lizzie J. knew when they were married, even though she'd always lived in town, the farm would be her life, too. Someday, when his dad retired, Andy wanted to take over the operation with his own son, Andrew Alexander Houston III. Lizzie J. knew her future.

"Maggie, thanks for asking me to join y'all," said Jake. "Do you mind if I go to the farm with Andy? I don't want to rush out and I do want to get to know you better, but I've missed being on a farm and I'd love to see Andy's place."

"I'm always watching Lizzie J. take second place to the farm, and I never dreamed I'd meet another guy who felt the same as Andy. Sure, go on. I'm glad you found a guy you have something in common with. I'll see you tomorrow at school." Maggie smiled at him. "I need to get to the hardware store anyway. I promised my dad I'd help stock after school today. Y'all have fun!"

Jake followed Andy outside and down the street to a black 1950 Chevy pickup truck. Though Jake had a license, he'd never had his own car or truck. The Chevy had a new paint job, new seats inside, and a radio.

"Hop in," Andy said. Jake was still standing outside the truck and looking it over with admiration.

"Man, this is great. How long have you had it?"

"We bought it a couple of years ago. It was rough and

needed a new motor, but the price was right. My dad and I worked on it whenever we had time. We finished it right before my sixteenth birthday. I have to say, this truck is my pride and joy."

"I can see why. The engine purrs like a cat," Jake said as he got in.

Andy eased into gear, turned on the radio, and after stopping by the bank, the two of them left town, heading out into the country to the farm. Two weeks ago, Jake and his dad had moved into their house and then returned to Marianna to celebrate Christmas with Cara. Jake hadn't seen much of the country outside of town and was taking in the landscape as they headed south. The fields lay barren in the cold days of January, and Jake knew in a few short weeks there would be the sound of tractors as the farmers readied their land for planting.

There were houses scattered here and there on both sides of the road. Those Jake could see in the distance looked as though they had sprouted up in the middle of the field. The main farm house usually could be identified by the surrounding tractor shed and outbuildings. Jake knew not to be impressed with what he saw. He'd been around farming and was aware you couldn't always tell which farmers were successful. Sometimes the farmers who drove the newest trucks or had the most equipment were the ones deep in debt and on the brink of bankruptcy.

They hadn't spoken since they left town. Jake was taking in the farmland, and Andy was wondering how it compared to the area Jake had recently moved from.

"My house is the one up ahead in the bend of the road," Andy said, breaking their silence.

"Looks nice. Looks new too. Is it?" Jake asked.

"Yeah, my mom saw the house plans in one of her magazines and had to have it. I think they call it a brick ranch. I guess it's the new thing — I've seen some houses like ours being built in town. The old farmhouse we'd been living in was destroyed by high winds. We think it was a small tornado, though it was never proven. I guess it doesn't matter what it was — it tore up the old home-place. My dad was heartbroken and sad about it; it was the house he'd grown up in."

"Well, though it may not be the same house, it's special because it's in the same place."

"Yeah, it is special. I plan to live in this house someday or build one of my own here on the farm," Andy replied as he turned off the dirt road onto the long driveway. Jake noticed that saplings had recently been planted on both sides and would someday make quite a statement.

"Must be great growing up on a farm. My dad's always been a banker and my mom was a school teacher. We always lived in town and my parents could never understand why I loved farming."

"Who did you work for back in Marianna?" Andy asked.

"My best friend, J.D. Spencer, lives on a farm, and I worked for his dad after school and in the summer. We've been friends since the first grade and I've spent many, many nights at his house. After my mom died, I liked going there even more. J.D.'s mom is a great cook. His dad treats me like a second son and taught me how to drive a tractor. I lived for the days in the summer when I could work there."

"I guess it was like saying good-bye to family when you moved."

"Yeah, it was. They offered to let me move in with them and graduate from high school in Marianna. If I'd stayed,

Dad would have moved here alone, and I couldn't do that to him."

"You'd be leaving him in a year and a half anyway, when you go away to college. Not a lot of difference," Andy said.

"You're right. As much as I love farming, though, I love my dad more. He and my sister Cara are all I have left. They're important to me, even if my dad wears a white shirt and tie every day instead of Levis," Jake said and laughed, lightening the mood and the conversation.

"So I'm guessing J.D. is like the rest of us, with a full name he doesn't use?" Andy asked.

"Yeah, you're right. I didn't think about that—his name is James David. When we were little and got rowdy in the house, Mrs. Spencer, like most moms, called him James David Spencer. I guess he'll have something in common with everyone when he comes to visit," Jake replied.

"Yeah, he should feel right at home with all of us who have nicknames, too. Come on in and meet my mom. You'll love her. She's a great cook."

Jake did like Andy's parents. They invited him to eat supper with them and he enjoyed every bite of the fried chicken, mashed potatoes and creamed gravy Mrs. Houston served. The biscuits she'd made weren't bad either. Andy was right, she was a great cook. Jake and his dad had been eating at the few cafes in town, and the food was okay, although it wasn't home-cooking like Mrs. Houston's.

Andy was the oldest of four kids. He had two younger sisters and a little brother, the baby of the family. Even though Jake had just met everyone, including Andy, he felt welcome in their home. Though it wasn't J.D.'s house, it felt a lot like it. Jake looked around the table, and as he listened to the banter going on among the family, he knew this was what he wanted in his future.

Mrs. Houston insisted on sending a plate of food with Jake for his dad. He said his good-byes, knowing he would be back, and often. The conversation between the two guys flowed freely on the ride back to town, as if they'd been friends forever.

CHAPTER THREE

*T*he following Sunday morning when Jake and his dad entered the sanctuary at Lake City Community Church, Jake was surprised to see Lizzie J. and Andy. They were already seated, so Jake nodded to them both and continued down the aisle with his dad until they found seats. The church building was on the small side, and Jake estimated it would seat about two hundred.

Jake tried to be discreet as he looked around the room searching for Maggie. He had no idea how many times he'd thought about her in the three weeks since he'd seen her the first time. In school this past week, he'd lived for drama class, and his heart had raced every time he'd caught a glimpse of her in the hallway between classes. He didn't see her in the sanctuary and wondered if she might attend a different church.

When the service ended, Andy and Lizzie J. wanted to talk to Jake. Many people came to welcome him and his dad, so they politely waited. Andy's parents, Alex and Mary Houston, were the last ones to speak to them.

"So you're Jake's father. It's nice to meet you, Mr. Martin. We enjoyed having Jake in our home a few evenings ago," Mary said.

"Please, call me Sal. And thank you, Mrs. Houston, for sending the plate of food for me. It was delicious. It's been a while since I had such good food," Sal replied.

"You're welcome, and thank you for the compliment. We enjoyed having Jake eat dinner with us, and please, call us Alex and Mary."

"Jake tells us you moved here from Marianna," Alex said. "He also told us how much he loves farming. Maybe in the spring he can help us when planting time comes — after school and on Saturdays."

"He'd love to, wouldn't you Jake?" Sal replied, but Jake, Andy and Lizzie J. had moved away from the adults and were involved in their own conversation.

"I didn't see Maggie here this morning. Where does she go to church?" Jake finally asked.

Lizzie J. and Andy exchanged looks. Jake noticed their hesitancy, neither wanting to answer his question.

"Maggie's family doesn't attend church regularly. They usually come here on special occasions, though. Maggie's parents want Sunday to be family time. Maggie usually practices the piano most of the day," Lizzie J. explained.

"Really? I heard her play at the Christmas program and I was impressed. She actually practices most of the day?"

"Yes, she does. She's quite serious about her music. Her dream is to be a concert pianist some day," Lizzie J. said. "We've been friends since kindergarten, and I've always been amazed at the dedication she has to her music. It's a part of who she is. I've tried to tell her that God gifted her with her talent."

"What do you mean you tried to tell her?" Jake asked.

"She says she doesn't see the need to come to church, though she says she believes in God. It isn't her fault. It's the way she's been raised. She has strong morals and so do her parents; they simply don't see the need to belong to a church. She's my best friend, and I keep hoping she will see something in my relationship with God that is missing from her life." Lizzie J. felt she shouldn't be saying these things about her friend, even though it was the truth.

"Oh, I see," Jake replied. He couldn't hide the disappointment in the tone of his voice. Jake's relationship with God was important to him.

"Hey, our youth group meets on Sunday evenings. We play games and eat, and eat, and eat. Want to come tonight?" Andy asked Jake.

"I'll check with my dad and let you know. What time?"

"It starts at six and is over somewhere around eight. Hope you can make it. If we don't see you tonight, we'll see you at school tomorrow."

"Yeah, sure. Thanks for the invitation."

ANNIE, MAGGIE'S MOM, was in the kitchen cooking their traditional Sunday dinner. Maggie had been at the piano for the past two hours playing some of her favorite pieces and practicing a few new ones. Right now the strains of Beethoven's "Moonlight Sonata" filled the air. Maggie loved this piece and had been playing it since she was ten.

Annie knew her daughter had talent, and she knew about Maggie's dream. As much as Annie loved her daughter, she didn't share the same dream. Annie and Oliver, Maggie's dad, cherished their only daughter. They'd tried to have more children but were always disappointed. Suffering through several miscarriages was hard on them both, and they finally gave up and focused all their energies on their only child. Like a lot of parents, they hoped to live vicariously through their daughter. They figured they would love grandchildren as much as the children they couldn't have, and they planned on Maggie to grant their wish. So when Maggie talked about going to a prestigious college in the northeast and living in a large city, they agreed only half-heartedly. They would try to talk her into going to one of the colleges close to home when the time came. They hoped she then would meet someone, fall in love, and give up her dream.

Neither Maggie nor her mom knew about the application Maggie's piano teacher had submitted to Carnegie Hall entering her in a piano competition. Mr. Davis knew it would be a long shot for Maggie to be accepted into such a challenging, world-renowned competition, so he decided to remain silent until he knew the results.

The phone in the hallway rang, and after the fourth ring Maggie stopped playing and went to answer it.

"Hello."

"Hi, is this Maggie? This is Jake."

"Oh, hey Jake, how are you?"

"I'm fine. Would you like to go with me to the youth group meeting at the church tonight?"

"Which church?"

"The Lake City Community Church. My dad and I went this morning and Andy and Lizzie J. invited me to come back tonight, and I thought maybe you'd like to go, too."

Maggie had gone a few times with her friends and had a good time, but it wasn't anything she would care to do every week. This time she had a different reason for thinking it was a good idea...Jake.

"Sure, sounds like fun. I need to check with my mom. Can I call you back?"

"Great, of course. It doesn't start until six this evening, so you'll have plenty of time. I thought I might come to your house about five to meet your parents. Would that be okay?"

"They would love to meet you. Give me your phone number and I'll call you back after I talk to my mom."

"Hold on, I have to check the number again. I still can't remember it. I keep thinking of our old phone number in Marianna. Here it is, 574-6621."

"Thanks, I'll call you back soon. Bye."

"Bye."

Maggie went through the living room where her dad was engrossed in the Sunday paper and entered the kitchen. Her mom was removing the pot roast from the oven and the aroma made Maggie's stomach rumble. She'd been so involved in her music she hadn't noticed how hungry she was.

"Who was on the phone?" Maggie's mom asked.

"Jake Martin—remember, I told you about him? He moved here from Marianna right before Christmas."

"Oh, what did he want?"

"He wanted to know if I would go with him to the youth group meeting at the church tonight. He went to church this morning and saw Andy and Lizzie J. They invited him, and he invited me. Do you mind if I go?"

"Will he come here to get you or are you meeting him there?"

"He wanted to come early so I could introduce him to you and Dad."

Maggie noticed the change in her mom and her sudden interest in what Maggie was telling her. She knew the reason for this. She was about to turn sixteen and her mom thought it odd that Maggie had never had a boyfriend. Lizzie J. was always going on and on about Andy and had been since third grade. Maggie's mom tried to sound lighthearted when she teased Maggie that the piano was the love of her life. Maggie knew the truth—her mom worried she would be married to her music. She'd never asked to go anywhere with a boy, and she could tell her mom was excited about this news.

"Oh, Maggie, we would love to meet him. How sweet. I heard Mr. Martin is the new president of Citizens First Bank. Do you know where they live?"

"Jake told me they rented a house on Park Street. They have a house in Marianna. Jake's sister recently married and she and her husband live there."

"Well, maybe Jake's mom wanted to have time to look around before buying a house," Maggie's mom replied.

"Oh, Jake doesn't have a mom. I mean, he did have a mom. She died," Maggie said.

"How sad. What happened and how long since she passed away?"

"Jake didn't give me a lot of details. I know she had cancer and he was only twelve when she died."

"How terrible it must be to grow up without a mother."

"Well, don't mention it to him while he's here. And don't start thinking you can mother him like you do Lizzie J. when she's around. Even though Lizzie J.'s mom didn't raise her, she does have her grandmother."

"I know she has her grandmother, but I still feel as though she's a second daughter. You have to admit she's spent half her life here with you. And you know your dad and I have enjoyed every minute she's been with us."

"I know, Mom, and I love Lizzie J. like a sister. I'll never understand how her mom can visit here from California with her husband and not take Lizzie J. home with them. And her mom won't tell her who her father is. How does a mom do that?" Maggie had said this to her mom more than once over the years. "Lizzie J. is always so sad after her mom leaves to go home to California or when she and her grandparents return after visiting there. Andy and I try to stay as close to Lizzie J. as possible, until she can readjust to the life she has with her grandparents. At this point in her life Lizzie J. realizes she will probably never live in the same house with her mom. Especially since it's been two years since she's even seen her. I never know what to say to Lizzie J.," Maggie said softly.

"I know this bothers you, Maggie. We don't know every detail and Lizzie J. doesn't either. Thankfully, she has her grandparents and they've done a great job of providing for her. And you and Andy have both been the best friends Lizzie J. could ever ask for."

"None of my friends or Gran could take your place, though. I love you, Mom."

"Aw, I know it hurts you to see your friend be without her mom and now you have another friend, Jake, without a mom, too. I love you too, Maggie Mae. Now, call your dad in here and let's eat. I'm starving."

"Me too. Dad, time to eat," Maggie yelled into the living room.

Jake hung up the phone and started pacing the floor, waiting for her to call back. He looked up and stared straight at the family photo hanging on the living room wall. Seeing his mom reminded him of all the conversations he'd had with her about God. She always told him God had a plan for his life, and if he listened and let God lead him, he would make far fewer mistakes. One of the things she explained to him was that when he chose a wife, she should be a believer too. Jake loved his mom, and they had an extremely close relationship. While she fought her war with cancer, they had many long conversations, and now it seemed to Jake she was trying to tell him all the things he would need to know. The phone rang and interrupted his thoughts.

"Hello."

"Hey, this is Maggie. I can go. It's not far, so do you want to walk?"

"Sure. I'll see you at five," Jake said.

"Perfect, see you then."

After lunch, Maggie excused herself and went to her room. She closed her door and let the excitement of Jake's invitation sink in. Since she didn't want her mom to know how thrilled she was, she resisted the urge to jump up and down and scream like a little girl. Maggie thought her mom didn't need any unnecessary encouragement; she was already too pleased about Maggie's date, her first date.

Jake was handsome, and she did love his brown eyes and dark curly hair. It was more than that, though. He was different from the other guys at school. He seemed older, and she wondered if it was because he'd been through the trauma of watching his mom get sick and die. Maggie thought every-thing Jake said and did was genuine and intentional, almost as if he always thought through everything with care. She liked that ... a lot. His good looks just happened to be a bonus!

Maggie wanted to call Lizzie J. — they discussed everything and she needed her advice. Maggie was in uncharted territory.

The doorbell rang and Maggie knew it would be Lizzie J. They were always joking that each knew what the other was thinking.

"Hey, what are you up to?" Lizzie J. asked, removing her coat as she came into the room.

"About to look for something to wear tonight," Maggie replied.

"Where are you going?"

Maggie twirled around and grabbed Lizzie J. by the shoulders. "Guess who called me? Guess!"

"That's an easy guess. Jake."

"How did you know?"

"Are you kidding? Can't you see the way he looks at you? And besides, I saw him this morning and he asked where you go to church."

"He did? Why would he care?"

"I guess he saw Andy and me and figured you would be there too. He didn't see you and asked if you went to a different church."

"What did you tell him?" Maggie asked. Suddenly she wondered if it would make a difference to Jake when he found out she rarely attended church. Obviously he went and was going back to the youth meeting tonight. She thought it must be important to Jake and wondered if he would be disappointed to find out she didn't feel the same.

"We told him you go to the same church we do, when you go. It wasn't a big deal. Were you excited when he called?"

"Of course! He's the best-looking guy I've ever seen. And he wanted to come early to meet Mom and Dad. I thought most guys didn't want to meet the parents unless they had to. He seems so nice. Though I don't know him well, my heart beats so fast when he's around I can hardly breathe. I guess that means I do like him."

"Yeah, I think it does," Lizzie J. replied with a grin.

"I've never felt this way before. My knees are weak, and my legs actually shake when he's around. Do you feel this way around Andy?"

"You won't always have weak knees. It's new and you don't know each other very well. And remember, I've liked Andy since we were in third grade. I love Andy and I know he loves me. I think we know almost everything there is to know about each other."

"I've never met anyone like Jake. Since the moment our eyes met at the Christmas program, I haven't been able to think about anything except him. It has even affected my piano practice."

"You really do like him! I never thought anyone or anything would interfere with your music. Mrs. Houston asked Jake to stay for supper the afternoon they went to see the farm. Andy said Jake acted like he'd known everyone forever. He thinks Jake is a great guy. I guess time will tell if he's as nice as he seems to be."

"It must be hard to move to a new place after living in the same town all your life. I wonder if he left a girlfriend behind in Marianna."

"He told Andy he left his best friend, J.D., behind. He didn't mention a girlfriend. Or if he did Andy didn't tell me."

"He had to have a girlfriend. He's too handsome not to have a girlfriend."

"Well, you look like you do and you've never had a boyfriend."

Lizzie J. was always telling Maggie how beautiful she was. She loved her gorgeous blonde hair and envied her slender figure, and Maggie loved Lizzie J.'s black hair and beautiful blue eyes. Maggie's mom was always telling them they should be happy with themselves and not envy the way others look. Sixteen is a hard age to be comfortable in your own skin.

"I'd never met anyone I cared to know more about until I saw Jake. I'm telling you, Lizzie J., my hands were shaking so much the day I saw him I didn't think I would be able to play the piano. I think about him all the time."

"Let me see, you can hardly breathe when he's around and you think about him all the time. And you wonder if you like him? Girl, you do need help!" Lizzie J. said.

"Well, I didn't know exactly how I would feel when I met someone I liked. And I'm not sure what to wear. What are you wearing tonight?" Maggie asked.

"I don't know. I haven't thought much about it. What were you thinking about wearing?" Lizzie J. asked.

"I was about to decide when you came in. Want to stay and help me?" Maggie pleaded.

"I can't—I've already stayed too long. I promised Nanny I would come back and clean my room. I left everything in a mess this morning because I slept late. You'll look great in whatever you choose. You always do."

"Yeah, sure. See you later at the church."

Lizzie J. left and Maggie sat on the side of her bed, not moving, daydreaming about Jake again. Finally, she pushed the vision of him away. Five o'clock would be here soon and she wanted to be ready.

Maggie pulled open her dresser drawer and the first thing she saw was her new green sweater she'd gotten as a Christmas gift from her parents. It matched the pleated wool skirt she loved to wear. People always complimented her whenever she wore green. She knew it accentuated her eyes and wondered if Jake would notice. It was cold outside, so she decided on her loafers and socks instead of her black flats. She hated having cold feet.

Leather jackets were the rage this season, but Maggie couldn't stand the cold leather touching the back of her neck. She remembered receiving a beautiful scarf that she figured she would never wear, and now she realized it went perfectly with her ensemble and would keep her neck warm.

Maggie wore make-up only on special occasions. She'd been blessed with beautiful skin even if she did have a few freckles. She'd decided she'd rather have freckles than the acne a lot of girls her age had to contend with.

She applied a little eye shadow and mascara to draw attention to her eyes, put on a little lipstick, brushed her hair, and stepped back from the mirror to see the effect of her efforts. At first Maggie liked the way she looked, then suddenly she began to feel unsure about her clothes, her make-up and her hair. She'd never before tried to please someone else with what she was wearing. These feelings were completely foreign to her.

She had worn her favorite perfume, Unforgettable by Avon, the first day Jake sat beside her in drama class. Now she wondered if he noticed it and, if he did, what he thought about it. How could all these thoughts running through her mind be so important today, when they'd never been important before? She smiled at her reflection in the mirror as the answer seemed to flash like a neon sign in her head ... Jake.

AFTER MAGGIE AGREED to go out with him, it was Jake who began to worry. What would her parents think? Would her dad be gruff and grouchy? He remembered all the conversations his own parents would have when Jake's sister, Cara, introduced her current boyfriend to them. Some of them passed the test; however, when one didn't, Cara would be forbidden to see him again.

Jake wished his mom were here. She'd always given great advice. He loved his dad, but he wasn't as easy to talk to about such things. Jake again stared at the photo taken the year before his mom died. Only eleven at the time, he was sitting beside her and she had her arm around him. He closed his eyes, remembering how that felt. Before he knew it, a tear slipped down his face. He missed her. He wiped the tears away and left the room without looking at her again. She wasn't here to encourage him and give him confidence ... he had to find that on his own.

He didn't know what to wear. He wasn't nearly as concerned about what Maggie thought as he was about what her parents would think. His hair was a little long, especially near the collar of his shirt. Would they think he wanted to be like Elvis Presley? He smiled as he pictured Maggie, the classical pianist, dating an Elvis Presley look-alike. Most parents disapproved of the singer's hip action and music. Jake thought it certainly wouldn't be good to be compared to Elvis.

Suddenly the words *just be yourself* popped into his mind. How many times had his mom told him to *just be yourself*? She'd taught him to never pretend to be someone or something he wasn't. He felt comforted and confident. He'd retained all those conversations with his mom, and they seemed to come to mind just when he needed advice. Unknowingly, his mom had prepared him for many things in the twelve years they were together.

Jake put on a clean pair of Levi jeans, his favorite boots, and a comfortable shirt, and decided to dress it up with a pullover sweater Cara had given him for Christmas. He stopped worrying about Maggie's parents and started thinking about Maggie. On his dresser he saw the Canoe cologne he'd also gotten for Christmas, and the memory of the first day he sat by her in drama class came flooding back. Often he remembered the scent of her perfume and how much trouble he had concentrating on what the teacher was saying. He would recognize the fragrance anywhere.

He hadn't opened the cologne since the morning he'd opened the gift. Now, though, he thought she might like it. He picked up the bottle, sat it back down, then picked it up again. He had no idea how much to put on or even where to put it. The last thing he wanted to do was wear too much, causing Maggie and her parents to choke to death when he went in their house.

He knew girls dabbed their perfume behind their ears, but somehow behind the ears seemed too feminine. Finally, he decided it should go on his chest, and that's where it went.

Jake looked in the mirror and hoped what he was wearing was appropriate. He wanted Maggie to like him, and he still thought he needed to impress her parents. At least, he thought, he would smell nice!

CHAPTER FOUR

1962

A LOT HAD HAPPENED since the Sunday Maggie and Jake
went out together the first time. All of Jake's worrying
had been unnecessary. Annie and Oliver Roberts had
fallen in love with him the first evening, even before
Maggie knew she loved him, too.

The school year ended in May. Jake and Andy worked long
hours on the farm during the week and on a few Saturday
mornings. Jake and Maggie had become as inseparable as
Lizzie J. and Andy, and the four of them were always together.

Jake was still a little bit in love with his car. The dream
he'd always had of buying a truck ended the day he saw this
gorgeous, candy apple red, 1957 Chevy. Jake thought one of the
reasons his dad was so agreeable to buy the car was because he
could never understand why Jake would want a truck. Didn't
make any difference to Jake what the reason was — he knew he
had to have that car and was happy his dad agreed.

He was driving back to Lake City from Jonesboro with
Maggie by his side, twirling her fingers in his hair, and Lizzie
J. and Andy in the back seat. The four friends had spent the
afternoon swimming at the Community Center, then stopped

at the new pizza drive-in to eat. It had been a good day after a week of hard work in the fields.

It was the middle of July and summer school would start next week. The crops were laid by and farmers waited for the hot summer sun to work its magic. Hopefully by October, the green bolls would mature and the fields would turn white with the harvest.

The four friends were looking forward to returning to school. Jake was seventeen and starting classes as a senior. The other three were sixteen and juniors. Jake had lived in Lake City for almost eight months and was surprised how much he felt at home. Maggie's parents and Andy's parents had welcomed him, and he loved being around both families. They had been the main reason for his easy transition to this new place.

At first Jake felt guilty about leaving his dad alone while he spent time with the other families, until he found out his dad had a girlfriend. She was nice enough. About ten years younger than his dad, she had never married and had no children. Jake had a hard time when he first found out, but he didn't want his dad to know how he felt. Jake knew his dad had been lonely, and could see she made him happier. It had been five years since his mom died, and Jake had always known his dad might re-marry one day.

It was a pleasant summer night, and with the car windows down the four were quite comfortable. With the radio tuned to Chicago's WLS, they were quiet, full of pizza and worn out from swimming all afternoon. Finally, Maggie broke the silence with a question.

"What time did you say J.D. would be here tomorrow?"

"He should be here early enough to go to church with me. Do you want to come too?" Jake asked, hoping she would say yes. He knew he was in love with Maggie, and almost every day his mom's words reverberated in his head. Jake knew Maggie was a good person, but, clearly, she didn't seem to have any faith or be interested in knowing more about God.

"Yes, I think I will. Can you pick me up? As hot as it is I'd be melted by the time I walked there."

"Of course, I'll stop by to get you. If we come early enough, I can introduce J.D. to your parents. I've talked a lot about them, so J.D. will probably feel as though he already knows them."

"Oh Maggie, I'm so glad you're coming tomorrow. We can all sit together. We're excited to meet J.D., aren't we Andy?" Lizzie J. knew Andy was a little anxious about his new best friend having his old best friend for a visit.

"Yeah, sure. Any friend of Jake's is a friend of ours, right?" Andy replied with as much enthusiasm as he could muster. No one seemed to notice the reticence in his reply and he was relieved. Andy didn't like the way he felt about Jake's old friend from Marianna, and he hadn't even met him yet. Jake and Andy were alike in so many ways, from their values to their love for God and their love for farming. And they had the same hopes and dreams for their futures. For some reason, Andy felt their friendship and close bond would be threatened with J.D. around. He didn't know their friendship wasn't the relationship in danger.

After church the next day, Andy discovered his fears were unfounded. The four friends and J.D. all gathered at Andy's house for lunch. Andy soon realized the reasons Jake and J.D. were such good buddies were the same reasons he and Jake had become friends. He was surprised how much alike the three of them were. While Maggie and Lizzie J. made fudge in the kitchen, at the invitation of Andy's mom, the guys went on a tour of the farm.

During the tour, J.D. noticed how clean the fields were of weeds, and all the outbuildings and equipment indicated a hard-working farm family in charge. J.D. liked Andy and was happy Jake had found a friend. He also was pleased because Jake seemed to be content in this new place.

J.D. thought he might be here often, because he'd been captivated from the first moment Lizzie J. turned to look at him when he entered the church. Her eyes were the most beautiful color of blue he'd ever seen. One minute they reminded him of the sky, then they seemed to turn as dark as periwinkle. He thought she was almost too beautiful. Her long dark eyelashes gave even more accent to her eyes, and her raven black hair framed her heart-shaped face, leaving him awestruck.

She was taken, he reminded himself many times throughout the day. J.D. thought how much easier it would be if Andy were a jerk, but he wasn't, and in fact J.D. liked him and knew he and Andy could become good friends. Besides, he said to himself, he could see they loved each other and had a long history together. So he would admire her from afar. She would never know he was attracted to her; he would not share those feelings with anyone.

J.D. was the star basketball player on his high school team. At seventeen he was 6'2" and still growing. He'd been on varsity since he entered the ninth grade. His body hadn't fully matured so he was still thin, which made him seem taller. He had green eyes, auburn hair and a ruddy complexion. His dad had always teased his mom about why he was the only member of the family with red hair. When the family was together, people who didn't know them always thought J.D. had to be adopted, until they looked closer at his dad. No doubt some ancestor from long ago had to be responsible for his red hair.

After returning from the tour of the farm, the five friends gathered in the living room with popcorn, fudge and soft drinks. Andy's parents were in the den watching TV, and the friends had a chance to get to know J.D., Jake's best friend, a little better.

"So J.D., what did you think about the farm?" Lizzie J. asked.

She and Andy were sitting on the floor with a bowl of popcorn between them. Her blue sweater made her eyes change to periwinkle again, and her skin seemed to glow. J.D. was having trouble comprehending her question. He finally found his voice.

"It's great. A lot bigger than ours — our farm is about half this size."

"Are you going to farm your family's land when you get out of school?" she asked.

Jake laughed out loud and almost spit out his coke.

"What's so funny?" Lizzie J. asked.

"J.D. won't ever be a farmer. As soon as possible, he'll be living in some big city as a high-paid lawyer working for a big-time corporation. Then he won't have to get his hands dirty ever again," Jake laughed.

"You don't like farming?" Andy asked.

"Farming's okay. Jake's giving me a hard time because I don't eat, sleep and breathe farming like he does. I don't mind getting my hands dirty. I just want to be an attorney and live in the city."

"The city will be quite a change from living on a farm," Maggie said. "I understand, though. I would love to live in

New York City for a while and have the experience of city life versus a small town."

"New York City would be a big change for you, too. Why do you want to live in the city?" J.D. asked her, noticing the change in Jake's facial expression.

"My dream has always been to be a concert pianist and to play in Carnegie Hall. I know it seems impossible for someone like me. A girl can dream, can't she?"

J.D. knew Jake better than anyone. They'd been best friends for years, and when Jake's mom died, Jake relied on J.D. They truly were like brothers. So the change in Jake's expression when Maggie talked about New York City was not lost on J.D. Before a word was said, he knew Jake loved this girl and was afraid he would lose her.

"We've been hearing about this dream for years, right Andy?" Lizzie J. asked.

"Yeah, years ago we didn't pay a lot of attention to what Maggie said about being a concert pianist, but in the last couple of years we've seen a change in her dedication to the piano. Now, I'm thinking if she wanted it bad enough she could make it happen."

"Thank you, Andy. I appreciate your confidence."

"Why do you think you have to move to New York City? Why couldn't you do the same thing somewhere closer to home? Why couldn't you play the piano for a symphony in Memphis?" Jake asked.

"To play in Carnegie Hall is every pianist's dream. There isn't another place to compare it to in all of America," Maggie explained in a soft, silky voice as her eyes took on the faraway look she always had when she spoke about her dream.

Jake watched her eyes and heard the softness in her voice,

and he knew he was fighting a losing battle. He believed what his mom had taught him about finding a wife, and he also believed he was in love with Maggie. Even though he was young, he'd known for a long time what he wanted in his life. He didn't understand why J.D. or Maggie had the desire to leave and start a new life in a city, especially so far from their families. Maybe his past, losing his mom, had shaped his future. He would trade places with J.D. or Maggie anytime. They had both parents who loved them, and they lived in communities where the people had known them their whole lives. Since his sister Cara was now married and still lived in Marianna, and his dad was spending most of his time with his new girlfriend, Jake felt as though he had no one.

Jake had never lived on a farm, though he'd spent many days and nights at J.D.'s. He always loved the early morning when the mist hovers slightly above the fields as the sun changes the landscape from dark to the tinge of first light. He could close his eyes and from his memory hear the rooster crowing, the birds singing, and the other animals coming awake, filling the air with the sounds of a working farm. He could see Morning Glories growing on the fence rows, vying for attention among the blooming Honeysuckle vines. Jake loved the wonderful scent of Honeysuckle carried on the light breeze of a summer morning. He always had a feeling of being at home, and an intuition in his gut that told him he was where he was sup-posed to be.

He always felt a deep connection with God's creation when the scent of the freshly turned soil wafted across the field as he plowed in the early spring. Seeing the seeds they planted poke through after only a few days left him amazed at how God had designed the earth and the perfect cycle of life. Jake's connection to the land ran deep in his soul, and the thought of living in a big city suffocated him.

Jake was brought back to the present when J.D. threw a pillow across the room at him. He tried to feel the same excitement of being with his friends he'd felt before the subject of Maggie's music came up. His mood had been altered, and as always, he wished life came with a clear set of instructions. Go here, go there, do this, don't do that, this is right, this is wrong; worrying about making a mistake that would change the course of his life made his head hurt.

Maggie and Jake had been dating for six months, and she knew his moods well. She felt him stiffen when the subject of the city and her music found its way into the conversation. She'd never known anyone like Jake. There were times he seemed as though he'd lived a lot longer than his seventeen years. Maggie knew Jake appreciated her music and her talent, and he always told her he admired her dedication. She was fascinated with his deep religious beliefs. They were not something he lived only on Sunday but every day. He didn't flaunt them or push them onto anyone unreceptive; they simply were part of who he was.

Worship on Sundays was hit or miss with Maggie's family, though they always attended on special occasions. Maggie believed there was a God, and she realized Jake knew him in a way she didn't understand, and for some reason, her lack of understanding frightened her. When she felt a tugging at her heartstrings, she quickly took her mind in a different direction. She didn't want to give in — give in to *what*, she wasn't sure about. Something inside her soul felt unsettled.

JAKE AND MAGGIE survived summer school and six weeks of stifling heat, fighting to keep the papers from blowing off their desks by the fans needed to avert heat exhaustion. It was Friday afternoon, and they were ready for a break, even if that meant field work. The cotton was ready to be picked and most of the school kids would be glad to make some spending money.

Jake loved farming when it involved driving the tractor or other machinery, but not when it meant pulling a cotton sack from one end of the field to the other all day long. But they'd all picked cotton in the fall since they'd been kids. Monday through Friday would find them in the cotton patch unless they woke up to the sound of rain. Those were the best days, when they knew there would be no work and they could roll over and sleep a little longer.

Maggie didn't like the work either, but she liked the money to buy extra clothes. Her parents said if she was willing to work, she could spend the money on clothes. She dreaded the soreness of her fingers — the sharp cotton bolls would tear the delicate skin around the tips. During cotton season she always got behind in her music studies.

On a very warm October Monday near quitting time, Maggie was about to cry. She was tired from the back-breaking, knee-bruising work, lagging behind the others and unsure if she could make it to the end of the field. She stood and stretched, then sat down in the dirt between the rows, the stalks heavy with leaves that almost covered her. The dirt felt cool under the canopy of leaves. Maggie heard rustling and looked up to see Jake standing above her. He knelt down and took her hands in his. Even though her hands were dirty from the field work, Jake didn't care as he turned them palms up and kissed the tips of her fingers.

"Are you okay?" he asked her tenderly. Even though he believed in hard work and felt it built character, he didn't like seeing her so tired and her hands so torn up. He was always in awe when her beautiful slender fingers flew over the piano keys.

"Yeah, I'm okay, and I think I'm finished for today. I know I have to drag my sack to the end of the row. I don't think I can pick another boll of cotton."

"You go on to the trailer and I'll finish your row, okay?"

"Thanks, Jake," Maggie replied, fighting tears of exhaustion.

She slowly walked to the end of the row, wondering how she would be able to see this last season of cotton picking to the end. After this year I will never, ever, pick cotton again, she thought. Never!

CHAPTER FIVE

New York City
1971

*M*aggie's sweet memories had occupied her thoughts for quite some time. Now they were tucked back into the recesses of her mind as the sound of the snowplow outside her apartment abruptly brought her back to the present. She watched as the plow cleared the street, appalled as the snow engulfed the parked cars, thinking it might be spring before they became visible again!

Some of her neighbors ventured out. Most everyone looked at the snow-covered cars, shook their heads and went back inside. The storm still raged, as the snow fell faster than the snow plows could move it, and the residents of New York City knew they weren't going anywhere. For most, on this Christmas Eve morning, the snow was a perfect excuse to stay inside and snuggle close to the fire. For Maggie, it meant a Christmas spent alone far from her family and friends.

She was unaware how long she'd sat in her chair daydreaming about the past until she took a sip of her cold coffee. She wrinkled her nose and forced herself to swallow. She rose from her seat, let the warm throw fall to the floor, and stretched her legs, grown stiff from sitting in the same position so long. The next few days seemed to extend out into eternity as she thought of spending Christmas stuck here in the city. Alone ....

When Maggie first saw this apartment, she fell in love with the high ceilings and large windows. The luxurious bathroom also was a selling point. Now, she stood in the marble shower under the hot water trying to wash away the regret she'd been dealing with the past couple of years.

Her mind went back to the beginning, when she was star struck with this big city, her eyes wide with excitement and disbelief as she realized her dreams had finally come true. She smiled at the memory of Mr. Davis, her piano teacher, coming to her home with the acceptance letter for the competition at Carnegie Hall. She was only seventeen. He was so excited, as was she; her parents, not so much. They'd finally given their permission and the rest, of course, was history.

Her first couple of years after college had been filled with hard work at the piano, earning her place in the concert halls here and in other cities across the country. She was renowned and highly sought after, and in the beginning she'd reveled in all the attention. As she felt the sting of the hot water on her skin, she tried to remember when all the glory had begun to fade and the feeling that she was missing out on life had taken up residence in her soul.

As usual, when she wasn't in a hurry to rush to another practice or performance, a yearning for home assaulted her; and before she could stop them, the tears began slipping down her face, mingling with the water swirling toward the open drain.

Most of the people she'd gone to school with and who still lived in Lake City would think she was completely nuts if they knew her true feelings. They all thought she was a star, and treated her like one when she went home for a visit. Her true friends, who knew her and loved her, knew the truth — except Jake. She never voiced her feelings, but she could see in their eyes they knew. Maggie believed she should be happier than she was, and was embarrassed her friends knew the truth. After all, this had been her dream and the reason for all the hard work.

She finished her shower, and with the regret still firmly in place, towel dried her long blonde hair. She stood in her closet trying to choose clothes to wear for the long day stretching out before her. The packed suitcase lay open on the floor ready for the scheduled flight, now canceled. Her sadness turned to anger, and she kicked the suitcase. It helped her frustration but hurt her foot. Finally she chose an old pair of jeans and an Arkansas State sweatshirt with a picture of an Indian on the front who looked as angry as she felt. She heard her phone ringing and hesitated, not sure she wanted to answer it.

"Hello," she said, struggling to sound happy and normal.

"Well, hello and Merry Christmas. I knew you would be there when I looked out and saw the snow. I'm sorry you didn't get to go to Arkansas for Christmas. I know how much you were looking forward to it."

Maggie was surprised to hear Miguel's voice; she was expecting to hear someone from home. As usual, her defenses immediately surfaced. She'd known Miguel since he first arrived in New York about a year ago. An accomplished pianist, he was from Spain and had come to America on a two-year tour, performing in large cities across the country, excited at the opportunity. Maggie and Miguel had their music in common, having met at a concert in New York City when

Maggie was the headliner and Miguel opened for her. They'd become friends, enjoying an evening out to dinner occasionally when both were in town.

Maggie found his accent charming when they first met; now it grated on her nerves. She knew he was attracted to her, and she'd tried to distance herself from him in the past few weeks. She had met many men since moving here, and several had tried to date her. She'd thwarted their advances until the past couple of years, having decided to start her life over and date again. Yet she never could move past the first few dinner dates, even though all the men were handsome and successful. By the third date, every time she looked up from her dinner plate the man's face had turned into Jake's. Those evenings couldn't end fast enough, and the next time he called for a date, Maggie turned him down.

"Hi Miguel, Merry Christmas. Yes, I'm disappointed I can't be home for Christmas."

"You mean be in Arkansas for Christmas. I thought your home was here in New York City."

"I never meant to make New York City my home. My home will always be in Arkansas."

"You *are* disappointed! If I could, I would come over and keep you company. I'm afraid I won't be going anywhere today."

"I wouldn't be good company anyway. I guess your Christmas Eve party won't happen now, huh?"

"Sure it will. Several people live in my building and others live close enough to walk. Maybe by this evening the cabbies will be out working and you can come, too. It'll be fun and the food will be fabulous."

"I'm sure it will be fun and the food will be great too. I'll get back to you later today."

"If you don't call me back, I'll be calling you. You won't get off that easy. Honestly, Maggie, you should get out and mingle. No reason to sit in your apartment and sulk. I'm sure the planes will start to get out as soon as the snow stops and they can get the runways clear. In the meantime, you should enjoy yourself," Miguel encouraged.

"I'll call you later, okay?"

"Okay, sure, talk to you then."

Maggie hung up the phone and went back to her chair by the window. The scene hadn't changed; the snow was still falling and the street still empty. If she hadn't seen the snowplow earlier she'd never guess it had already been down her street.

Giving up on clearing skies, she went to the stereo and tuned in to a local station playing Christmas music. Her melancholy mood was magnified as she listened to Elvis crooning *Blue Christmas*. She thought about the Christmas of 1963, and how sad they all were after everything had changed so tragically and drastically. Trying to push those memories aside, she hoped the next song would be better. She couldn't believe it when they played *I'll be Home for Christmas*.

She had taken her anger out on the suitcase; now she felt only sadness, the tears coming again. Somehow, while striving for this successful life, she had weaved a web of isolation. As always, her music became her solace in her alone times, which seemed to be more often than not. Maggie quickly turned off the stereo, went to her piano and began to play. As much as she'd hated the piano earlier, after her dream of Jake, she now loved the familiarity of the keys beneath her fingers.

Arkansas

JAKE HAD BEEN in the tree stand since before daylight and now felt cold and stiff. It was a beautiful Christmas Eve morning. The sun, rising above the trees, lit the valley below and caused the mist to rise from the tall grasses and hover above the ground, creating a magical scene. He loved this time of morning and sat completely still, mesmerized, his discomfort now gone from his mind. Jake didn't come out in the early morning for a kill. His true reason was his love of witnessing the dawn of another day in the woods.

Feeling the closeness of God gave him pause, and he prayed, thanking Him for the privilege of living the life he loved. And as usual, Jake prayed for Maggie. He knew Maggie had been searching all these years for God. During their time dating, he began to realize her dream of becoming a success in New York City was partly to fill the emptiness in her soul. Though her talent was God-given, she clung to the talent itself for fulfillment instead of the God who gave it.

The past two years had been difficult for Jake. All the years he'd invested in his and Maggie's relationship seemed to be a waste. Even though she was physically out of his life, emotionally she was still as much a part of him as ever. He tried to move on and date other women, but after a few dates he knew it wasn't fair. He didn't have anything left to give. He'd already given everything to Maggie, and she held his heart whether she knew it or not.

About a year ago, Jake had flown to New York to surprise her and try one more time to make their relationship work.

He parked the rental car across the street from Maggie's apartment, but before he could get out of the car, he was stunned to see her emerge with a handsome man, arm in arm. He felt nauseous as he watched them laughing and talking in a way that seemed to him very intimate. When they were out of sight, he started the car and headed back to the airport, defeated once again. He was too late ...

As Jake got down out of the tree stand, he tried to push away the memories of Maggie. At times he could forget and think about something else. At other times, like now, her presence seemed to be everywhere he turned. Jake had heard through the small-town grapevine Maggie was coming home for Christmas, and if the gossip was true, she would arrive in Memphis today. The last time he'd seen Maggie and talked to her had been a few days after her father's funeral. Their fight before she went back to New York was what started the two-year separation. He pushed aside those ugly memories and let other, more pleasant ones, come to mind.

He walked across the valley to his old truck, started the motor, and let his mind go where he knew it would. As luck would have it, Rod Stewart's new song, Maggie Mae, was playing on the truck radio. He'd heard the song many times before, and even though the lyrics didn't exactly fit his and Maggie's relationship, there were lines in the song that seemed perfect. Jake felt the last three lines of the song were written for him. *You made a first-class fool out of me, but I'm as blind as a fool can be. You stole my heart, but I love you anyway.*

He knew the pain that would result from giving in to these memories of better days. But on this beautiful morning in December he missed her so badly that the pain could not be avoided anyway.

He had loved Maggie Mae Roberts since the day their eyes first met as she was moving toward the piano to play Christmas carols. He had prayed for guidance, taking seriously his mom's words about finding the right person. He first prayed for God to change her heart so she would be a believer, too. But the tragedy they experienced when he was a college freshman and she a high school senior had turned her heart further from God. His prayer since his trip to New York last year was for God to take away his feelings for Maggie.

Jake would sometimes feel immature and foolish for being in love for so long with someone who could not commit to him. He didn't understand why God hadn't answered at least one of his prayers over the past few years. He was twenty-seven. He had wanted a wife and family for several years. Waiting for Maggie was futile, so now he'd decided to pray for God to help him be content to be single. Was that God's plan? Jake knew if God planned it, He would have to give him contentment, because it wasn't Jake's idea.

Going to Lizzie J's always drove home to Jake how alone he was, and tonight at Christmas Eve dinner would be no different. If it wasn't for little Maggie expecting him, he might call and cancel. Jake would never, ever disappoint her. At least there was one Maggie who wanted him in her life, even if she was only two. Jake was unaware the other Maggie was supposed to be there for dinner, too. Lizzie J. had not given up on them and was playing matchmaker unbeknownst to both of them. But the call from Maggie earlier in the day about the blizzard in New York City was delaying her plans to bring two of the most important people in her life back together.

CHAPTER SIX

Lake City, Arkansas
1963

*I*T WAS A PERFECT DAY in May 1963. The severe storms two days earlier had cleared the heat and humidity away, and left in their place sweet spring weather with skies of deep blue and not a cloud in the sky. The graduates believed that this *not a cloud in the sky* kind of day was an omen for their futures.

Jake knew his name would be next. He scanned the faces in the audience and found his dad sitting next to his new wife, both of them beaming with pride. Sitting on the other side of his dad was his sister Cara and her husband Mark, along with Maggie and her parents. J.D couldn't be there—his own high school graduation was the same evening in Marianna.

Jacob Matthew Martin was now a high school graduate. As he accepted his diploma and crossed the stage he saw the pride in his dad's eyes. Jake was happy his dad had found someone to share his life with, but when he saw her sitting beside his dad, it made him think about how proud his mom would've been to see his accomplishment.

Jake was heading to Arkansas State College in Jonesboro

in the fall. With the scholarship money he'd been awarded, he'd decided to live on campus. He still felt a little uncomfortable living with his dad and Lillian and was ready to try living on his own. He was excited — J.D. had chosen to go to the same school and they would be roommates. The two guys had never stopped being best friends, and both could hardly wait for August and move-in day.

Lillian had no children of her own, and she'd genuinely tried to get to know Jake. She and Sal had planned a graduation party for later in the afternoon, and Jake promised them he would be there at least an hour before the guests. First, he wanted to spend time with Maggie.

"Can you go for a ride with me?" Jake asked her.

"Are you sure? Your party will start in two hours."

"I know. I promised Dad I'd be back home at least an hour before. Want to go for a ride in the country with the windows down?"

"Sounds perfect."

Holding hands and walking to Jake's car in the parking lot, they waved to classmates and yelled congratulations. The blue sky, no clouds perfect day had gotten even better with a light breeze. Jake was almost giddy with happiness. He was deeply in love and believed his graduation today was one step closer to asking Maggie to marry him.

As much as Jake wanted to talk about the future, he knew Maggie wasn't ready. They'd been dating for almost a year and a half. Though they were young, seventeen and eighteen, he knew she was the one he wanted to spend the rest of his life with. He knew Maggie loved him, but she hadn't given him her whole heart. He had only half of it, and her music had the other half.

They left the school and drove south down the dirt road toward the prairie. Jake thought about the first time he'd gone down the same road with Andy to see the farm. In some ways it seemed only yesterday; in other ways, as with his relationship with Maggie, it seemed a lot longer.

Jake looked over at Maggie and watched as she took a headband out of her purse and pulled her long blonde hair up into a ponytail. The windows were down and the wind had been blowing her hair across her face. Now with her hair pulled back, he could see the sprinkling of freckles across her nose that he loved so much. He stared until she felt his gaze and turned and smiled at him. Only Jake's resolve to God about abstinence was keeping him from touching her all over. Sometimes, after their dates, he took long cold showers and had trouble falling asleep when all he could think about was Maggie.

When the houses in town were in his rearview mirror, he pulled over to the side of the road. He left the motor running, put the gear into park, and pulled her across the seat and into his arms. He loved how she felt and he kissed her, lightly at first, then deeply. Maggie responded and wrapped her arms around him a little tighter. Hormones raged through both of them, and thankfully, a car approaching in the distance pulled them apart.

"Maybe we should go back to town. How about parking at the Root Beer Stand and having something to drink before we go back to my house for the party?" Jake asked her, breathing hard from the desire their kisses had aroused in him.

"Yes, I think so," Maggie replied breathlessly.

Jake was an eighteen-year-old young man, virile, handsome and in love. When he was a young boy, and old enough to understand, his mother had explained to him that God had a girl for him, only him. Jake would know when he found her—he was to be patient, pray and be sure she was the one. She also told him when he found her, he was to honor her, and that included waiting to be intimate until their wedding night. Of course when Jake agreed with his mom, he had no idea what she meant. *Now he did!*

The graduation party was a huge success. When the last guests departed, Jake and Maggie finished the evening on the front porch swing. Maggie had been waiting for the right time to share her good news she'd known about for several days. She hadn't wanted to steal Jake's spot in the limelight on his graduation day. Now, she thought she'd better tell him.

"I'm so happy for you. I know you're anxious to start college and move to Jonesboro. The party was great. A lot of people love you ... like me," Maggie said softly. Jake had told Maggie he loved her, but when she didn't tell him she loved him too, he'd never said it again. Now, he wondered if he'd heard her right.

"What did you say?" Jake asked.

"I said your party was great."

"No ... did you say you love me?"

"Yes." Her reply was almost a whisper.

"Aw, Maggie, you know I've been waiting to hear you say you love me, too. I never said it again because I didn't want to scare you away if you didn't feel the same."

"We're so young Jake, and there are so many things I want to do. You have four years of college in front of you, and I have another year of high school and then college. I don't want to be like Andy and Lizzie J. All they talk about is getting married."

"I know we're young, but I also know you're the person God chose for me," Jake told her hesitantly, knowing she wouldn't understand what he meant.

"How do you know?"

"Maggie, you know I believe in more than an idea that there is a God. I believe he loves and cares for me in every decision I make, including who I fall in love with."

"I've never understood the way you think about God. It's not only when you're in church, it's every day. Why?"

Jake was quiet for a few seconds before answering. He'd been waiting for a moment like this when he could try to explain his faith. He didn't want to mess this up.

"Because a long time ago I realized I was a sinner and only through Jesus, God's son, could I have a relationship with God."

"You don't sin. You're one of the best people I've ever known. If anyone could make it to heaven, it would be you."

"Maggie, being good is not the answer. Trusting in Jesus Christ is the answer, the only answer," Jake said with conviction.

"Well, I think being good and nice to people should be enough. I don't want to talk about it anymore. I do have something exciting to tell you, though!"

"Okay, we won't talk about it anymore. Now . . . what did you want to tell me?" Jake asked, deciding he'd said enough for tonight.

"I didn't want to tell you until after graduation and your party. Guess where I'm going in July."

Jake could tell she was excited and happy. He wondered where she could be going and suddenly was filled with dread.

"Where?"

"Are you ready for this?" Maggie scooted to the edge of the swing and turned to face him.

"Yes . . . I think I'm ready. Where are you going?"

"New York City!" Maggie squealed with delight as she clapped her hands together like a little girl.

"What for?" Jake finally asked.

"A piano competition at Carnegie Hall! I'm so excited!"

"I'm confused. Did you apply to be in the competition?"

"Mr. Davis sent in an application for me last year, didn't tell me, and they've invited me to participate. I can't believe it. It's like a dream come true!"

Jake was quiet. This was worse than he'd thought. He'd always known Maggie was talented, but he'd always thought her dream of performing at Carnegie Hall was just that...a dream. He waited too long to respond.

"You aren't happy for me, are you?" Maggie's eyes were wide with disbelief and disappointment. The one person she wanted to share this with, and he wasn't excited for her.

Jake wanted to be happy. He knew he was supposed to be. He was afraid and he didn't know how to tell her.

"Maggie, of course I'm happy for you. I'm also a little afraid."

"Why are you afraid? My parents are going with me to New York City, and of course Mr. Davis will go too. I'll be fine."

"I don't mean I'm fearful for the trip, I mean afraid for what this means for our future. I know we're young and we still have college ahead of us, but I know I want to marry you."

"Oh Jake, I can't think so far ahead. There are so many things I want to do and so many places I want to see. This is an opportunity of a lifetime, and I've studied and practiced hard to be able to qualify for something like this. How could I not go?"

"You're right, you should go. I am happy for you. I know this is something you've been dreaming about and you deserve the chance." Jake tried to keep the disappointment out of his voice, but he knew he'd failed.

"You sure don't sound happy."

"Maggie, I love you and I'll always want what is best for you. We might disagree, though, about what the best might be."

"How can success not be the best thing for me? Sometimes I don't understand how you can sound so much like my parents and some of the things they say to me. Why is everyone so against my desire to live and work in New York City someday?"

"Success can be many different things, Maggie. You've linked success to New York City. You can have a successful musical career in many other places. God gave you musical talent, and you need to find out why."

"What are you talking about? What do you mean I need to find out why?"

"You can find many places to use your talent—until you find the place where God intended you to use it, you won't have complete contentment. God has a plan for each person's life. Very few find it because they go their own way without asking God to show them the right way," Jake said with conviction.

"There you go again! You sound like a preacher! Can we leave God out of this? Please!" Maggie got up and walked to the edge of the porch. She crossed her arms and took a defiant stance with her back to Jake.

In the past, Maggie had somehow turned the conversation away from Jake's beliefs when she began to be uncomfortable. Tonight he was pushing. And he was trying to tell her that what she wanted to do wasn't right for her. She was angry, and also conflicted. She loved Jake and respected and admired his faith, and the fact he was that way every day, not only on Sunday. But for some reason, when their conversations became serious about faith, she wanted to run. Maggie didn't want to discuss it and felt resentful toward Jake at this moment.

She continued to stand. Silently. She stared out into the darkness as if searching for what to do or say next. Was this their first fight? Jake continued to swing, staring at her intently, as if he could will her to turn back to him.

The lingering quiet between them felt heavy with anger from her and frustration from Jake. The only sound was the creaking of the swing chains and the loud croaking of the spring tree frogs in the monkey grass around the porch. The sounds seemed to grow louder with each passing moment.

"I'm sorry," they both said at the same time.

"No, I shouldn't have said some of the things I said. I know this is something you want to do and I can't tell you what's right for you. I know we're too young to talk about marriage and I'll try not to mention it again, at least for awhile. Forgive me?" Jake asked.

"Yes, I forgive you. Thank you for agreeing with me. Do you forgive me for being so angry?"

"Yes, of course I do. Will you come back and sit down? I promise to stop talking about the future, unless you want to talk about college," Jake said.

"No, I don't want to think about college, either. Can we simply sit and swing? Just be together."

"Of course we can. Now come over here and sit by me."

And that's the way Maggie and Jake's first fight started and ended.

CHAPTER SEVEN

THE SCHOOL YEAR started with a continuous nine-month curriculum, beginning in August and ending in May. With her summers free, Maggie had begun spending them working full-time in her dad's hardware store. She was certainly not sad she would no longer be picking cotton in the fall. Field work, thankfully, was no longer a part of her life.

It was the second week of an extremely hot August in 1963, and on the coming weekend Jake and J.D. would be moving into their dorm rooms in Jonesboro. They were as excited as two little boys about to go to their first major league baseball game. Maggie couldn't remember if she'd ever seen Jake as happy as he'd been while preparing to move out of his dad's house and finally be on his own. She understood his excitement; this time next year would be her turn.

Maggie, Lizzie J. and Andy came to help. After moving Jake and J.D. into their dorm room, the five friends went to have dinner and see a movie.

Somehow, when they took their seats in the theatre, J.D. wound up sitting between the two couples and next to Lizzie J. When Jake had moved to Lake City, J.D. was sure he would visit his friend often. But since the first time he'd visited last summer, he'd been back only twice. Even though he'd only been in the presence of Andy and Lizzie J. briefly, he realized right away he didn't want to do that again. He had hoped the old saying *out of sight out of mind* was true—he'd found out over the past year it was a myth.

J.D. had dated a few times during his senior year in Marianna and had taken a girl he liked to the prom. He didn't like her enough. The last time he took her home after their date, and his thoughts immediately turned to Lizzie J., he knew it wasn't fair to continue to ask her out.

Tonight was the longest time J.D. had been in Lizzie J.'s presence since the Sunday afternoon at Andy's house when he'd met Jake's new friends. Sitting across from her at dinner was difficult. He wanted to stare at her and knew he shouldn't. Her blue eyes were as he'd remembered. Her hair was longer now, still black and lustrous. He was fascinated that being in the same room with her caused such strong emotions in him he'd never experienced before.

Suddenly, J.D. thought, maybe going to college in Jonesboro was a little too close to Lake City. Excited about being with Jake again, he failed to think about the close proximity to Andy and Lizzie J. Sitting close to her in a darkened theatre was something he didn't want to do again, especially having to watch her and Andy holding hands. It was a reminder; she was off limits. He was glad when the evening was over.

Maggie felt lonely riding in the truck with Andy and Lizzie J. back to Lake City, leaving Jake and J.D. in Jonesboro for their first night on their college campus. When Jake had offered to drive Maggie home, she told him it wasn't necessary. She had tried to prepare herself for the change in their routine and didn't realize until tonight how different the year ahead would be.

The heat and humidity had been building all afternoon, with thunder rumbling in the distance. Now, as they left Jonesboro and headed east on Highway 18, the skies grew angry with low-slung clouds, sending down jagged streaks of lightning, almost constant, coming closer and closer. Maggie didn't like storms. Jake would tease her about her fear then reassure her and comfort her that everything would be okay. Obviously, she would miss Jake in a lot of different ways.

"Man, that lightning was close," Andy said. Thunder was no longer rumbling—it crashed immediately and shook the truck.

"Oh, my gosh Andy, hurry! Drive faster!" Maggie could feel the wind against the truck and knew they were caught in the storm. The heavy rain and strong winds were so intense, the road was hardly visible. Andy could hardly see to stay on the highway.

"I can't go any faster. I can't see the road now!" Andy yelled to make himself heard over the roar of the storm.

"I'm so scared!" Maggie cried.

"It's okay, it's just a storm. We'll get home, I promise," Lizzie J. tried to reassure her friend, even though a little worried herself.

Andy slowed to about thirty miles per hour, and without telling the others, he began to pray God would guide him to stay on the road and out of the ditch, quickly filling with rushing rain water.

That was the last thought Andy had. The bright headlights seemed to come out of nowhere and happened so quickly he didn't have time to respond. The sound of the head-on collision could be heard over the sounds of the storm. Another pickup truck, the driver no longer able to see the road, lost control, then crossed the center line and hit the three teenagers. The impact spun the truck around and it overturned on the slick roadway.

Maggie sat on the side of the road in the pouring rain. She felt numb, no longer afraid of the storm and intense lightning. She didn't know where she was or why she was sitting outside in the mud next to the highway. Struggling to remove the mud from her face, she didn't realize most of it was blood, her blood. Maggie saw Andy's truck and wondered why it was upside down. Slowly her brain began to function, and as it did, she felt the screams start in her throat as she saw Andy and Lizzie J. both lying a few feet from her ... neither one moving.

Cars stopped and people ran toward the terrible scene. Residents in the house across the highway had heard the sounds of the accident and called the police, and advised ambulances would be needed.

The next morning, the photo on the front page of the *Jonesboro Sun* newspaper stunned everyone as they looked at the horrific scene of the accident. The driver of the other truck, Charlie Chandler, walked away from the accident with only a few cuts and bruises.

The article reported that all three teenagers were hospitalized, with one in critical condition. Andy, Lizzie J. and Maggie had all been thrown from the cab of the truck. Andy had landed on the asphalt roadway, and only inches away Lizzie J. had come to rest in the mud, like Maggie. Andy was in a coma with severe head trauma. After being taken to Jonesboro, he'd been transferred to Memphis to a larger hospital.

Jake and J.D. slept late on Sunday morning. A loud knock on the dorm room door brought both guys to their feet in an instant.

"Jake! It's me, your dad! Open the door!"

Jake opened the door and immediately knew something was wrong.

"What are you doing here, Dad? What's wrong?"

"I think you and J.D. both need to sit down. I have some bad news."

Jake felt sick in his gut, knowing something was seriously wrong, and each person he loved crossed his mind.

"Please, tell me!" Jake demanded.

"Andy, Lizzie J. and Maggie were in a terrible car accident last night as they drove home in the storm. Another truck crossed the center line and hit them head on. I didn't hear about it until this morning, and I wanted to get here to tell you before you saw the morning paper."

"Are they okay? How bad were they hurt? Where are they?" Jake asked.

"Maggie and Lizzie J. are at St. Bernard's, and I know their injuries aren't life-threatening. Andy wasn't so fortunate."

"No! Please no! Tell me he didn't die! Please ...."

"Jake, Andy has head injuries and he's in a coma. They transferred him to a Memphis hospital last night. I haven't heard anything else this morning. I know he's in critical condition. I'm so sorry, son."

J.D. sat down, his face drained of color with the shock of the news. Jake turned away from his dad and stared out the window at the people walking around outside, their world normal while his suddenly seemed shattered. He wondered how he'd slept so well during the night when one of his best friends was fighting for his life. Sal walked up behind his son and touched him on the shoulder. Jake turned, and as his dad hugged him both men cried.

"Why don't you and J.D. get dressed and we'll drive over to the hospital to get more information. I'm sure Maggie's parents are there and Lizzie J.'s grandparents, too."

Jake and J.D. were both silent on the drive to the hospital. Sal glanced over at his son from time to time and could see the pain in his features. He remembered watching Jake go through the pain of his mother's illness when he was a boy, and thought it was not nearly so painful to go through tragedy yourself as it was to watch your children experience pain and not be able to change it. Right now, Sal wanted to make this difficult time go away, rewind back to yesterday, and change the course that caused this terrible accident. Sal prayed for the parents and grandparents of the three teenagers and thanked God his son was sitting next to him, whole and healthy.

Jake's thoughts were chaotic and desperate. He was thankful his dad had come to get him and was by his side, and he realized as glad as he was to go away to college, he still needed him. That revelation surprised him. He was afraid of what he might see when they arrived at the hospital. They didn't know how badly injured Maggie and Lizzie J. were. He blamed himself for not driving Maggie home. He was angry at the man who caused the accident. Truthfully, he was mad at God. His angry turmoil surprised him. Jake had a lot of faith, but right now his faith was being tested.

J.D. was still stunned. He couldn't believe the weekend that was supposed to be so happy had turned into such a nightmare. He and Jake had been excited to be at college and on their own. All he could think right now was how much he wished his own parents were here. Suddenly, J.D. felt very young. He'd watched Jake go through the tragedy of his mother's illness and ultimate death but had never had a similar experience. Even though he didn't know Andy, Lizzie J. and Maggie like Jake did, he still considered them friends and felt like someone had punched him in his gut.

J.D. began to think about his attraction to Lizzie J. and his decision to bury those feelings because he liked and admired Andy. From time to time he had wondered if he could have a chance with her should something happen to break Lizzie J. and Andy apart. Guilt began to surface that somehow his feelings for her, and the wish that Andy were not in the picture, caused this accident.

Checking at the front desk, they were told Maggie had been released and Lizzie J. was still there. When they stepped out of the elevator they saw Maggie and her parents in the hallway outside Lizzie J.'s room.

Maggie began to cry when she saw Jake. She had a bandage on her forehead above her right eye, and other than scratches on her arms, no other injuries were visible.

"Maggie, I'm so sorry. I was so afraid for you. Why didn't you go home? Why are you still here?" Jake asked her.

"Because I wanted to see Lizzie J. before I leave. We're waiting while the nurses change her bandages. Her leg is broken and she has lots of cuts and scrapes. She hit part of the pavement, and I was thrown clear into the mud. I have to see her."

"Do you know anything about Andy?" Jake asked softly.

Jake's question caused Maggie to weep uncontrollably, so he drew her to him and held her close. The mood in the group became somber. Maggie's mom began to cry too, and Jake and J.D. realized how bad the accident had been.

"This morning we were told Andy is in a coma and his head injuries are critical. We met in the hospital chapel with Lizzie J.'s grandparents and prayed for him," Mr. Roberts said.

"I spoke with our pastor early this morning and the church was planning a prayer vigil. I know there are many prayers being offered up for Andy and prayers of thanksgiving for Lizzie J. and Maggie," Sal replied.

"Dad, do you think we can drive to Memphis and see Andy?"

"Jake, I know you want to see him, but I think under these circumstances we should wait until we can speak to his parents or get another update," Sal said.

"Can we wait until the nurses are finished with Lizzie J. so we can see her? I would feel much better if we could at least see her and talk to her," Jake pleaded.

"Of course we'll wait."

Lizzie J. had been heavily sedated to ease her pain, and also because she was so distressed about Andy. All Maggie could think as she looked at her best friend was how young and tiny she looked in that big hospital bed.

It took only one look for all of them to see Lizzie J.'s injuries were much worse than Maggie's. Being thrown into the mud without hitting the paved road had saved Maggie.

Sal suggested they pray, and the group gathered around Lizzie J. Maggie felt the same tugging at her heart that always made her want to run; this time she pushed those feelings away, grabbed Jake's hand and bowed her head. She loved Lizzie J. and Andy, and right now if there was a God, they needed Him to hear this prayer and heal her friends. Suddenly, she was thankful for the people in this room who believed so fervently in the God of the Bible.

Maggie was well enough to start classes on Monday, but Lizzie J. remained in the hospital for several days. As soon as Lizzie J. could travel, Maggie's mom drove them to Memphis to see Andy.

None of them were prepared for the scene in that hospital room. Andy looked lifeless, hooked up to machines that were doing the work for his body he could no longer do himself. Lizzie J., leaning on crutches with Maggie by her side, stopped right inside the door, seemingly stuck to the floor, both of them unable to go any further. How could this be Andy?

Lizzie J. was the first to move. She went over to his bedside and tentatively touched him. She stood still for a few minutes, her back to the others in the room. Slowly she turned as tears ran down her face, and she lost her balance and would have fallen to the floor except for Maggie and her mom rushing to catch her. They lowered her to a chair and she buried her face in her hands and sobbed.

Mrs. Houston knelt in front of Lizzie J. and gathered her into her arms and let her cry. Andy's mom had already shed many, many tears over the past several days, and she understood Lizzie J.'s shock on seeing him for the first time since the accident.

"Shh, it's okay, we must keep praying. Andy needs all of us to be strong. I'm so sorry you have to see him like this. We have to believe he'll get better," Mrs. Houston whispered.

"I knew he was seriously injured ... I didn't think he would look like this."

"Do you think you feel like going out to the hallway for a few minutes?" Mrs. Houston asked Lizzie J.

"Yes, I guess," Lizzie J. responded quizzically.

Once they were all outside of Andy's room, Mrs. Houston told them the doctors had advised them to be positive and upbeat because they weren't sure what Andy could hear and understand.

"Maybe if everyone could talk to him as if there was nothing seriously wrong and be encouraging, it might help him get better," Mrs. Houston explained.

"Oh, I didn't think about it that way. I'll try."

Lizzie J. opened the door and was again appalled by the whooshing noises of all the machines hooked up to Andy as he lay motionless in the hospital bed. The door closed quietly behind her and she was alone with him, the others waiting outside in the hallway, giving her privacy. Lizzie J. stood completely still, looking around the room, her eyes coming to rest on her best friend, the person she'd planned to spend the rest of her life with. When she felt faint again, she leaned on her crutches, closed her eyes and tried to visualize the way he'd looked their last night together.

"Hey Andy, it's me, Lizzie J. I've missed you and I've wanted so badly to come see you. I had to get better before the doctor would allow me to ride in the car for long. Classes started and everyone misses you. We talk about you a lot. They are praying for you, too—we need you to get better and come home. The guys down at the agricultural building can't keep things straight without you there. They told me to tell you to quit lying around in this bed and get back to work." Lizzie J. grew quiet. She reached out and touched his hair and then his face as her tears began to fall. She struggled to regain her composure. "Andy, I love you and I need you. Please try to get well."

Maggie had quietly slipped into the room. She came up behind Lizzie J. and placed her hands on her friend's shoulders. They stood together for several minutes, then turned away and left the room.

"I don't think he heard me. I'm sure of it. It's like he's not there anymore." Lizzie J. looked lost, and everyone around her could see her grief.

Maggie was sure those images would never leave her memory. It had been heart-wrenching to watch Lizzie J. talking to Andy, hoping the sound of her voice would get through to him and cause a response. That had not happened.

Andy's parents had been taking turns staying with him, and they looked exhausted and drained. They, too, had tried to get through to Andy, talking to him about the farm and playing his favorite music, to no avail. They, too, felt he was absent from his body, but they knew God was in the miracle business, so they kept praying.

CHAPTER EIGHT

New York City
1971

REMINISCING CAN LEAD to painful memories. Maggie had been trying to assuage her pain and loneliness at the piano. However, as she started to play the theme song from *Love Story*, which she loved, she began to think about the movie, and suddenly sadness overwhelmed her. Before she could stop the memories, tears were running down her face and she was once again transported back in time.

The accident in the terrible thunderstorm was a pivotal intersection in all their lives. It changed everyone and everything. Nothing was ever the same.

Maggie stopped playing; she couldn't bear to hear it any longer. As a professional pianist her repertoire was extensive, and sometimes she didn't even think about what she was playing and most of the time it didn't matter. Today it did.

She went into her bedroom and reached to the top shelf of her closet for her old photo album. The tears changed to smiles as she looked at the four of them sitting in Jake's 57 Chevy. She remembered the day they posed for the camera like it had happened yesterday. They were leaving to go to a movie, and she asked her mom to take the picture. They were young, happy and carefree.

Her breath caught in her throat as she looked at a photo of Andy and Lizzie J. sitting on the tractor at the farm. Lizzie J. was barefoot and wearing shorts, with her beautiful hair tucked up into one of Andy's old ball caps. They looked as though they belonged together.

She laughed out loud at the next photo of the four of them dressed in costume for a Halloween party. They didn't look scary, just silly. In farming country, going to a party dressed like pigs was predictable, she thought.

There were more photos and many that didn't include Jake. A class picture, taken when Maggie, Lizzie J. and Andy were in second grade, showed all three of them missing front teeth. Maggie was already several inches taller than Lizzie J., her freckles standing out like specks of dirt, her knees knobby and her hair in pigtails.

Maggie smiled as she looked at Andy. Somehow, even as a second grader, he looked like a farmer. Lizzie J. was a cute petite little girl, and though the old picture was in black and white Maggie could envision her beautiful blue eyes. Just a year later the two would announce that someday they were getting married.

Maggie reluctantly closed the album and stored it back on the top shelf of her closet, out of sight. She glanced out the window as she returned to the piano. She remembered Lizzie J. begging her to play her favorite melody, over and over. "Please Maggie, play it one more time, I want to practice." Then Lizzie J. would walk down the pretend aisle while Maggie played the Wedding March. Andy and Lizzie J. had been married many times in the living room of Maggie's house when they were growing up. Andy was never there, because people in pretend play never are.

Maggie finished playing with a flourish, turned around and said, "there you go, Lizzie J., that was for you." No one was there to hear the music or Maggie's words, and the memories from her past assaulted her throughout the long day. She was lonely.

CHAPTER NINE

Lake City, Arkansas
1963

THE SCHOOL GYMNASIUM was filled to capacity, standing room only. There was no other place in town large enough for the funeral of Andy Houston.

It had been two long weeks since the tragic accident. His family and friends had no chance to say goodbye because Andy never woke up from the coma. He'd left home on Saturday evening a happy, healthy young man with his life planned and his future bright. He was the oldest child of Alex and Mary Houston, and had been a model son and sibling to his two sisters and younger brother.

Lizzie J. and her grandparents were invited to sit with the family. Lizzie J.'s broken leg was in a cast up to her hip, and she struggled to sit comfortably in one of the chairs on the gym floor. The bruises had faded, and the cuts that required stitches were now healing as well. The worst injury she'd suffered was her broken heart, and it was the most visible. She'd been unable to stop crying as the grief consumed her. The future had been stolen from her, and she wrestled with wondering why. She fought going to sleep because she dreamed of Andy, and when she first came awake, everything seemed the same until she remembered the reality of her life now.

Maggie and her parents were seated behind the family. The stitches had been removed from the cut above Maggie's right eye, the scar still red and raw. She'd experienced a complete range of emotions since the accident. She'd settled on anger.

This God they had prayed to after the accident had been completely absent as far as Maggie could tell. Before, she'd had doubts; now she felt sure there was a God because of her rage. Why would she be so mad if there was no God and nobody was in control of this world and things only happened by chance? When she thought about it, she became angrier. Why did God allow this to happen?

While most everyone had tears of grief as they sang the old hymn *"Amazing Grace,"* Maggie felt her heart harden. She'd witnessed no grace during this tragic time, and while the others sang, she silently scoffed.

Jake had considered himself a believer with a firm faith in God. Now, doubt flooded his soul. What good would or could come from taking Andy at such a young age?

J.D. had gone home to Marianna the weekend after the accident and returned for the funeral. He'd suddenly felt the need to be with his family and worship with them. His faith and beliefs also had been shaken, and he needed help to accept what had happened.

Death was supposed to happen to old people, not teenagers. If this could happen to Andy, could it possibly happen to one of them, too? Like most young people, they thought they had many, many years before they would ever think about dying. They were alarmed when they had to acknowledge that their own death could come at any time.

Jake had talked with Maggie about seeking God's plan for her music, and he knew she didn't actually understand. Now he wondered if he understood that concept himself.

The minister's words at the funeral service gave them a different perspective on life. *Psalm 138:8: The Lord will fulfill his purpose for me. Lord, your love is eternal; do not abandon the work of your hands.* After reading this verse, he went on to explain God has a purpose for each one of us, and when our purpose is finished our life on this earth is done. We look at earthly lives and measure in time how long we think one should inhabit this place. God, however, works in the big picture of eternity. *Isaiah 55:8–9: "For My thoughts are not your thoughts, and your ways are not My ways." This is the Lord's declaration. "For as Heaven is higher than earth, so My ways are higher than your ways, and My thoughts than your thoughts."*

Each person at the funeral had to come to terms with the fact that regardless of their relationship to Andy Houston, the plans God had for them, from this day forward, didn't include Andy. Each one had to move on. They would grieve and God would comfort them, and someday sweet memories would surface and they would be surprised to realize their grief had subsided. The four friends Andy left behind matured in a lot of ways because of his passing, and each had a new appreciation for life, but in different ways.

Everything changed. Lizzie J.'s physical injuries healed and were no longer visible. But her emotional injuries surfaced and became obvious in her features. She'd believed she knew what

God wanted for her life; now she questioned why she'd believed that. Instead of being angry at God, she began to seek Him. She wanted to *know* her purpose in this life.

Maggie went in a completely different direction, much to Jake's disappointment. Maggie now believed there was a God, but she wanted nothing to do with Him or His church. Jake could no longer even bring up the subject; she was emphatic she didn't want to hear it.

With their parents' help, both J.D. and Jake were strengthened in their belief of a loving God, and the scriptures read at Andy's funeral settled deep inside their hearts. Our days are ordained by God and when they are finished, they are finished. Both of them were determined to live their lives honorably. Andy had lived honorably, so as somewhat of a tribute to their friend, they were determined to honor God in everything they did. They knew they weren't perfect, but they knew they could rely on God's Word to guide them through this earthly life.

The change experienced by the four young people was in fact an acceleration of the life each was already living. With more purpose, the three believers grew more committed to their faith, and the lost one pulled further and further away.

The other driver in the accident, Charlie Chandler, changed too. He had lived in Lake City for only a few years and was a loner. No one knew where he'd come from or anything about him. He would sometimes play a game of pool at the local pool hall next door to the post office. He wasn't mean or unfriendly, just quiet and a little mysterious.

The investigation determined that both vehicles crossed the line into the opposite lane. Since both were at fault, no charges were filed. Anyone who came in contact with Charlie saw his deep suffering over the death of Andy Houston. Most people figured his grief was payment enough. The vehicles were at the mercy of the storm, and neither driver could have changed the circumstances.

At the funeral, Charlie had slipped inside the back door of the church and tried to be invisible. He was grieving. Although he knew in his heart it was an accident, he felt so responsible. Not having any children of his own, he could only imagine what Andy's parents were going through. And watching Lizzie J. was heart-wrenching. A long time ago he'd also lost the love of his life, so he knew what she was feeling. He'd always believed in God — now he began to feel the need to know Him. On Sundays he started slipping into the back pew of the church after everyone was seated, and left before the service ended so he wouldn't have to speak to anyone.

Many people didn't know Charlie had paid a visit to Andy's parents and been so relieved to know they didn't blame him for their son's death. He was stunned when they welcomed him into their home and treated him like a friend. He would not have been able to visit church without their forgiveness. He came knowing they had forgiven him for any part he'd had in the accident. He never spoke to any of the teens, though, and tried to avoid eye contact with them.

One Sunday he was quietly leaving church and was almost to the street when he heard his name.

"Mr. Chandler, wait a minute. Can I talk to you?"

Before he turned, Charlie knew it was the young lady who had been Andy's girlfriend. His heart sank as he realized he couldn't get away.

"Sure," Charlie replied hesitantly.

"I want you to know I'm not angry with you. You won't look my way and I know you've been in church the past couple of weeks. I've been watching you slip out early so I was ready to follow you out this morning," Lizzie J. explained.

Charlie hadn't seen her up close and was surprised at the periwinkle color of her eyes. It was not what one expected to see with such raven black hair. He felt awkward and didn't know what to say.

"I'm so sorry about the accident. I see the cast is off—how is your leg?"

"It's fine. I believe you're sorry about what happened, but I also know it wasn't totally your fault. I remember the accident as though it just happened. The storm came on so fast and Andy couldn't see the road." Tears welled up in Lizzie J's eyes and she struggled to maintain her composure.

Charlie watched her, and it made him think about the one person he'd loved and lost so long ago, who had suddenly disappeared from his life. The pain he saw in this young lady's eyes brought to the surface the memories of his own pain he'd experienced back then.

"Thank you for telling me this. If I could change things, I would."

"We know." Lizzie J. reached out and touched the man on his arm. She felt such compassion for his grief and hoped he could forgive himself and realize it was simply an unavoidable accident on a darkened highway in a fierce storm.

"I've got to go. Thanks again. I hope the days will get better and better."

"Okay … well … goodbye," Lizzie J. said as she watched him walk away. She never knew his abrupt departure was so she couldn't see the tears running down his face as he turned away from her.

CHAPTER TEN

*L*IFE MOVED ON. Maggie and Lizzie J. were high school seniors, and like the rest of the class were experiencing their senior year with a new perspective on life. Andy Houston had been a classmate to almost everyone since kindergarten, and his death left a huge hole in every activity.

Lizzie J. continued her search for more of God. Maggie continued to run from Him, and as a result, she focused on her music even more.

Jake and J.D. settled into college life. All the instructions Jake's mom had given him before her death became even more important as he realized how crucial it is to make the right decisions.

J.D.'s attraction to Lizzie J. dissipated since Andy's death. Before the accident, he often had to suppress thoughts of her. Now, he would go for days without thinking of her, and then only because Jake brought her name into their discussion for one reason or another.

As the semester ended for Christmas, J.D. headed home to Marianna. Jake went home to Lake City. Since the accident, he'd re-evaluated his feelings about his dad and Lillian and was ready to be around them. He also wanted to see Maggie.

"Dad, I'm home. Hello, anybody home?" Jake yelled as he went through the front door of his dad and Lillian's new house.

"Jake, is that you?" Lillian replied as she came from the kitchen with her apron on, drying her hands on a red-checkered dish cloth.

"Yep, it's me. Think you can put up with me for about a month?"

"Absolutely. We've been looking forward to it."

"This place looks great. It's hard to believe y'all moved in a couple of weeks ago," Jake said. Looking around, he realized they had new furniture in the living room.

Lillian noticed him taking in his surroundings, and she could tell he felt awkward and a little uncomfortable in this new house that he would never call home.

"I hope you don't mind — we took a lot of the furniture that belonged to your mom and dad to Marianna and gave it to Cara. Your dad was happy for her to have it, and felt it looked right at home in the house where you grew up," Lillian replied softly.

"Oh, no, that's fine. I'm happy to know it's back where it belongs, and I'm sure Cara appreciates having it. Thank you."

"Your dad and I thought we should start our new home with our own furniture. Your bedroom furniture is in the first room on the left at the top of the stairs. Of course, it's yours to take someday when you have a place of your own. For now you have a bedroom here anytime you want to come. Your dad is excited you'll be here for a whole month."

"Well, it's good to be here. I think I'll take my bags upstairs. When will Dad be home?" Jake asked.

"He said to tell you to come to the bank and he'll take you to lunch at Rogers Café. Friday is catfish day, remember?"

"Sounds great. I'm starving...you want to come?" Jake asked.

"I have some other things I need to do; you two go on and catch up. We'll have dinner together tonight and you're welcome to invite Maggie. We'll have plenty."

"Thanks. I'll call her."

Jake hoisted his bag onto his shoulder and started up the staircase. Everything smelled new — the wood floors, the curtains and even the walls had that new paint odor. The hallway floor was covered in plush wall-to-wall carpet, and Jake realized everything he'd seen was the best money could buy.

The first door on the left stood slightly ajar and Jake softly pushed it open with his foot. The room looked exactly the same as it had in Marianna and in the rental house he and his dad had shared. All the wall pictures were hung the same way and the picture of Maggie sat on his bedside table. Finally, something felt familiar, and Jake breathed a sigh of relief as he threw his bag onto the bed and sprawled out beside it.

It had been almost four months since Andy tragically died, and Jake still thought about calling him now and then. Living at college in Jonesboro had helped because it was a completely different routine.

Jake hadn't worked for Mr. Houston since the accident, and as hard as it might be, he knew he should visit Andy's family. He would have to drive out to the farm, and he wasn't sure he was ready for that trip. Too many memories.

He looked over at the picture of Maggie and was overwhelmed with desire to see her. First, he wanted to have lunch with his dad. He got up and opened the closet to find plenty of hangers for his clothes, then decided to wait until later to unpack. He was anxious to get to town. Lake City was a small town, and Main Street was the place to be—you could see almost everyone if you hung around long enough, especially during the lunch hour.

In the hallway, Jake was stunned when he noticed the family picture from long ago hanging beside several others of himself and Cara when they were younger. He figured those memories had been stored away, and was pleasantly surprised that Lillian chose to display them. Since the master bedroom was downstairs and only Jake and Cara would ever occupy these upstairs bedrooms, it seemed to be the perfect place. Jake felt it was a message from Lillian that though she was married to his dad, she wasn't trying to take his mom's place. He liked her even more for that.

MAGGIE WAS COUNTING down the minutes until the last bell of the day sounded. Her Christmas break would be only two weeks, unlike Jake's; he would be home for a month before his classes resumed in January. She knew he'd be waiting for her, and the closer it got to three o'clock the more excited she became.

All week Maggie had worried about Lizzie J. She knew Lizzie J. would feel excluded if she and Jake were together the whole weekend. The last couple of months Maggie had begun to feel pulled between the two of them. She loved both Jake and Lizzie J. and wanted to be there for them, but with Andy gone the foursome was now an awkward threesome.

Maggie's problem solved itself, however. Lizzie J. was gone with her grandparents for the weekend to visit relatives in Mississippi. Maggie felt a sense of freedom as she threw her books into her locker, slung her purse over her shoulder and hurried down the hall, avoiding eye contact with anyone who might delay her. She pushed open the door and the first thing she saw was his candy apple red Chevy. It was a warm day for the fifteenth of December, and Jake was leaning against the back of his car waiting for her.

She felt the desire for him assault her senses. They'd dated for almost two years, and abstaining from sex had been Jake's belief, not hers. Maggie had recently turned eighteen and Jake would be twenty on his next birthday. He was no longer a lanky young man of seventeen. She watched him walk toward her and noticed how his body had changed. In a good way, she thought, and no longer able to contain her excitement, she ran to him and threw her arms around him. Jake picked her up and swung her around. He didn't kiss her—there were too many teachers around, so he would have to wait. He opened the car door for her, then went around and slipped into the driver's seat.

"I've missed you. Let's go for a drive." Jake took her hand and pulled her closer to him.

"I'd love to take a ride with you. Maybe we'll run out of gas or have a flat tire," Maggie teased.

"Sorry lady, I have a full tank of gas and I know how to change a tire. However, we might get stuck in the sand down on the prairie—now wouldn't that be a shame!" Jake teased back as he felt his own desires rage out of control. He would marry her today if he could talk her into it. They were both old enough to get a marriage license. Then he could have all of her. At times like this he wondered how he would ever have enough self control for both of them. He knew Maggie didn't understand his reasons for waiting until marriage, and anytime he asked, she would be a willing partner.

They didn't get stuck in the sand, but they did stop on a side road. They did get a kiss, actually a few kisses, then things got out of control. Jake was the one to stop it, and he was the one to start the car and head back into town. Neither one spoke, and Jake found himself repeating *Psalm 119:9 over and over: How can a young man keep his way pure? By keeping Your word.* It was one of the first verses he'd memorized, and it had come in handy since he'd met Maggie.

"I love you Jake," Maggie said softly as she stroked his arm.

"Aw, Maggie Mae, you know I love you too, and you know I would marry you today. And before you go getting all mad, you know you feel the same way. Why won't you talk about getting married? You only have a few months of school left. We could get married and live on campus together in Jonesboro."

"My parents would kill me, and your dad would probably have a heart attack. You know we can't get married. Please don't ruin today talking about something we can do nothing about right now."

"I know we can't get married right now, it's just that ever since Andy died I keep thinking we need to live now! I don't want to be without you, even for a day. Each day that goes by and I can't see you, touch you, and love you, feels wasted."

Maggie was quiet and didn't respond. Jake looked over and saw a single tear slip down her face. He could feel his own tears trying to surface; the emotion of Andy dying was still so raw. Jake reached over, squeezed her hand, and suddenly their physical passion for each other subsided, but mentally and emotionally they were closer than ever.

They spent many days together during the Christmas

season of 1963. Maggie kept her secret from Jake, though it was difficult. She loved him, but she still held on to her dream. Her music still occupied half of her heart and soul, and Jake was solidly entrenched in the other half. Maggie still didn't understand why she was always so torn between the two. Jake knew why she struggled. Her anger still burned toward God, and she still wanted no part of Him.

CHAPTER ELEVEN

New York City
1971

IT WAS ONE O'CLOCK in the afternoon. Maggie had been playing music for so long she'd lost track of time. When she noticed the framed certificate of her graduation from the Manhattan School of Music on the side table, she was abruptly brought back to the present.

She rose from the piano bench and walked to the window. The snow had stopped and there was a slight break in the clouds. The weak winter sun was somewhat visible, as if mustering up the energy to shine and stop this nor'easter that had sabotaged her Christmas. Maggie laughed at the thought.

Realizing she was hungry, she went into the kitchen and made a sandwich. Coming back to her chair by the window, she promised herself she would call Lizzie J. as soon as she finished eating. Lizzie J. would be disappointed, but Maggie knew her house would be full of friends and family tonight and tomorrow. Lizzie J. was happily married and had the cutest little two-year-old girl Maggie had ever seen. She still felt so honored that Lizzie J. had named her daughter Maggie.

Thinking of Lizzie J. and how happy she was caused Maggie to remember the Christmas that Jake wanted to get married during his first year of college.

They had been dating for two years, and it was the second time Maggie had kept something from him. It wasn't a minor thing, either, and became a turning point in their relationship. Maggie tried to tell him several times during those weeks in December, but she could never find the words.

Maggie glanced over at the certificate again. She was still proud of her accomplishment, though it didn't seem so important today. She'd been ecstatic when first accepted to the Manhattan School of Music. That was the secret she'd kept from Jake. Instead of hearing from her that she was going away to college, he heard the news from someone in town while he was home on Christmas break. He was angry with her and also disappointed that she'd not told him, and that made her feel even worse. After all this time, thinking about it still caused her distress.

Two years ago, when she bought this expensive apartment few people could afford, having made a name for herself in the genre she'd pursued for so long, she thought she would finally experience true happiness. Thinking back over the past two years, she was not happy, not even remotely happy. Since her daddy had died, Maggie had begun to slowly know in her heart that she was missing something vital in her life. Her soul felt empty, as though she was dry inside . . . thirsty. Maggie knew in her innermost being that God was the vital something she was missing.

In a bookstore a few months earlier, Maggie found herself in the section on religion. As she tried to move away and find the book she'd come for, she felt as if a mighty force held her back. She began to look at the books and was surprised at how many there were, on many different subjects. Whatever you were going through, it seemed there was a book to help you through it. There was even a Christian fiction section. Maggie was amazed. When she left, she was the proud owner of a Bible and a book about finding your purpose in life.

She began to read the Bible and discovered passages that sounded like things Jake had said to her through the years, those conversations that always caused her anxiety, fear, and most of the time, anger. She began to understand Jake's deep faith, and Lizzie J.'s too—even through all her trials. Maggie found herself hungry for the words she was reading and longed to find the strong faith her friends had enjoyed for years.

She could have married Jake anytime, up until two years ago. Is that what she was missing? If she'd married Jake, would she have found God? Maggie doubted that. Before she'd started reading the Bible, she thought she needed counseling. She'd felt completely confused, and thinking back over the past several years, she realized she'd been that way since Jake walked into her life.

Maggie suddenly lost her appetite, so she rose from her chair and took her plate with the half uneaten sandwich back into the kitchen. She was trying to get her emotions under control before she called Lizzie J. They'd been best friends since they started school, and Maggie knew hearing Lizzie J.'s voice might push her over the edge. Maggie didn't want to ruin Christmas for Lizzie J., and she didn't want anyone to feel sorry for her, not even her best friend.

Returning to the living room, she sat in her chair by the window and reached for the phone on the side table. The clouds finally parted and revealed a brilliant blue winter sky, and within seconds the sun burst through, directly overhead, shining on the fresh snow. Immediately the scene lifted her spirits. There was hope, she thought — maybe the flights would begin by tomorrow after all.

Maggie dialed the familiar phone number and waited for an answer.

"Hello," Lizzie J. answered.

"Merry Christmas! It's me, Maggie."

"Hey, I thought you would be in the air by now. Was your flight delayed?"

"Do none of you watch the news? You haven't heard about this huge snowstorm that hit last night here in the city? I'm snowed in."

"Liar, Liar, pants on fire! You are not — I know you. You probably got out early and now there isn't anyone at the airport to pick you up," Lizzie J. scoffed.

"Hey, watch out calling me names. You know I don't lie! Honestly, Lizzie J., I'm in my apartment and I'm snowed in. The sun came out awhile ago, though, so hopefully if the storm has passed they can begin to clear the runways. I haven't checked with the airline yet, but I'm hoping for a flight tomorrow, even if it's a late one. I'm so sorry I will miss having dinner with you tonight."

"I thought you were teasing me. You're serious aren't you? Oh, Maggie, you'll be all alone on Christmas. That doesn't seem fair. Are you okay?"

"Don't go feeling sorry for me or I might start crying."

"No, no, don't cry. We'll have Christmas when you get here whether it's tomorrow or a week from now. Little Maggie is only two — she won't know the difference." Lizzie J. tried to sound encouraging and not let her disappointment come through. She wanted so badly to get Maggie and Jake together, and now her plans had gone awry again.

"I would love to be there and see her face in the morning when she opens her gifts. She'll love that. I have a special gift for her and it will be like having Christmas over again. Sure hope I can get out of here sometime tomorrow. Of course, so will everyone who is snowed in."

"Well Maggie will miss you and so will her brother. You know he is a little bit in love with you. Like most little boys, he acts completely innocent and says he has no idea why I would say that," Lizzie J. laughed. Maggie noticed the change in her friend's voice when she spoke about her children.

"Tell them both that I have special presents for them and as soon as a plane can leave this big city, I'll be headed home," Maggie replied. The thought of missing Christmas Eve dinner at Lizzie J.'s was so disappointing.

"Call me as soon as you know when you'll be here. I love you and we can't wait to see you!"

"Love you too! Hug the kids, okay?"

"You know I will. Bye now."

"Thanks, bye. Call you soon."

After the call was disconnected, Maggie sat holding the phone, reluctant to face the remainder of the day alone. She thought about how different Lizzie J.'s life was from her own. Lizzie J. had two children she loved beyond measure. Both had their mother's beautiful blue eyes, and each had features from their father, too. Lizzie J. was blissfully, happily married.

It hadn't always been that way. Maggie could vividly remember the year Andy died and all that had transpired in the months after. Those memories still haunted Maggie from time to time. All alone today, her memories seemed to be everywhere she turned, and with the sound of Lizzie J.'s voice resounding in her mind, she remembered that difficult Christmas of 1963.

CHAPTER TWELVE

Lake City, Arkansas
1963

A S MAGGIE AND JAKE drove through the subdivision where Jake's dad had built his new house, she noticed the many Christmas decorations. Even though it was only five o'clock, the falling darkness accented the Christmas lights, transforming the neighborhood into a scene beautiful enough to grace the front of a Christmas card.

Jake had asked Maggie to have dinner with him tonight. He wanted to be with her, and he also hoped her presence would help to ease any awkwardness. The thought of staying in the new house for an entire month made Jake feel like an intruder. Though he had lived with his dad and Lillian in the old house, this new house was theirs, and he felt like a visitor.

The dinner went well and Jake began to relax, deciding maybe the next month wouldn't be so bad after all. He was happy to be back in Lake City where he would continually see faces he knew and had missed. When his dad and Lillian said goodnight and retired to their bedroom for the evening, Jake and Maggie had a chance to be alone.

"We didn't talk about Lizzie J. today. How is she?" Jake asked.

"Okay, I guess. When Andy first died, all she wanted to do was go to church, study her Bible and be with his family as much as possible. In the last few weeks she seems different … changed. I've asked her about it, and even though we are more like sisters than friends, she won't talk to me," Maggie answered.

"I can't imagine the feelings she's been having for the last four months. I know they loved each other and were also best friends. She actually lost two different relationships."

"Maybe visiting relatives in Mississippi will take her mind off things for at least the weekend. I know she's dreaded Christmas this year. It was always her favorite time of year, and she and Andy always gave each other special gifts." Maggie's voice grew soft, and Jake noticed her eyes becoming dark with emotion.

"Let's change the subject. I've missed you and I want to know what's going on with you. Have you sent all the paperwork to the college for your admission? You only have a few months of school left and I can't wait until you are on campus with me," Jake said, his voice rising with excitement.

At the mention of college, Maggie felt her heart race. She'd known for a long time she'd been accepted to the Manhattan School of Music in New York. She knew she should've told Jake a long time ago, but she'd locked the words away and was struggling to set them free. Maggie knew Jake wanted her to go to Arkansas State and be with him. She wanted so badly to pursue a musical education at the most prestigious school that would accept her.

Maggie got up from the couch and walked over to the Christmas tree. A moment ago she was about to cry thinking about what they'd experienced the past few months, and now she was full of dread and fear. She had let Jake think she was planning to attend ASC. She hadn't outright lied about it, but she'd been able to skirt the issue, much like she'd always done about their relationship. Her mind raced as she tried to come up with yet another conversation that would protect her secret for a little longer.

"I did send in the paperwork, and I'm sure it will all work out. I want to be with you and enjoy Christmas break. Can't we talk about this later?"

"Come back and sit with me. It's getting late and I'll have to take you home soon." Jake felt the familiar sensation in the pit of his stomach that always came when deep down he knew Maggie was trying not to discuss whatever she didn't want to face. He loved her so much, yet constantly felt as though their relationship was held together with strands of thread. He knew he might never have her, yet he continued on, striving to get her commitment. She had deftly avoided the college issue and that worried him. As usual, he decided not to think about that right now. She was here and he was happy.

Maggie sat down, scooted closer to Jake and rested her head on his shoulder. She thought about how much she missed him when he was away at school, and how much she loved him. She knew he would be disappointed to know she was going to college in New York, but she felt confident she could make him understand. After all, she'd finally convinced her parents this was an opportunity of a lifetime, so surely she could manage Jake. Not tonight, though. Maybe she would tell him tomorrow.

"How is J.D.?" Maggie asked suddenly, trying to change the subject.

"He's fine. He was happy to go home for a month. I think living in the dorm in Jonesboro and being somewhat on his own wasn't as great as he'd thought. Actually it wasn't that great for me either."

"None of us had a great start to the school year. If the accident hadn't happened, everyone would be in a very different place right now," Maggie replied.

"I should go out to the Houstons' farm this weekend and visit with them. Have you seen them or has Lizzie J. mentioned them to you? I can't imagine the grief their whole family has experienced."

"For a month or two after Andy died, Lizzie J. spent a lot of time with the Houstons. That's changed too. I'm telling you Jake, something is wrong with Lizzie J. I'm worried about her. It seems her whole personality is different; it's almost as if she is withdrawing from everyone."

"I think the first few weeks after my mom died I was a little bit in shock, and I do remember that the grief became overwhelming. Maybe that's what's happening with Lizzie J.," Jake said.

They were both silent for a few minutes, each lost in their own thoughts. Even though a few minutes ago they'd tried to change the subject, here it was again. Death...

To Maggie, it seemed to have permeated every facet of her life. If she was at school, Andy's absence was a void that couldn't be filled. When she looked at Lizzie J., it was as though half of her was missing. It had been Andy and Lizzie J. since the third grade; now it was just Lizzie J. Maggie dreamed about the accident and Andy's funeral, and whenever she dreamed about it or thought about death, her anger was aroused again toward the God she wanted no part of.

Jake never knew when the yearning for his mother would come to the surface. It seemed to always be at the most inopportune times. Here it was again. He was with Maggie, the lights low, the Christmas tree beautifully decorated, no parents around, and all he could think was how much he missed his mom. Their romantic mood had dissipated.

"What are you thinking about?" Maggie finally asked.

Jake didn't answer and Maggie turned to look at him. His eyes were filled with tears as he struggled to control his emotions. Not wanting to break down and cry, he abruptly stood and walked to the window with his back to her.

Maggie misinterpreted his sadness. She had no idea how much he still missed his mom; it was never discussed.

"Jake, are you okay?" Maggie asked as she came up behind him and wrapped her arms around him.

"Yeah, I'm okay. Talking about Lizzie J. and thinking she might be grieving made me think of those months and years after my mom died. It was a tough time for our family. I know you might not want to hear about that, though."

"If you want to tell me about it, then I want to hear about it."

They stood together for several minutes, Jake staring out the window and Maggie behind him with her arms wrapped tight around him and her head on his back. Maggie was aware Jake was letting her into a place where only his family and J.D. had ever been allowed.

"Some days I don't think about it, and others are especially difficult, even after all these years," Jake said, pulling Maggie around beside him.

"I have no way to understand what you've been through. All I can do is try to imagine what my life would be like without my mom or my dad. It makes me want to cry to think about it," Maggie replied softly. "How long was she sick?"

"About three years. At first I didn't realize how serious it was. They told me she would be in the hospital for surgery, and that she would be okay. Of course, at the time that's what they believed."

"I can't remember either of my parents ever being sick—maybe a cold or stomach bug, never anything serious." Maggie remained completely still beside him, hoping to encourage him to keep sharing.

"I remember when she began to have serious conversations with me. I'd recently turned twelve and started to go through puberty. I think she willed herself to live that year to give me all the information about life that she'd previously thought would happen through my teen years. Slowly, over that year, I started to realize she might not live." A single tear coursed slowly down Jake's face. He was transported back in time with his memories that he'd been unable to share with Maggie until tonight.

"What were some of the things she told you?" Maggie asked, sensing his need to talk. She realized Jake was being completely vulnerable, and she wanted to understand the things that had happened to him to make him such a spiritual person. She wanted to understand how, after losing his mom and now a good friend, his faith seemed to be stronger than ever. She, however, remained angry. Tonight, she was determined to hear him and not voice her opinion or show her bitterness.

"Are you sure you want to know? Some things you may not understand, and usually you don't want to hear about it."

"You can tell me anything. I might not understand, but I promise not to do anything but listen," Maggie said with conviction.

Jake took her hand and guided her back to the couch. They

were quiet again, Jake thinking about where he wanted to start in his story.

"Do you remember I told you my mom called me Jakey when I was little?"

"Sure, I remember. That was the day we met and you told me she'd died. After our conversation was interrupted, when the class started, that was all I could think about."

"When I was about nine, I began to be embarrassed if she called me that in front of other people. I'd give anything to hear her call me that today. Her voice always became tender and gentle when she called me Jakey."

"My mom always tells me that no other person can love you like your parents, and that one day I'll understand when I become a mom."

"Yeah, I think that's probably true," Jake replied.

"What was she like?" Maggie asked.

"Since I'm truly biased about what she was like, I'm probably not the right person to describe her," Jake said and smiled for the first time.

"I don't care what other people might have thought. I want to know about her from you."

"The first thing I think about is how much my mom loved Jesus. My earliest memories include listening to her tell Bible stories and sing hymns when she tucked me in at night. I cut my teeth on the pews at church." Jake laughed at what he said and so did Maggie.

"So you've always gone to church?"

"Yes, but it's more than that. My mom and dad lived each day as followers of Jesus. It was a way of life in our home. Have you ever heard the saying the family that prays together stays together? We were that family."

"I don't know what that's like. Even though my parents are wonderful people, they aren't religious."

"It's hard to explain because, honestly, it isn't about religion."

"I don't understand—what do you mean it's not about religion?" Maggie asked, sounding confused.

"Maggie, people can be religious about a lot of things. Being religious doesn't mean much, but being a believer in Jesus as the Savior of the world means everything."

Maggie had heard this before and it always caused her anxiety. Tonight, she was determined to hear Jake.

"Well, I guess you're right. I'm religious about practicing the piano. Is that what you mean?" Maggie asked.

"Exactly. It can be a lot of things for different people. It's anything that becomes more important than worshiping our Creator."

"So what did your mom teach you?"

"That God loves me more than she did. She told me there were times when she didn't know how that was possible, but she knew it was true. She explained that God has a plan for my life because he loves me so much, and if I follow God's plan, life will be much easier. Not perfect, but a life lived with the assurance that God would help me through the difficult times."

"That sounds pretty deep. How do you know it's true?"

"By reading the Bible, God's Word; I call the Bible the "how to" book on living life."

"What else did she teach you?" Maggie asked.

"To be kind to others and always try to see things from the other person's perspective. She had a gentle spirit."

"She sounds wonderful. She must have been loved by a lot of people," Maggie replied.

"She told me she'd not always been kind. I think she grew up with parents who spoiled her, and she said she'd been selfish until she became a believer and began to study about Jesus and His teaching. I remember telling her I sure was glad that had happened before I came along," Jake said and laughed.

"Do you actually believe people change when they believe in Jesus?"

"If you believe and follow His teachings, absolutely. It means living each day striving to do what Jesus would want us to do, not what we want," Jake explained.

They became quiet again, Maggie trying to grasp an understanding of all the things Jake had told her, and Jake trying not to give her too much at one time.

Maggie was wondering if God loved *her*. She sure had been mad at Him over the past few months. God had always seemed like someone big and scary out there in the Heavens somewhere. She'd never thought that God might love her. And to love her more than her mom and dad was hard to understand. She *knew* Jake believed every word he was saying to her.

"I remember you told me that you believed God would direct you to the person you should spend the rest of your life with. Why do you think that person is me?" Maggie suddenly asked.

Her question caught Jake off guard, and he didn't answer right away. After thinking about it for a few seconds, he hoped his answer would make sense to her.

"I love you, Maggie, almost from the first moment I saw you. Of course, when I saw you walk out onto the stage in the Christmas program, your physical beauty caught my attention. Then when you began to play the piano I was mesmerized by your talent. I realized you had a God-given ability for music.

The beauty that is inside of you comes out when you play," Jake said.

"Thank you for all those compliments. Now, can you answer my question?" Maggie pressed.

"Honestly, I don't know if you are the person God has for me. I know that I love you and I hope it's you. I also know circumstances change, people change, and I'll wait on the future to see how our relationship unfolds," Jake told her softly.

"Why do you think God cares about who you marry? Did your mom tell you that?" Maggie asked.

"One of the verses she taught me during the year she was giving me so many instructions was *Jeremiah 29:11–13: "For I know the plans I have for you,"* this is the Lord's declaration, *"plans for your welfare, not for disaster, to give you a future and a hope. You will call to Me and come and pray to Me, and I will listen to you. You will seek Me and find Me when you search for Me with all your heart."*

"You actually know that without looking it up in the Bible?" Maggie asked, astonished.

"Yeah, I do. Actually I've memorized several verses that are important to me," Jake admitted. "That's one of my favorites, though."

Maggie was quiet again, and Jake knew she was thinking about what he'd said. The words were powerful and he hoped they would help Maggie understand why he believed that God loved her more than anyone.

"But I don't understand. It says He has plans for your welfare and not for disaster. When your mother died, I would think that was really harmful. And Andy's death harmed his family and Lizzie J. and a lot of other people. How can you explain that?" Maggie asked.

"That verse also says He will give us hope and a future. The hope is that I will see my mom and Andy again someday in Heaven, and that in spite of losing them, I still have a future. If I pray and call upon God to help me, He will guide me to make right choices. Maggie, these verses and these teachings have been instilled in me since I was a little boy. You can't expect to understand everything the first time you hear it," Jake advised.

"Earlier today you tried to convince me to marry you, and now you say you aren't sure I am the one God has for you."

"Yeah, well, I'm human and I don't always wait on God. I stop thinking about what He might want for me and hurry to grab the things I want right now. You are the person I want. Maybe God is using your hesitancy about marrying me to keep me from making a mistake. Maggie, all the people in your life are there for one reason or another. Some journey alongside you for years, others for months, some only for moments, but they all serve a purpose."

"Lizzie J. told me she'd always thought God's plan for her life was to marry Andy and raise a family together. When he died, she told me she was confused about why she'd been so sure about that."

"That's where faith comes in. Trusting that what happens to us might not be what we want, and having faith that someday we'll look behind us and see a bigger plan," Jake explained.

"I wish I could have met your mom. What was her name? All I've ever known was Mrs. Martin."

"Her given name was Sadie Elizabeth. My dad always called her Sadie Beth," Jake told her softly.

"That's a beautiful name. She sounds like someone I would have liked. Do you have a picture of her that I could see?"

"Sure, I'll be right back."

Jake hurried up the stairs and removed the family photo hanging in the hallway right outside his bedroom.

"This was taken the year before she died and it's the way I remember her," Jake said as he handed the photo over to Maggie. She studied the picture and the people in it. Jake was eleven and his sister Cara sixteen. They looked happy, all of them. Maggie knew that Jake's mom had already been sick for a couple of years when the photo was taken. She looked strong and confident. Without warning, Maggie began to cry. Her emotions took both her and Jake by surprise.

"Hey, it's okay, don't cry," Jake consoled.

"I'm sorry. It seems so sad. I'm looking at this happy family that was torn apart only a year after this was taken. I'm only a little older now than Cara was at that time. And I think how much she must've missed your mom on her wedding day. That's the most important day in a girl's life."

"Cara would be the first to tell you it was hard, and she'd also tell you some good came out of that terrible time as well."

"What was that?" Maggie asked with disbelief.

"Mark," Jake replied.

"Her husband?" Maggie asked.

"Yeah, that's when they met," Jake said.

"How did they meet?" Maggie asked, confused.

"When Mom was in the hospital in Memphis, Mark was working there part-time while he was in college at Memphis State. He was an orderly, transporting patients from place to place."

"So, what happened?"

"I'd seen Mark several times while I was visiting Mom. It seemed Cara was never there when Mark would come to take Mom for one test or another. Then one day he came into the room as usual and stopped in his tracks when he saw Cara. Those of us in the room could tell there was an instant attraction between them," Jake smiled, as he remembered that day.

"Sounds like love at first sight."

"Well I don't think I believe in love at first sight, though I do believe in attraction at first sight. That's how I felt about you the first day I saw you, remember?" Jake reminded her.

"Yeah, I remember," Maggie replied softly. "So did they start dating?"

"No, not right away. When Mark showed up at my mom's funeral, Cara knew he was a special person. Actually, he was more of a friend to her in the beginning. He was there during the grieving process and was patiently waiting until the day came that Cara could start to be happy again. Mark is a special, special man."

"So you are saying that if your mom hadn't been sick and in the hospital, Cara and Mark would never have met. And you believe God planned that?" Maggie asked.

"I believe God uses events in our lives to bring people together. God didn't make my mom sick or cause the accident that took Andy's life, but He did know those things were going to happen," Jake explained.

"If you believe that, do you believe that you moved from Marianna to Lake City so we would meet?" Maggie asked.

"Maybe, but maybe not to marry you," Jake replied tentatively.

"For what then?"

"To share my faith with you and help you know how much God loves you."

Maggie was quiet...reflective. Jake wondered what she was thinking.

"I'm only one person in this huge world with so many people, and it's hard for me to believe God loves everyone in the whole world. How is that possible?" Maggie finally asked.

"Maggie, when you believe in God as the creator of the world, you begin to realize how magnificent He is. If God can create the world and every living thing in it, He can surely love all of us," Jake explained.

Their time alone was interrupted when they heard Jake's dad open his bedroom door, walk down the hall and enter the kitchen. They heard the refrigerator door open and close and a bar stool scrape against the wood floor. Their conversation was over. Tonight she'd allowed Jake to tell her about his relationship with God. She'd listened. Now, Maggie would have to decide if she believed the things Jake had shared with her.

CHAPTER THIRTEEN

T o Maggie it seemed the weekend went by way too quickly. However, she was ready to see Lizzie J. Maggie was genuinely worried about her friend and hoped the trip to visit relatives had lifted her spirits.

Since it was Christmas break, Maggie slept in on Monday morning. She woke up around nine and continued to snuggle down under the quilts, relishing the fact she didn't have to get dressed and go to school. The day was hers to do whatever she wished. She planned to ask her mom if she could invite Lizzie J. to go shopping in Jonesboro for Christmas gifts. Staying in her pajamas, eating a late breakfast and visiting with her mom was the order of the morning.

A soft knock on her bedroom door interrupted her thoughts and plans.

"Come in," Maggie said.

The door opened and her mom came into the room and sat on the side of Maggie's bed. Immediately, Maggie sensed something was wrong.

"What's wrong?" Maggie asked as she sat up and reached for a hair band on the nightstand. She searched her mom's face as she swept her hair out of her eyes and up into a ponytail. Suddenly, she was wide awake.

"Mrs. Raines called and wanted to talk to me about Lizzie J. this morning. I'm afraid I have some bad news."

"What do you mean bad news? Is Lizzie J. sick? I've been worried about her—I knew something wasn't right! What is it?" Maggie pleaded.

"Lizzie J. isn't sick, Maggie...she's pregnant."

Maggie struggled to comprehend her mom's words.

"That's not possible! Not for Lizzie J. She hasn't been dating or seeing anyone. Besides, Lizzie J. wouldn't do that—I know she wouldn't! Her Nanny told you that?" Maggie couldn't believe what her mom was saying, and she certainly didn't think it could be true. She would've known if her best friend was pregnant. They were as close as sisters. Her mom was wrong, and she needed to talk to Lizzie J. and get this straightened out.

"Maggie, it's true. It's Andy's baby and should arrive sometime in April," Annie said softly to her daughter as she watched Maggie trying to process the words. Annie was told earlier and had already taken the time to think about this unwelcome news. Could things get any more complicated for Mr. and Mrs. Raines? This had happened to their daughter and resulted in the birth of Lizzie J. Now they were reliving that time all over again. Annie felt such compassion for what they were going through.

Maggie began to cry. Lizzie J. was pregnant with Andy's baby? He'd died and would never see their child. All their plans for the future had ended in that car crash, and now this? Maggie thought she might be sick.

Her mom wrapped her arms around her. They sat, not moving, until Maggie was able to stop her tears and get out of bed. Her mom guided her to the living room couch and they sat down together, neither speaking for a while.

"What will happen to Lizzie J.? She's halfway through her senior year. She's only eighteen. She was going to go to college—how can she do that with a baby?" Maggie's mind was spinning with all the unanswered questions.

"Mrs. Raines told me they are encouraging Lizzie J. to give the baby up for adoption," Annie said quietly.

"No! They can't be serious! Lizzie J. would *never* do that. I *know* she wouldn't! Why would they even say something like that?"

"Maggie, you know that Lizzie J.'s grandparents loved her enough to give her a good home when her mother couldn't. I imagine at their age they can't think about raising another child."

"They wouldn't have to. Lizzie J.'s mom didn't want to take care of her, and who knows if her dad would have, since her mom would never tell anyone who he was. I know, without a doubt, Lizzie J. won't feel that way. All she's ever talked about was getting married to Andy and raising a family out on the Houstons' farm."

"Maybe Mrs. Raines has watched Lizzie J. mourn the absence of a father—and a mother that was absent as well. That can be a painful thing to watch someone you love as much as they love Lizzie J. and be unable to provide what she's always wanted . . . parents," Annie explained to her daughter.

"This baby *will* have a mother—Lizzie J. I have to help her, Mom. She needs someone to help if her grandparents won't," Maggie said, sounding desperate.

"Maggie, these are decisions that Lizzie J. and her grandparents will have to make. No matter how much you want to help, this is a decision that involves a baby and his or her future. After their emotions are under control and the truth of the situation has been accepted, the decisions will be easier. You will have to be patient and give them time," Annie said gently.

"She will *never* agree to give up her baby. I know she won't. I need to get dressed and go see her," Maggie said as she started to get up from the couch.

"Lizzie J. isn't at home — she stayed in Mississippi for a few days," Annie said as she reached out and pulled Maggie back down beside her.

"Her grandparents left her there? How could they do that? I have to call her. Mom, I have to talk to her!"

Maggie didn't get to talk to Lizzie J. until after Christmas. Annie tried her best to comfort her daughter, though inside she struggled as much as Maggie. Lizzie J. was almost like a daughter to Maggie's parents, and they wanted to help as much as Maggie. Annie knew it wasn't their decision to make and they would have to be patient.

When Jake found out about the baby that Andy would never know, he reacted just as Maggie had. He also wanted to help, and like the others, he didn't know how. It was a somber Christmas.

School was starting back in a couple of days and Maggie found out she would be returning without Lizzie J. The school administration agreed that Lizzie J. could complete her senior year with at-home studies and could graduate with her class in May, since by that time she would no longer be pregnant.

When Maggie was finally allowed to visit her best friend,

they cried together and talked until the wee hours of the morning. Only a year ago their conversations consisted of boys, college, and their futures — bright and happy futures, not a cloud in the sky. Now, ominous dark clouds hovered over their whispered words during that long night.

"Maggie, Andy and I knew God didn't want us to make love, and I realize most people probably wouldn't believe that. After the first couple of times, we promised each other we wouldn't be together again until we were married. That promise was harder to keep than we thought. We kept telling each other that someday soon we would be married, and we'd never be with anyone else. We never thought about something like this happening to either of us. Even if I had been the one to die, Andy would have shared with me something that was meant for someone else. We had no idea I was pregnant. If we'd known, we would have immediately gotten married. We were both already eighteen, and we wanted to do what our families wanted us to do. I'm so embarrassed and ashamed."

"I still can't believe everything that has happened, and I can't believe I didn't notice your weight gain. Why did you keep the truth from me? I tried so many times to find out what was wrong," Maggie asked, her feelings of isolation from her best friend coming through in her voice.

"Because I was so ashamed, and I didn't want that to affect the way you think about God. I always wanted you to believe in God and how much He loves you. I wanted you to see something in me that would make you want the same relationship. Andy and I went against what we knew God would want for us and let our desires take over instead. We were lying and hiding what we were doing, not thinking that God could see," Lizzie J. said sadly.

"Lizzie J., you're more like my sister than my best friend. I've watched you over the years and I do want to have faith like yours, but something keeps me from accepting that. I can't understand your deep faith after all you've been through."

"Maggie, my faith is exactly what has kept me going since Andy's death. And all the time I've been distant with you, I've been spending time alone with God, asking Him to forgive me for the sin I committed and give me guidance. I don't know what will be best for the baby. Nanny and Poppy think maybe I should give the baby up for adoption to a couple who can't have their own kids. I don't think I can do that. If they won't help me until I can find a job that will support us, I may not have any other option." Lizzie J. was trying hard not to cry again. She was still trying to cope with her situation, seeking to do the right thing, but she wasn't completely sure what that was.

"Lizzie J., somehow we'll find a way for you to keep your baby. I just know it. This baby will be part of Andy — you must keep this baby. Andy would want you to. Have Andy's parents been told?"

"No, we're going to see them tomorrow. Nanny and Poppy didn't want to tell them before Christmas. They knew Christmas would be difficult enough since Andy wouldn't be there."

The tears came, and before Maggie realized what was happening, Lizzie J. was sobbing — big gulping sobs that wracked her little body. Maggie wrapped her arms around her best friend and cried with her. Two young women on the cusp of adulthood, sitting on Lizzie J.'s bed, grieving and confused. The future that only four months ago seemed so bright now could only be seen through the darkness of consequences. God had forgiven Lizzie J. of the sin that was giving her a baby outside of marriage. He would not, though, eradicate the consequences. Those had to be dealt with, and they might be difficult and painful.

CHAPTER FOURTEEN

$\mathcal{N}$OW IN THE LAST semester of her senior year of high school, Maggie could think only about Lizzie J.'s pregnancy and what would happen to her and her baby. Ever since Maggie and Jake had learned about her situation, each conversation seemed to be about finding a way to help.

The knowledge of a baby on the way that was unplanned and unexpected cooled the temptations Jake and Maggie sometimes experienced in their own relationship, especially for Maggie. She didn't want to get married anytime soon, although she did love Jake, and she definitely didn't want a baby.

With their thoughts occupied with Lizzie J., the subject of college had not come up again. As the time grew nearer for Jake to return to ASC, Maggie began to worry. She still had not been honest with him about her acceptance to the Manhattan School of Music. As a result of the worry, she tried to avoid being alone with him and kept the conversation in safer areas. Still, she knew she had to tell him. That was on her mind when he called.

"Hey, you want to go see a movie tonight? Before I leave and get busy with classes again, I thought we might want to do something fun," Jake said.

"Sure, what time?"

"I have to meet my dad at the bank to change some things on my account at 4:00, but that shouldn't take too long. How about 5:30 and we can grab a bite to eat before the movie?"

"Sounds good. I have a bit of homework, and I think I can finish it before you come."

"Okay, bye."

"Bye."

Maggie slowly walked back toward her bedroom, deep in thought about what she *must* tell Jake tonight. She knew he wouldn't be happy about it, but she would feel much better revealing the secret she'd guarded for so long.

As Jake walked through the bank lobby, he was stopped by Mr. Davis, Maggie's piano teacher.

"Hi Jake, how are you? Your dad told me you're about to go back to school. Have you enjoyed your time at home?" Mr. Davis asked.

"Yes sir, I have. When you're having a good time around all the people you want to be with, it doesn't seem to last long enough," Jake said wistfully.

"I know what you mean. It seems like yesterday that Maggie was a little five-year-old girl swinging her legs on the piano bench and trying to stretch her little hands over the piano keys. Who would have guessed then that she would be accepted to such a prestigious school," Mr. Davis said with a big smile full of pride stretched across his face.

Jake felt sick, struggling to comprehend what he'd heard. Everything felt surreal. He stood there trying to regain his composure and not give away the fact that he had no idea what the man was talking about. Before Jake could reply, Mr. Davis continued.

"That girl will have to buy some heavier coats and lots of boots to live in New York City. Lake City will be proud to boast that one of their own was accepted to the Manhattan School of Music. What an accomplishment! I know you're proud of her and happy for her."

"Yeah, sure. Hey, I have to go. My dad is waiting for me. Good to see you," Jake replied and hurried away, leaving Mr. Davis standing there with the same smile on his face that Jake couldn't bear to see.

Instead of going into his dad's office, Jake rushed into the restroom and shut and locked the door. He rested his hands on both sides of the sink and hung his head, trying to regain his composure. His mind reeled. How could she have kept this from him? She had lied to him, or if not outright lied she'd certainly not been honest with him. How long had she known? How long ago had she applied? What else had she not told him? Fortunately, there was a chair in the room and Jake slowly sat down. Someone finally knocked on the door, and Jake had to step out into the real world of their relationship — not the relationship that obviously existed only in his mind, but the one that existed between him and Maggie. One thing he knew it was lacking ... honesty.

After Jake met with his dad, he went home and called Maggie. He cancelled their date, saying something had come up and he would call the next day. Instead, Jake packed his clothes and went back to the dorm. Only a few students had returned, and his floor was almost deserted. That was fine by him. He sat and stared into space for so long that hunger pains brought him back to the present. He walked across campus and bought a hamburger and fries at the cafeteria. He didn't see anyone he knew and was glad for the solitude.

THE NEXT DAY Maggie went for her weekly piano lesson. Even though she was now an accomplished pianist, she still needed the security of Mr. Davis and his affirmation that she was good enough to go to the school she'd dreamed about for so long.

"Hey, Maggie, come on in," Mr. Davis said as he opened the door.

"Go ahead to the music room. I'll be right there."

"Sure," Maggie replied.

She entered the music room and walked over to the piano, the same piano she'd started lessons on thirteen years before. She remembered how she felt when she memorized her first piece and how proud she'd been at her first recital. Other students she'd known over the years had complained about having to practice. They said it was hard work and most of them had stopped taking lessons. They would leave and new students would take their place. Maggie was one of the few who had stayed so long. She never felt it was work — she loved the way learning to read music and finding the placement of her fingers could result in beautiful melodies. She loved music and felt happy when at the piano.

"Hey, ready for your lesson?" Mr. Davis startled her.

"Oh, yes, I'm ready," Maggie replied.

"Guess who I saw yesterday at the bank?"

Mr. Davis' question took Maggie by surprise. She suddenly knew why Jake had cancelled their date, and she immediately felt nauseous.

"I don't know, who?"

"Jake. I told him how proud the whole town would be when

they find out you've been accepted to such a prestigious school. He was in a hurry, though, and I'm guessing he's known about this for awhile. I'm still so excited and happy for you," Mr. Davis gushed.

So, there it was...her secret...told to Jake by someone other than her. Maggie didn't know how to reply, so she didn't. She sat down and somehow got through her lesson. When she left Mr. Davis' house, the tears came and she cried all the way home. She felt like a deceitful, terrible person. She loved Jake and she loved her music. She had always felt torn between the two; now that tear felt more like a huge wound. She had no idea how to heal the damage she'd done to their relationship.

CHAPTER FIFTEEN

New York City
1971

MAGGIE LOOKED OVER to the side table where she kept her new Bible. She stared at it for a few minutes as if willing the words on the pages to be imprinted in her mind so she could recall her favorite verses as quickly as Jake had done. The October day she'd gone to the bookstore would be an indelible memory forever. As she'd read the passages from her Bible over the past three months, she'd been assured over and over that the trip to the store that day had happened for a reason. Maggie realized her heart was changing. As she read and studied, she no longer felt the old fear and anxiety but a new sense of being drawn to the words.

Remembering her conversation with Jake about his mother's guidance brought to mind Jeremiah 29:11–13. That Christmas in 1963 was the first time she ever heard Jake quote scripture, and she still remembered the awe she felt that it came to him so quickly.

She underlined those verses in her new Bible. She read them often. After speaking with Lizzie J., Maggie thought about the hard times her dear friend went through after Andy's death and during her pregnancy. At that time, Lizzie J. had no idea about her future, or the happiness she now enjoyed. God had provided a husband for Lizzie J. who loved and cherished her. When Maggie thought about how that transpired, she knew deep down it wasn't by chance. As Jake had always said, God puts people in our lives for a reason — some for only moments, and some for days, weeks, months or years. God had given Lizzie J. a husband for a lifetime.

The past three months had been a reflective time for Maggie. As she pondered the fact that everyone she knew had impacted her life in one way or another, she thought back as far as she could remember to the ones who had affected her the most.

Maggie's parents were good people, but they never taught her about God and only touched on being "church" people. But after Maggie moved to New York City, they accepted the fact they needed a Savior. They began to study God's word and tried to persuade Maggie that she needed to do that too.

Even though Maggie had been resistant to their urgings, when her dad died she realized she was happy her parents had made that decision. She found that she did believe in heaven and hell, though she still fought making a decision about her own eternity.

Then there was Lizzie J. — sweet Lizzie J., the best friend anyone could ever ask for. She lived out her beliefs each and every day. When she sinned, she admitted it, asked for forgiveness and tried to do better. Lizzie J. had never made Maggie feel like a bad person. Maggie would never know the many prayers her best friend had prayed for her over the years.

And Jake. He was like no other man she'd ever known. She remembered their conversation at his house the Christmas she was a senior and he was home from college. They discussed whether God plans things and makes them happen, or if things happen and God uses those things for good. Maggie could still remember how surprised she was when Jake said he came into her life possibly to share his faith and show her God. She *knew* he would have married her right then if she'd agreed. Yet he honestly admitted he wasn't sure why God had brought them together or whether marriage was the right thing for them. Maggie no longer questioned why. She knew God had used Jake and his influence to draw her. As stubborn and resistant as she'd been, Jake had never faltered in his faith or his witness to her about how much God loved her.

God's love for her was made clear when she stumbled across Psalm 119:73: *Your hands made me and formed me: give me understanding so that I can learn your commands.* That verse was powerful for Maggie. She loved making music with her hands, forming the notes so that beautiful melodies delighted her listeners. As much as she loved her music, she knew there was no comparison to forming a person. When she finally made that connection, she felt overwhelmed knowing how much God loved her.

Maggie finally picked up the Bible. She turned to Luke chapter two and began reading the Christmas story. She thought about all the Christmas programs she attended at the church in Lake City as she was growing up. While reading the Bible recently, she began to realize how little she had comprehended in church. Now she wondered how in the world that could be. Her ringing phone interrupted her thoughts.

"Hello," Maggie answered.

"Hey, you never called back. The party is still on and I think there will be quite a crowd since all the restaurants are closed. How about I call and see if I can get a taxi to come pick you up?" Miguel asked.

"I think I'll pass. I'm thinking about going to church tonight," Maggie replied.

"Church? Did you say church?"

"Yes, it is Christmas Eve, you know. What's wrong with wanting to go to church?" Maggie asked, sounding a little irritated.

"Well, nothing is wrong with church," Miguel replied, sounding confused.

"I don't feel much like partying. Hope you have fun, and thanks again for inviting me."

"Well if you change your mind, we'll probably be here until the wee hours of the morning. Hope you can get a flight out soon. Merry Christmas."

"Thanks, Merry Christmas to you too," Maggie replied and hung up, glad that conversation was out of the way. For some reason, a party like Miguel was having seemed wrong today. She knew that the last thing on anyone's mind at the party would be the celebration of a Savior's birth.

It was late afternoon and the sun was still shining. The weather system that had created one of the largest snowstorms in many years had thankfully expended all its energy, leaving a crippled city in its wake. On an ordinary day, Maggie would call a taxi. This wasn't an ordinary day, and she realized if she was going to leave her apartment and go anywhere, it would be by foot. She began to think about the churches she'd seen close by and wondered if any of them would have Christmas Eve services.

CHAPTER SIXTEEN

Lake City, Arkansas
1963

AFTER CRYING ALL the way home from her piano lesson, Maggie dried her tears, rushed into the house and went straight to the phone. Without even thinking through what she might say, or how she might explain herself, she hurriedly dialed the number to Jake's dad's house. Lillian answered. Maggie felt heartsick when she heard Lillian explain that Jake had left and gone back to Jonesboro to school. Not wanting Lillian to think she didn't know he'd left, she told Lillian she'd forgotten.

The tears began again and Maggie went to her room, closed the door and fell across her bed. How did she get in this mess? Why didn't she tell Jake from the beginning instead of letting him think she was going to Arkansas State? Looking back, she knew that would have been much better, and now it was too late; she couldn't change the circumstances. Maggie knew that letting him think something that wasn't true was the same as if she'd voiced the lie.

"Maggie, can I come in?" Annie knocked softly on the door.

"Sure," came Maggie's muffled reply, her face buried in her pillow.

"Are you okay? What's wrong?" Annie sat on the edge of Maggie's bed. She reached out and pulled the hair away from her daughter's face. Maggie rolled over and buried her face in her mom's lap.

"I never told Jake I was going to New York to go to school, and he found out from Mr. Davis yesterday. Jake called and cancelled our date last night and I didn't think anything of it until Mr. Davis told me about seeing him in the bank. Mr. Davis told Jake how proud he was that I'd been accepted to a prestigious music school. When I called to talk to Jake about it, Lillian told me he'd returned to his dorm."

"Oh, Maggie, why didn't you tell him? We thought he knew. You knew he would find out sooner or later," Annie admonished.

"I've been meaning to tell him — the words simply wouldn't come out. I knew how much he wanted me to go to college with him. I don't want to lose Jake, but I really, really want this opportunity. What should I do, Mom?"

"Maggie, you shouldn't feel bad about wanting to go to school where you think you will learn the most. You should have been honest with Jake. Honesty is so important in a relationship of any kind," Annie said.

"Okay, I admit I should've been honest, and I know to Jake it seems I lied about it, but I just didn't tell him. That's not the same thing."

"Who are you trying to convince, me or you? The only advice I can give is to try to explain to Jake how torn you were about your situation and ask him to forgive you."

"This has been the worst year of my life. And it's my senior year of high school. In my wildest imagination, I never could've dreamed up the things that have happened since last August," Maggie said as the tears slipped down her face and she crumpled into her mom's lap again, like she had as a little girl.

"Have you tried calling him at his dorm?"

"No, not yet. I don't know what to say, and anyway, I want to talk to him face to face, not on the phone. Can I drive to the college tomorrow after school and see if I can find him?" Maggie pleaded.

"I don't know, Maggie. Maybe Jake needs time to think about it. He's always known about your dream; this can't be a surprise to him."

"Please, Mom—I have to see him and try to explain."

JAKE'S CLASSES WERE scheduled to begin Thursday morning, and in the past he'd returned the night before. This time was different; Jake felt the need to get away. Other students, including J.D., had not yet returned. All alone in his dorm room, Jake slept late and then spent the day being angry, then sad, and finally confused. It was now late in the day and the walls were beginning to close in on him.

The phone rang in the hallway. Someone answered it and called his name. Jake was told he had a visitor downstairs in the reception area. He didn't want to see anyone but thought it might be his dad. When he opened the door into the lobby, he was surprised to see Maggie.

She looked beautiful, and Jake noticed a couple of guys staring at her, which dampened his anger and made him feel possessive. He could tell she'd been crying and was visibly upset.

"Hey, let's go outside where we can talk," Jake said, taking her by the arm. The campus was still somewhat deserted and they were able to find a bench in an out of the way place.

"Jake, I'm so sorry I didn't tell you about New York. I wanted to tell you so many times, but I knew you would be disappointed and I kept waiting and waiting. I know you won't believe this, but I was planning to tell you the night we had a date. Then Mr. Davis saw you in the bank that afternoon and told you before I had a chance. I'm so sorry."

"Before you had a chance? How long have you known this, Maggie?" Jake asked, his voice rising with skepticism.

"About two months. No one else knew except my parents and Mr. Davis," Maggie replied quietly. Saying out loud how long it had been sounded dreadful, even to Maggie.

"I honestly don't even know how to reply. All this time I thought you were coming here to school. You let me believe that, Maggie. You deceived me," Jake challenged.

"Again, I'm sorry I didn't tell you. That was wrong of me. Jake, you've known since you met me that I wanted to pursue a musical career. Why can't you support me?" Maggie asked, her eyes searching his face for some sign of understanding.

"Maggie, I love you, but I think we want two different futures. All I've ever wanted was to get married and have a family. Arkansas and farming is my dream, New York and playing classical music in concert halls is your dream. I don't see how this will ever work out."

"I know you want to get married, and I don't want to be single the rest of my life, but Jake we're so young. Marriage can come later. Why can't marriage come in a few years? I do love you, and I don't feel it's fair to have to choose between you and my music."

"I hear you, Maggie, but have you actually thought about how hard it will be to come back here and live if you become successful? Can you give up fame and money to come back here to the life I want? I don't see that happening," Jake said sadly.

Maggie tried not to cry. Jake's last comment stung. Deep down, she knew they were at a crossroads and decisions needed to be made. They were quiet, each lost in their own thoughts about what they wanted in life, how they wanted each other and how it seemed an impossible situation.

"Jake, I love you, and you're also my best friend. I don't want to lose that. With Andy gone, I see Lizzie J. struggling with the loss of not only the person she wanted to marry, but her best friend as well. I don't want to be in the same position. After what we've experienced with Andy's death, we should realize today is all we have. My musical career might not happen, and your dream of farming and having a family might not happen either. Can't we enjoy today? Continue in school and see what happens?" Maggie implored.

"Maggie, that sounds easy, but the longer we have a relationship the more I love you, and the more it will hurt if we don't end up together. I don't know what to do or how we can work this out."

"Are you breaking up with me? You are, aren't you?"

"Maggie, I'm not breaking up with you—I'm trying to come to a solution. I'm aware, and you should be too, that our dreams and future plans are going in opposite directions."

"I need you in my life, Jake, even if we don't see each other often. This has been a year of losses and I don't think I can stand another one. Andy had been my friend since we started school—not only have I lost him, in a way I've lost Lizzie J. too. I'm the only one of the four of us still in high school. It's lonely, and I'm anxious for the year to be over. This isn't the senior year I imagined I would have." Maggie could no longer keep her tears at bay. She was miserable.

Jake was moved by her tears, and he was miserable too. He put his arms around her and she laid her head on his shoulder. They sat, not moving, both of them thinking how right it felt and confused about what to do. Even though Jake felt she'd deceived him, he accepted her apology, and they decided to wait to make any further decisions. As much as Jake hated to admit that Maggie was right, he finally agreed she should get her education where she chose, and marriage would have to wait.

WITH JAKE IN COLLEGE, Lizzie J. at home waiting on her baby to be born, and Maggie in school, their lives had changed so drastically that all three seemed to be swimming upstream. Jake did have J.D. at school with him, but with different schedules they rarely saw each other.

Maggie either studied or practiced her music, determined to graduate from high school with honors. What little free time she allowed herself was spent with Lizzie J. By the first week in March, Lizzie J. was becoming uncomfortable. She was short—or petite, as she often reminded Maggie—and there was not a lot of room for a baby.

After Christmas break, when school had resumed and Lizzie J. didn't return, it hadn't taken long for word to circulate through their small town that she was pregnant. Some of the known gossips in town had speculated all kinds of things, but for the most part, people were sympathetic to her situation. We all make mistakes. Lizzie J.'s would soon be for the world to see, though. Pregnancy could only be concealed for a brief time.

Charlie Chander had become somewhat of a family friend to Lizzie J. and her grandparents, precipitated by his conversation with Lizzie J. as he was leaving church not long after the accident. He remained a mystery to everyone else. No one seemed to know where he came from, most couldn't remember how long he'd lived there, and the rest didn't care. When talk of the accident died down, things went back to the way they'd been, and Charlie became a fixture in town that most people didn't even notice. That was exactly the way he wanted things, and one of the reasons he'd chosen to settle in this small, rural farming town.

Charlie had been the owner and CEO of a textile mill in Memphis. He inherited the company when his parents were killed in a plane crash in the company jet. Charlie was the only heir of his family's fortune, and the tragedy of losing his parents turned him into a multi-millionaire before he was ready for the responsibility.

He'd been in love once in his life, and she'd broken his heart. He became incapable of managing his business and decided to sell it before he lost it all. Charlie invested his money with a financial firm in Memphis, owned by personal friends he knew he could trust, and became somewhat of a recluse. He was known in Memphis as James C. Chandler, so he dropped his first name and started using his middle name, Charles, and eventually started introducing himself as Charlie. He felt it was less formal, and Charlie Chandler didn't sound like someone with a lot of money.

Growing up in a wealthy family and being an awkward kid yet extremely intelligent, he soon came to realize people liked him because he was rich, not because of the person he was. So he began to isolate himself. He was an adult before he made true friends he felt he could trust. They were also wealthy and didn't care about his money. He'd never wanted anyone to know who he was or what he had — hence, the reason he'd always been somewhat of a mystery to the people of Lake City. Everyone in town would be shocked to know his net worth. Actually, Charlie probably would be too — it was something he never worried about.

Charlie didn't know Mr. and Mrs. Raines before the car accident, and he was certainly unaware they were raising their granddaughter. Since the Sunday Lizzie J. stopped him outside of the church to tell him she didn't hold him responsible, he felt drawn to her and her grandparents. A lot of the reason was guilt. Even though he was forgiven and never charged with any traffic violation, he still struggled with Andy's death. Somehow he felt responsible to watch over Lizzie J. for Andy. Though he knew people would think that weird, he couldn't shake the feeling.

Lizzie J.'s grandfather and Charlie became friends. Mr. Raines loved to fish, and so did Charlie. An old dugout that Mr. Raines had inherited from his dad was their source of travel on the St. Francis River. They would haul it on the back of the truck, fill it with their fishing gear and oars, and slip it into the waters not far from the bridge. They would paddle into the old channel of the river where they would fish until the mosquitoes chased them home. Mr. Raines never questioned

Charlie about not having a job or how he supported himself, another reason their friendship developed.

Charlie was invited to eat supper with them many times. He would come in and leave by the back door. He went through their living room a few times when he sat on the front porch, but it was always a brief pass through on his way from the kitchen.

When the news traveled through town that the Raines girl was pregnant with Andy Houston's baby, Charlie heard all about it, and some of the things he heard made him angry. He also heard some talk about the Raines' daughter who had gone away to live with relatives in California and never returned. Most of the people who lived there knew Lizzie J. had been born to that daughter, and they admired Mr. and Mrs. Raines for providing her a home. Charlie heard the people in town say Lizzie J.'s mom had married. They speculated about the reasons she'd never taken Lizzie J. to live with her in California.

When Charlie heard these conversations in various places of business, he always pretended not to hear or be interested. He was actually listening to every word, and it broke his heart for Lizzie J. He had begun to feel like part of their family. He'd protected his heart for so many years that it was hard for him to trust and care. He'd recently had his forty-eighth birthday, but no one knew that — only his friends in Memphis who remained faithful to him and his secret.

Charlie drove to Memphis late in the evening a couple of times a month to have dinner with those friends. They'd stopped trying to understand why he'd chosen to live in Lake City and be someone other than the person they knew. Unlike Charlie, his friends enjoyed their wealth. They still lived in expensive homes in the best areas of Memphis and served elegant dinners reminiscent of Charlie's former life.

Reading an article about Lake City in a Memphis newspaper almost seven years ago was the reason Charlie lived in this small town. He remembered opening the paper that Monday morning in September of 1957 and becoming intrigued with the place. He studied the photos of Main Street and the Eastern District Courthouse with a few workers taking a break on the front steps. He was exhausted from living in Memphis and felt that small town calling his name. Here he was seven years later, never having regretted the move. He'd come to love the laid-back atmosphere and the hard-working people, and he'd learned to appreciate the cotton fields that had given his family their wealth in the mill. Charlie was living comfortably between his two worlds. However, the life he'd carved out for himself in this small town was about to change in ways he could never have fathomed.

CHAPTER SEVENTEEN

New York City
1971

AGGIE'S FRONT DOOR was frozen shut, but with effort she managed to get it open enough to step out with her snow shovel to try to clear her steps. The day had actually passed more quickly than she'd thought it would. The sun had dropped behind the high-rise buildings and twilight was fast approaching. The temperature had climbed to only about twenty degrees, even with the sunshine, and now she could feel the cold seeping into her bones. She expected it would fall below zero by midnight.

Back inside, she decided to bundle up and take a walk to find a church. She knew there were several in her neighborhood but had never paid much attention to the names. She hoped one of the closer ones was a Christian church — if so it should be having Christmas Eve services.

Maggie pulled on her snow pants, a fleece-lined hooded parka, snow boots, and completed her attire with warm gloves. Right before going out the door, she grabbed a ski mask in case her face got too cold. Outside, she gingerly went down the steps, taking her time and holding tightly to the railing.

Looking out from her window earlier, she knew the snow was deep, but until she tried to walk in it she didn't realize that this snowstorm would probably go down in the history books as one of the worst.

Finally, at the end of the street she turned to the right, hoping the church she was thinking of was only another block or two away. After trudging through the deep snow for another two blocks, she arrived in front of First Presbyterian Church. The stone architecture and huge stained-glass windows were breathtaking. Maggie stood still and took in the details of the building, as if seeing it for the first time. And in a way, she was.

Standing there in the middle of Manhattan, on Christmas Eve, 1971, Maggie's spirits began to soar. Earlier in the day she'd felt so alone, experiencing many emotions, even anger. Now she felt more at peace than she could ever remember. She would've been embarrassed to try to explain her feelings, but she felt she was on the precipice of something life-changing. She stood staring at the church, unaware of the time, until the frigid air brought her back to reality. Christmas lights in the buildings around her grew brighter in the growing darkness, reminding her she was all alone. She suddenly didn't care. She knew she was where she was supposed to be.

The front door to the church opened and a man approached her. He'd been watching her for several minutes and thought she might be in need.

"Merry Christmas! Can I help you with something?"

His voice startled her; she'd not seen him coming. She noticed his robes and figured he must be the pastor.

"Oh, hello, and Merry Christmas to you too. I was wondering if you were having services this evening," Maggie replied.

"Yes we are. Not sure how many people will be able to

attend, but we've never cancelled a midnight service in the history of this church, and that's been over one hundred years. We don't want this to be the first!"

"I'll be here. I only live about three blocks away."

"I'm Reverend Thomas," he said as he reached out to shake her gloved hand.

"I'm Maggie, Maggie Roberts. It's so nice to meet you."

"Well, Maggie Roberts, I'm happy to meet you too, and I'll not keep you in the cold any longer. See you in a few hours," Reverend Thomas replied and quickly went back through the church door.

As Maggie turned toward her apartment, the scene before her took her breath away. She'd walked there in the twilight, but it seemed darkness had suddenly descended. The stars in the sky cast a twinkling canopy over the neighborhood, illuminating the heavy snow with a radiance Maggie had never seen before. Or maybe she'd never noticed.

The usual heavy traffic was absent on this special night, and the snow crunching beneath Maggie's steps were the only sounds she could hear in the silence of her world. All of the bricks, concrete, asphalt and cacophony of a city teeming with millions of people had been miraculously transformed as if preparing for the birth of the Savior. Maggie stopped walking. Looking up into the night sky, she asked for forgiveness—for all she had done and all she had failed to do. Jesus had died for her, and after all these years of denial, she now wanted Him to live in her heart. She felt whole...complete, and for the first time in her life she knew God.

She *knew* God!

Walking slowly back to her apartment, Maggie felt transformed and free. No fear or anxiety, only a sense of surrender.

Why had she fought for so long? Pride, control, fear—maybe a little of all of these had kept her from God all those years. Now she understood Jake, Lizzie J., Andy, and all the other Godly people in her life. Even though she'd been on the outside looking in, they had accepted her, loved her and forgiven her when she failed them. A new emotion she'd never experienced before surfaced...humbleness.

She looked in awe at the beauty of the night and wondered if it resembled the night of Jesus' birth. Maggie had heard the Christmas story many times and thought she knew it. Tonight, for the first time, the real meaning took up residence in her soul, and she knew she was changed.

Back in her apartment, she removed her coat and boots and hurriedly went to the closet where she kept her Christmas decorations. It was too late to purchase a tree, so she strung lights and hung ornaments on a tall plant in her living room.

Maggie, like a lot of people, hadn't given much thought to the reason Christmas Day was celebrated. Her parents had given her a crèche a few years ago, but it had remained in the box. Now she couldn't wait to open it and display it on her fireplace mantel. As she placed the figurines in position in and around the manger, she felt an overwhelming longing to be in Lake City. She knew that within the hour their Christmas Eve service would begin, and all the people most important to her would be there. Instead of allowing that longing to depress her, she let it settle inside of her as she thought about each person, one by one.

Then there was Jake. Her Jake. Even though they'd been estranged over the past two years, she still thought of him in those terms. She loved him, she'd always loved him, and she knew he loved her. But right now she had to focus on her new salvation and what that would mean in her life. This was solely between her and God.

Jake would have to wait ... again.

THE TEMPERATURE IN Arkansas on Christmas Eve, 1971, was a balmy forty-five degrees. At least it was cold enough to wear sweaters. A white Christmas was a rare occurrence in the south, so people scattered fake snow around their Christmas tree or sprayed it from a can. White Christmas, by crooner Bing Crosby, was still a favorite, as well as Jingle Bells, even though no one down south had ever ridden in a one-horse open sleigh. The lack of snow didn't dampen the Christmas spirit, and there was plenty to go around at Lizzie J.'s home that evening.

Everyone loved Lizzie J.'s parties, always full of love and warmth. The fragrance of evergreens filled the air and beautiful ornaments adorned the Douglas Fir, especially those made by the children.

As Lizzie J. looked around the room, she felt blessed with her family and friends who always gathered with her on Christmas Eve. But she couldn't stop thinking about Maggie, snowed in and all alone in New York. Lizzie J.'s husband walked up behind her and wrapped his arms around her, and she leaned back into him, blissfully happy. That's what she wanted for Jake and Maggie — that's all she'd ever wanted for them — and her efforts at getting them together tonight had failed miserably.

"Great party Lizzie J., and as always, the food is excellent," Jake said.

"Thank you, glad you could make it. Maggie has talked of nothing else all day. How did you get a break from her?"

"She left me in the dust for that other guy over there," Jake laughed as he watched little Maggie following a cute four-year-old boy.

"Oh, I should've warned you. Marcus goes to her preschool and she is quite in love with him," Lizzie J. explained.

"Well you know, I never could hold on to a girl named Maggie."

They were both stunned that Jake brought Maggie into the conversation, and awkwardness settled over them for a few seconds. Jake was as surprised as they were and already regretted his remark. Thankfully, neither Lizzie J. nor her husband commented.

"Hey, I have to shove off early. I promised to help with the Christmas Eve service at church. Y'all are coming, aren't you?"

"We sure are. Merry Christmas, Jake," Lizzie J. said as she reached up to give him a hug.

"Merry Christmas to you two, and thanks again for having me. See you at church tonight," Jake replied.

THE CHRISTMAS EVE service at the Lake City Community Church had been the same as long as Jake had lived there — the same order of service, the same carols, and the same Christmas story. The only changes each year were the children and youth who played the various parts. Jake liked the tradition and familiarity — after all, the Christmas story never changes.

As always, the sanctuary was packed, with many faces seen only on Christmas and Easter, so Jake wasn't surprised when his dad and Lillian called him over to meet a family he didn't know.

"Jake, this is Caroline and her children, Greg and Kristen," Sal said as Lillian stood by beaming.

"Hi Caroline, Greg, Kristen. It's nice to meet all three of you," Jake said as he shook Caroline's hand.

"Caroline is my niece. She's moving here from Tennessee," Lillian explained. "She'll be staying with your dad and me until she can get settled in her own place."

"Well you can't find a better place to stay. Are you already moved in or are you coming after the holidays?" Jake had never heard anything about this lady, and he'd certainly not been told she would be staying with his dad and Lillian. He was confused and trying not to show it. He wanted to ask more questions but felt as though he would be prying.

"We won't move until after the holidays. We came to visit, and the idea of moving here, close to Aunt Lillian, seemed to be right for us. Our story is complicated — maybe later we can explain," Caroline said, sensing his confusion about who she was and where she came from.

"Jake, remember about two years ago I told you about my niece whose husband died in Viet Nam? Caroline is the niece I was speaking about," Lillian said as she looped her arm through Caroline's and pulled her close.

"I'm sorry for your loss," Jake said and didn't know what to say after that. He wished Lillian hadn't brought that up right here in the church. "So I guess I'll see you at dinner tomorrow night?"

"Yes, we'll be there. We're leaving the day after to go back to Tennessee to have our furniture put in storage until we find a place here. It was nice to meet you. I'll see you tomorrow."

He noticed the look on his dad's face—an apologetic look—and realization dawned on Jake that Lillian might have instigated a move for her niece thinking he needed a wife. She wasn't beautiful, but she was attractive. She wasn't Maggie though. Great—another single female that someone was trying to fix him up with. And this time it was his stepmother. Now he dreaded going to Christmas dinner tomorrow night.

CHAPTER EIGHTEEN

Lake City, Arkansas
1964

Charlie Chandler knew the relationship between Madeline and Paul Raines and their daughter, Rita, was tenuous, at best. She was never mentioned in casual conversation. He didn't know how Lizzie J. felt about her mother leaving her with her grandparents, but he was about to find out.

Paul and Charlie had an established fishing day every Thursday, first thing in the morning, weather permitting. This Thursday morning in mid-March was going to be perfect for a day on the St. Francis, Charlie thought to himself as he leaned his fishing pole against the back porch and sat his tackle box down beside it. He was about to step up onto the porch when he heard yelling coming from inside the house. He froze and stopped his ascent.

"I don't want her to come here! She's never cared before. This is none of her business!" Lizzie J. screamed.

"Now honey, we had to let her know. We waited as long as we could. The baby will be here in a few weeks — we had to call her," Madeline said to her granddaughter.

"Poppy, make her stay away. You know she doesn't care about me, and she certainly won't care about a baby," Lizzie J. said sarcastically.

"Lizzie J., your mom does care about you." Poppy had told her the same thing many times through the years.

"Poppy, I'm no longer a little girl; you can stop telling me that. I cannot believe you haven't told me before this morning and she will be here any minute. I don't want to see her!"

"Your mom knows a family that lives close to her that wants to adopt a baby. We thought maybe you might consider their offer. Then you can go on to college and make a good life for yourself," Nanny said.

"A good life? Without my baby? I have said this over and over—I am not giving up this baby. If y'all won't help me, I'll find someone who will. I know Maggie's parents will help me. I'll get a job. I'll go to college later. I am NOT leaving my baby with anyone! Do you hear me? I will not!" Lizzie J. ran from the room sobbing and slammed her bedroom door.

Charlie couldn't move. Though he wanted to, his feet wouldn't budge. Before he could become mobile again, Paul came through the back door and caught him. Charlie felt as though he'd been eavesdropping and hoped he could explain why he was standing there with his mouth gaping open.

"Good morning, Charlie. I guess you heard all the screaming—sorry you had to hear that."

"I didn't mean to eavesdrop. I guess we aren't fishing today. I overheard that your daughter will be here any minute."

"Yeah, Rita should be here any minute. She's coming alone this time, though, and I'm glad. We love Lizzie J. as if she was our daughter instead of our granddaughter. I won't bore you with the details of what our lives have been like the last eighteen years. Lizzie J. has a lot of anger toward her mom, and honestly, I can't blame her. We've all made mistakes when it came to making decisions about where Lizzie J. would live. Maybe someday I'll tell you all about it; now is not the time."

As if on cue, and before Charlie could reply, a car turned the corner and came to a stop in front of the house. Both men turned their attention to the car. After a few seconds, the driver side door opened and a beautiful woman emerged and waved.

Paul stepped down from the porch and started to the street to meet her. Charlie couldn't believe he was caught in the middle of the Raines family drama and there seemed to be no escape.

Charlie picked up his fishing pole and tackle box and was trying to be invisible, but knew he couldn't be rude and would have to at least say hello.

Paul and his daughter were walking toward him so he looked up in greeting. As they came closer, Charlie thought he was seeing a ghost from his past, his long-ago past. He could see the moment she recognized him.

"Katie? Katie Griffin?" Charlie said.

"No ... no, my name is Rita," she replied, her eyes begging him to accept what she was saying.

"Sorry, you reminded me of someone I knew a long time ago. Rita ... it's nice to meet you." Charlie reached out to shake her hand, and he could feel her trembling as she accepted his handshake. He held her hand a little longer than he should've, and Paul sensed something between them.

"You certainly have a beautiful daughter, Paul," Charlie said. "It was nice to meet you Rita. Paul, I'm going to shove off."

"Wait, you didn't tell me your name," Rita said.

"Oh, I didn't, sorry. My name is Charlie. Maybe I'll see you again."

"Maybe we can get that fishing trip in sometime tomorrow," Paul said as he watched Charlie hurry away. "Maybe you can come to dinner while Rita is here, okay?"

"Yeah, maybe," Charlie responded over his shoulder as he kept walking at a fast pace. He wanted out of there. His heart was racing and he felt physically ill. He didn't care what name they called her—to him she was Katie!

The last time he'd seen her was a few days before Christmas in 1945. For months after she disappeared, he tortured himself reliving the months they'd known each other and trying to figure out what he'd done wrong. At the time he was twenty-nine and still grieving the loss of both of his parents a year earlier. He was also struggling to manage the mill that had been left to him in his parents' will.

Charlie met her at a friend's house. Katie was a friend of a friend, and later thinking back on their introduction, he realized he never knew a lot about her. Now he was totally confused how someone he'd known as Katie who lived in Memphis could possibly be Paul's daughter, Rita. And Lizzie J.'s mother ... Lizzie J's mother ... Lizzie J's mother.

He dropped the fishing pole and tackle box, and if the tree he leaned on for support had not been close by, he would've been on the ground too. Was it possible he was Lizzie J.'s father? He tried to remember and calculate the months, but he wasn't sure when Lizzie J. had turned eighteen. Memories that had remained locked away, because he would never allow them to surface, came rising like a flood.

His house was on the last paved street in town. The Raines lived on the other side of town near the cemetery. Charlie usually walked there on Thursday mornings and Paul would take him home after they returned from fishing. Charlie walked today and couldn't remember making any of the turns that brought him home. After unlocking his front door, he dropped his fishing pole and tackle box in the middle of the living room floor, went into his bedroom and fell across his bed. The day Andy Houston died from the car accident was the first time Charlie Chandler had cried in many years, since he'd shed every tear he thought he had when he couldn't find Katie. Seeing her today caused the floodgates to open again and Charlie wept.

RITA'S DEMEANOR WAS translated by her dad to mean she was apprehensive about seeing her eighteen-year-old daughter pregnant. He figured she was reliving her own bad choices when she was only a couple of years older than her daughter was now. He had no way of knowing that Rita, like Charlie, felt like she'd seen a ghost from her past. Her mind was reeling as she tried to act normal.

Where did he come from? How in the world did he know her family? Why was he using the name Charlie and not James? Most importantly, did he know he was Lizzie J.'s father? No, she didn't think so or he wouldn't have been so shocked to see her. She was sure he was as surprised to see her as she was to see him. As she entered the back door of the house she'd grown up in, she pushed all those thoughts away to concentrate on the problem she'd come here to help solve.

After the conversation with her daughter ended in tears

for both of them, she left Lizzie J. and went out to the front porch where her parents sat together on the porch swing. Now, without a husband, she suddenly felt like a child again.

Rita had been a beautiful young girl and was still a beautiful woman. She'd grown up longing for more than this small town could offer her. As a result, she'd made many mistakes, and two of her earliest ones were deceiving Charlie, or James, as she knew him, and allowing her parents to keep Lizzie J. with them. It seemed to Rita that every time she made a mistake, by the time she realized the mistake had been made, it was too late to do anything about it.

She loved her mom and dad and knew they were disappointed in her. They could never understand her desire to be an actress, and they never understood why she had not given that up and gotten a "real" job, as they called it. They were about to hear another change in Rita's life, and none of them would believe what she was about to do.

New York City
1971

THE LIVING ROOM was aglow from the lights on Maggie's makeshift Christmas tree. She'd covered each table with candles and hung wreaths in her front windows. It might be a little late to decorate since it was already Christmas Eve, but that was okay, she thought—she might leave everything out until the end of January!

Maggie rummaged in her freezer for something to cook that would be worthy of a special dinner. She might be alone, but she was determined to celebrate before attending the midnight church service. She found a steak in the freezer and took it out to thaw. She had salad left from a take-out dinner a couple of nights ago and found part of a loaf of French bread. She realized as she looked in the almost empty refrigerator this would have to do.

The radio station that earlier made her so homesick now filled the air with the Christmas Carols she loved so much. Knowing her life had been eternally changed that day gave her joy and hope for her future. Now she understood Jake, and she felt in her bones that even though she didn't know *how* they would be together, they eventually *would* be together.

Looking through her closet for something appropriate to wear for the church service, she decided on a red velvet dress. She made her choice as though she was in Lake City with her family and friends. She would take her dress shoes in her shoulder bag and put them on once inside the church. She chose her diamond earrings and decided no other jewelry was needed.

Over the years as she matured into a woman, she learned to dress simply. She knew what to wear and how to wear it, and as a result, when she entered a room all eyes were on her. She laid her clothes out on her bed and went back to the kitchen to start her dinner. It was only seven and she had to fill the time until she should leave for her walk to church.

Maggie opened her cabinet to find the seasoning for her steak, and her eyes came to rest on her daddy's collection of jars that held the spices he always used when grilling. When he was suddenly taken away from her and her mom, Maggie begged her mom to let her bring them here to her apartment. When she used them, she loved wrapping her hand around the outside, turning them upside down and shaking out the goodness onto whatever she was cooking.

She stood still, staring at the jars as if she'd never seen them before. She felt as though they were giving her a message. Confused about why she couldn't look away, the realization came over her that she would see her daddy again…in Heaven. He'd given his heart to Christ and had encouraged Maggie to do the same, though at the time she'd resisted. As she stood there in her beautiful kitchen, staring at some old jars that had belonged to her daddy, the tears started and wouldn't stop. She laid her head on the kitchen counter and sobbed, big gulping sobs from deep within her soul.

She'd felt such guilt since her daddy died so suddenly and without warning. For the past two years, Jake's words to her after her daddy's funeral played over and over in her head. Her anger toward Jake had caused their break-up. During their heated argument that quickly became a shouting match, she knew Jake was right but couldn't admit that at the time.

When she finally stopped crying, she felt better than she could ever remember. She finished cooking and ate with a hearty appetite. It seemed to Maggie, on this snowy Christmas Eve, that it was the best dinner she'd ever had—almost as if fairy dust had been sprinkled on her food. Then she smiled to herself—she didn't believe in fairies, but she did believe in angels.

While singing along with the radio, Maggie cleaned the kitchen and brewed a cup of tea. Then she went back into the living room and sat in the same wing-back chair she'd sat in that morning while sad, lonely and angry over her confinement. Now as she looked around at her Christmas decorations, she felt happy and satisfied and couldn't wait to go to church.

Even though she was alone, she picked up her Bible and read the Christmas story aloud. Any other time she would have felt childish reading aloud when no one was there. But Maggie *knew* she had an audience of one on this night—she knew God was listening. When she finished reading, she turned off the radio and went to the piano. Immediately, Jake's words came crashing down on her from long ago, words that at the time she didn't comprehend.

"Maggie, you can find many places to use your musical talent, but until you find the place God intended for you to use it, you won't find complete contentment. God has designed a plan for each of us, though few find it because they go their own way without asking Him to show them His way."

The concert in her apartment that night was solely for the Creator who had given Maggie her gift for music.

Lake City, Arkansas

WHEN THE CHRISTMAS EVE service was over and Jake had said goodbye to his dad and Lillian, he mingled with others for a few more minutes. He was aware that Lillian was making the rounds, introducing her niece, Caroline, and her children to all her friends. Suspicious that Lillian had other motives for bringing Caroline to Lake City, he found himself discreetly watching her. She had auburn hair about shoulder length, and he had to admit she had beautiful brown eyes. Her height fell somewhere between Maggie and Lizzie J., not tall or short, just average. She was also friendly and had a nice smile. He was watching her and trying to carry on a conversation at the same time when he overheard a more interesting conversation between Maggie's mom and another member of the church.

"Annie, I thought Maggie was coming home for Christmas. Where is she?"

"She called this morning and told me she's snowed in. All the flights were cancelled. I know she wanted to be here… I was so disappointed. She tried to sound as though she wasn't disappointed too," Annie replied.

"I know you were looking forward to having her home for Christmas. I'm so sorry that didn't work out. Is she doing well?"

"She hasn't been home since she helped me move to my new house, but I went to see her back in the summer. She stays on tour most of the time. Her agent is working on a concert date for Memphis early in the new year."

"You'll have to let me know if that works out. I would love to see her, especially in concert. Have a Merry Christmas and I hope Maggie can get a flight out soon."

"Merry Christmas, and I hope she can too!"

Jake had heard through the grapevine she was coming home, but he figured it was another rumor. He couldn't believe the sound of her name could make his heart race and his knees go weak.

He finally broke away long enough to get to the door. Before leaving, he turned back toward the group of people still milling about and saw Caroline watching him. Caught off guard, he waved and quickly left.

Out on the street in front of the church, a group of teenagers had gathered around to admire Jake's new car. As a Christmas present to himself, he had splurged on a silver Chevrolet Camaro, new and fully loaded. He'd had it only about a week and was still surprised at the attention it brought whenever he drove it. Jake had decided that if he was going to accept being a single male, then he would look the part.

Most of the time Jake drove his farm truck, but when he went out socially he wanted something nicer. He'd traded in his old 57 Chevy, finding it difficult to say goodbye to his first car. Letting the Chevy go seemed to Jake a step in the direction of letting Maggie go.

Jake talked to the guys and showed them the interior of the car, then started the motor. As he drove away, he was amused at the admirers he could see in his rearview mirror, watching the car until he turned the corner. He wondered if Maggie would admire his new possession. That thought made him a little angry, so he pushed her from his mind and suddenly thought about Caroline, who piqued his curiosity.

Going home right now seemed like a lonely idea. It was only nine, and he dreaded the emptiness he knew he would feel at home alone when so many other families were celebrating together. Though Jake had many friends and a busy life, he couldn't rely on friends to constantly keep him company. These times were the hardest and drove home to Jake that this life he was living had never been his plan.

He wondered about Caroline and what it must feel like to lose your husband and the father of your children in war. She looked happy, but so did he, proof that looks can be deceiving. He felt compassion for her and her children; he knew what it felt like to grow up without both parents. Caroline's children were much younger than Jake had been, though, and he wondered if they had any memories at all. As Jake grew older his memories of his mother became more and more dream-like, fuzzy around the edges.

Jake drove slowly through town, still in no hurry to get home. He had bought an old fifty-acre farm right outside of town, intending to demolish the dilapidated house. Instead, he'd become attached to the house and its history and renovated it, adding a large front porch supported with heavy, thickset posts that he felt gave the house a manly charm. When he bought the property, he had visions of building a new modern house that might tempt Maggie to want to live there with him. That was not long before her daddy died, and they'd been estranged since, so that dream was still just a dream.

Jake passed the road leading to his house and continued on

Highway 18 heading toward Jonesboro. As he neared the place of the fatal car crash, he thought about all that had occurred since his teenage years.

He had continued working on the Houstons' farm during college, and at the invitation of Andy's dad had even joined him as a partner. Jake's degree in Agriculture from Arkansas State coupled with Mr. Houston's years of experience gave them the right combination for success. Their cotton and soybean crops were the envy of every farmer in the region, and together they secured more acreage, growing quite large over the past three years. Jake was grateful for the opportunity Mr. Houston had given him.

He realized that in some ways he'd taken Andy's place. He trusted that Andy would be happy to know he was farming with his dad. Jake and Andy's friendship had begun with the conversation, that long-ago day in the drugstore, about farming. He thought about Andy's plan to marry Lizzie J. and live on the family farm. He also remembered Andy wanting a son to name Andrew Alexander Houston III. Jake thought about seeing Trey tonight at Lizzie J.'s and felt sad for his old friend who died unaware of his son. But Jake knew Andy was in Heaven and if given the chance to return, he wouldn't be interested.

Now Lizzie J. was happily married and the mother of that little boy along with her little girl, Maggie. She and her husband had agreed from the beginning that Trey would use the last name of Houston and understand who his father was. Jake admired the way the Houstons had accepted Lizzie J.'s husband and the relationship they enjoyed with Trey.

Jake felt as though he was the only person on the road; he'd passed only a couple of cars and was now entering the city limits of Jonesboro. He crossed over the railroad tracks and continued onto Highland Drive, looking for something open so he could at least get a coke. He finally gave up, pulled in to a service station and got a bottle drink out of a machine.

As he got back into his car and turned back toward Lake City, the longing for Maggie assaulted him. He wondered what she was doing. He figured she was at some Christmas Eve party with all the people in her circle that he had no desire to know. When he had returned home from New York the year before, after seeing Maggie leave her apartment with a man, he had insisted to Lizzie J. and everyone else that anything to do with Maggie was not to be discussed around him. Lizzie J. tried to reason with him, saying he didn't actually know who the man was or why they were together. But Jake was done, finished, and he didn't want to hear about her from anyone.

New York City

It was around eight and Maggie decided to rest for awhile before getting dressed for church. She snuggled under her favorite down comforter on her bed and quickly drifted off to sleep.

Maggie dreamed that Jake had married and no one had told her. He was working for her dad in the hardware store and living next door to her parents. In her dream, her parents treated Jake's children as if they were their own grandchildren. His wife and Lizzie J. were best friends. They were all laughing at her because she was in the cotton patch picking cotton all alone. Her hands were hurting, and Jake wasn't there to care.

Her phone rang and she sat straight up in bed, crying. That wasn't a dream—that was a nightmare! She tried to remember what Jake's wife looked like in her dream and how many kids they had. But like most dreams upon awaking, already the images were vague and hazy.

She didn't know what prompted her to cry—Jake being married, her daddy's presence, or Lizzie J. with another best friend. It made sense she would dream of all of them, as her whole day had been full of memories, and the mere sight of her daddy's spice bottles had made her cry while preparing dinner. She didn't understand, though, why she'd dreamed that Jake had gotten married.

She ignored her ringing phone. It was ten o'clock and she wanted to shower before dressing for church. She didn't feel like talking with anyone and she figured it was Miguel. She didn't care that the phone was still ringing when she stepped into the shower.

Maggie wasn't conceited, but she did know she was a beautiful woman since she'd been told quite often. She was blessed with thick shiny hair the color of corn silks that had not darkened over the years. She always wore it swept up off her neck and shoulders in some sort of bun when she was performing. Tonight, she weaved a French braid around the front of her head and left the rest long and flowing down her back.

She slipped into her dress and struggled to zip it up without help. Once finished, she saw that it accentuated her slender body and was pleased with the effort. The diamond earrings sparkled from the light above her mirror and added a touch of glamour. It was exactly the look she wanted, elegant and classy. She tucked her dress shoes into her leather bag, tugged on her snow boots and the rest of her attire that she'd worn earlier, and was ready. It was 11:30 and she had just enough time to walk to the church.

A blast of cold air took Maggie's breath away when she opened her front door. The snow on the ground seemed harder and slicker than it had earlier, and she fought to keep her balance. She hoped she could get there in thirty minutes, or she might freeze to death.

Her street could've been the front of any Christmas card, and Maggie quickly forgot about the cold as she admired all the decorations. An aura still enveloped the neighborhood, and the stars above seemed even brighter. She made good time and opened the door of the church with about ten minutes to spare.

Never having been there before, she was relieved to find someone right inside the door to give her directions. She was a nice elderly lady, and Maggie wondered how she had managed to get there in this snow-covered city.

Maggie took off her snow boots and reached into her bag for her dress shoes. She left her boots in the cloak room and hung her parka with all the other coats. She walked into the sanctuary and was surprised at the number of people who had come out on such a night as this. She realized that it must be an important part of their Christmas celebration to put forth such an effort.

After choosing an aisle seat, she began to look around, awed at the beauty of the interior. She realized that all the attention to detail on the exterior, which she'd noticed for the first time that day, had been lovingly lavished on the inside as well. She gazed at the high ceilings and beautiful stonework of the walls, but her interest in the architecture was interrupted when she noticed a group of people in quiet discussion at the front of the church. They began to disperse and started down the center aisle, stopping at each pew and quietly speaking to the person at the end. That person said something to the next one, and the whispered message was carried all throughout the congregation.

Finally a gentleman stopped, leaned in toward Maggie, and said, "Miss, do you play the piano? Our pianist fell ill this afternoon and we have no one to play music."

Really, Maggie thought—the first time I venture into a church as a new believer and they ask me if I can play the piano. She didn't know God had a sense of humor.

"Yes, I can play the piano. I'm not prepared, though."

"We have the music—it's simple, traditional Christmas music. I'm sure you'll do fine. We've asked everyone and you're the only person who has said you can play. We need you. Won't you consider it?"

Maggie hesitated, her mind rushing through all the reasons she should say no. Instead, she replied, "Sure I can do that." She rose from her seat and followed the gentleman down the aisle to the front of the church. It seemed to take forever to get to the piano, and a hush descended over the people as they watched her.

Reverend Thomas met her at the piano and immediately recognized her from earlier that afternoon.

"Maggie, right? Maggie Roberts? You came to the church this afternoon."

"Yes I did. It's nice to see you again," Maggie replied.

"So you play the piano?" he asked.

"Yes, but I've never played in church before," Maggie told him.

"Well, I know it will be a little different playing for an audience. You can pretend they aren't there," he reassured her, not realizing who she was. If Maggie hadn't been so polite, or hadn't wanted to remain incognito, she would've laughed at what he said.

"Do you have an order of service along with the music you want me to play?"

"Yes, here is the program, and the music book our pianist uses should be in the bench. I hope the music isn't too advanced—our pianist is quite accomplished."

"Well, I'll do my best," Maggie said, and smiled sweetly.

"Thank you so much. I'm sure this takes you out of your comfort zone, and I know the people here will appreciate your efforts. Honestly, you look as if you dressed for the part," Reverend Thomas said.

"You're welcome, and I promise you I had no idea when I dressed to come here that I would be asked to participate in the service. I guess God had other plans for me tonight," Maggie said, and turned toward the piano. It was a beautiful Steinway Grand and she couldn't wait to play it.

"Do you think you could find a few pieces in the book that you could play until we start? It shouldn't be more than a few minutes. And our pianist usually plays something at the end of the service as the people are leaving. You can choose whatever you would like."

"Sure," Maggie said as she took her seat.

Reverend Thomas patted her on the shoulder to reassure her and walked away. Maggie looked over the program, found the music and decided she wouldn't need the book. She hoped the church had kept the piano in good repair; she'd never before played for people without first listening to see if the piano was in tune. All she could do was begin playing.

As soon as she played the first note, she knew she was going to love this instrument. It was an expensive piano and she could tell it had been lovingly cared for. Maggie was a performer, and it took restraint for her to play with a casual demeanor. She played several simple songs and then followed the program.

The minister delivered a Christmas message and served communion. The service ended with a closing prayer. As soon as the minister said amen, Maggie began to play the Hallelujah Chorus with all the talent God had given her. Just because she'd never played in church didn't mean she hadn't played Handel's Messiah.

People who were leaving stopped, turned toward her, and found their seats again. All the well-wishing came to an end as a hush descended on the congregation. All eyes were on Maggie — they knew they were hearing someone special. Suddenly, throughout the church, people here and there began to recognize her and whispered her name to those around them.

Maggie didn't care — she wasn't playing for them but for her Heavenly Father, and when she hit the last note tears ran down her face and she knew she'd experienced His sweet Holy Spirit.

She remembered Jake telling her that people are placed in our lives for a reason; some for only moments, some for days, weeks or years. God had used her, *her*, for a few moments to bring all those people in the church that Christmas Eve of 1971 into worship.

JAKE FINALLY WENT to bed early on Christmas morning. He was glad Maggie had not answered her phone the evening before when he'd succumbed to the memories and the loneliness and called her apartment in a moment of weakness. He promised himself he wouldn't do that again.

CHAPTER TWENTY

Lake City, Arkansas
1964

L IZZIE J. PUSHED herself up into a sitting position on her bed, no easy task with the child she was carrying in her petite little body. She felt as though she'd had a visitor in her room the last thirty minutes, not her distant, uncaring mother. At least to Lizzie J. she'd always seemed that way. She dried her tears and thought back over their conversation.

Could her mother honestly mean the things she'd said? Lizzie J. was about to become a mother herself. She'd yearned for her mother through the years, and had accepted the fact that she would never be a part of her life. Now … Lizzie J. was skeptical. She had been disappointed and had her hopes dashed so many times growing up that she felt cynical and distrustful toward her mother. Her heart couldn't be broken again — she wouldn't allow it.

After talking to her daughter, Rita knew it was time to talk to her parents about her plans. She knew that none of them would believe she was serious. Rita was sadly aware of the distress she'd caused her parents through the years and the hurt she'd caused her only child. Her plan was the reason she'd come home to Arkansas. Now was the time.

Even though it was the middle of March, a weather system from the Gulf swept warm air into the region and the temperature that day was well into the seventies. In a few days the calendar would show spring arriving, but Mother Nature seemed to be bringing it now. Tiny buds were evident on some trees and the yellow bell bushes were in full bloom. Rita pushed open the screened door and walked out to the porch where her parents still sat in the swing. She pulled a chair up and sat down.

"I need to talk to both of you. Is now a good time?" Rita asked.

Her mom and dad looked at each other, then slowed the swing to a stop and looked at their daughter with a questioning expression.

"Sure, we can talk now. Are you okay?" her mom asked, noticing her daughter had been crying. "Is Lizzie J. okay?"

"Yes, I guess she is. I've already told her the things I want to tell you. I felt like I should tell her first." Rita felt like a naughty child caught in a terrible situation. She noticed her parents looked tired. They were wonderful, hard-working people — good neighbors and good parents.

"What's going on?" her dad asked.

"I want to come back. I want to move home," Rita said quietly.

Neither her mom nor her dad said anything for some time. They stared at their daughter for so long that Rita looked away; she could no longer look them in the eyes. What if they said no? Where would she go? What would she do?

"You mean to live here with us?" her mom finally asked.

"You want to leave California and move back here to Lake City?" her dad asked, surprise clearly in his voice. "Why?"

"Honestly, I'm tired. I'm tired of trying to get acting parts. I'm tired of trying to make a living on my own. I need help."

"What about Clark? What does he want? What do you mean, make a living on your own?" her dad asked.

"Clark left me almost two years ago for a younger woman. Our divorce was final several months ago. I haven't been able to find the words to tell you. I'm so embarrassed that I'm forty years old and need help. Now you know the truth."

Rita looked down at the floor, afraid of what she would see in her parents' eyes. They had the right to be smug and unforgiving. They could also say, "I told you so." Her tears began to fall again. Madeline went to her daughter and wrapped her arms around her. Rita hugged her mom and hoped this was an indication they could forgive her and help her.

"I'm so sorry for all the hurt I've caused you both through the years. When Lizzie J. was a baby and I left her with you, I had plans to come for her. But it never seemed to be the right time. When I felt that I could support her, she was so attached to the two of you and you both loved her so much that I didn't see how I had the right to do that. Days turned into weeks that turned into months that turned into years. When you called me and told me about Lizzie J., I knew I had to take a long hard look at my life. I was living in a furnished, seedy apartment barely surviving and I want more than that."

"What happened to all the assets that you and Clark had? What happened to your house and the business you owned together?" Paul asked his daughter.

"The business fell apart while Clark was off doing other things. He ignored the business, and by the time I realized what was going on, it was too late. Like all the mistakes in my life, by the time I realize the mistake has been made it's too late to correct it. He left me and moved in with his new girlfriend, and we lost the house." Rita was twisting her hands together, still not able to look up. Admitting to what she'd been going through the past couple of years was painfully embarrassing.

"Are you asking to move in with us and live here? Are you planning to get a job?" her dad asked.

"I've worked office jobs in the past and I think I can find something in Jonesboro, and yes, I would need to live with you until I can save a little money. I know I'm asking a lot, and I promise I'll pay you back as soon as I can."

"What did Lizzie J. say when you told her you wanted to move home?" Madeline asked.

"She didn't say anything. She wouldn't look at me. I know I've hurt her over the years, and I know I may never be able to mend our relationship. I'm happy and grateful she's had the two of you as parents. You probably did a much better job than I could have anyway."

Rita continued staring at the floor. Her parents were so stunned they didn't know what else to ask or what to say, so they remained silent.

"*Please*," Rita finally said, quietly.

"Of course you can stay. You'll need a job, though, and quickly. What about all your possessions? Your clothes?" Madeline asked her.

"Except for the clothes I brought, I sold it all. It wasn't much, but it brought enough money for me to get here. I don't have a lot of money left, though."

"We can help you until you get a few paychecks, but it is a loan and you'll have to pay us back," Paul told her.

"I will, I promise—and thank you. You won't be sorry. I'll work hard and I'll make you proud, and I will make it up to Lizzie J. for all the lost years. I will!"

LIZZIE J. HAD come into the living room and through the open door heard the conversation between her mother and grandparents. She needed to talk to Maggie, so she left a note on the kitchen table and quietly left by the back door.

Andy was the one she wanted to talk to. Though he'd been gone only a few months, it seemed forever since she felt his touch and heard his voice. By now they should be married and living on the farm as they'd always planned. She missed him so much that sometimes she thought she might actually die from her broken heart. The only thing that kept her going was the baby. It seemed every time she thought she couldn't go on, the baby would move, kick, or sometimes get the hiccups. It always made Lizzie J. smile. She felt that somehow this baby was reminding her that in a few weeks she would be needed.

Knocking twice, loudly, Lizzie J. stood on Maggie's porch waiting for someone to come to the door. She suddenly realized it was a school day. Maggie wouldn't be home for hours, and her parents were probably at the hardware store. Lizzie J. didn't want to go back home, and she didn't think the Roberts would mind if she went around to their back porch. She and Maggie had spent many hours on their porch swing, and right now it felt like the best place in the world to be.

THE HOUSE THAT Charlie had bought and paid for with cash was modest. Since he'd grown up with and was accustomed to elegant surroundings, he'd furnished his house with fine furniture — not ostentatious, just sturdy and well-made. Over the past few years, he'd slowly remodeled the interior. He did all of the work he knew how to do and only hired others when he didn't. Usually he would find someone from Jonesboro, Monette or Caraway to do the work he needed. Someone coming into his home from another town kept the gossip to a minimum. The workers were the only people who had been inside his house, except for a few visitors from Memphis.

Charlie lay on his bed, staring at the ceiling and trying to comprehend everything that had happened that day. It almost seemed a dream, but he knew it wasn't. Over and over he kept thinking about Lizzie J. Was it possible he might be her father? From the first time he met her, he felt a connection. All this time he thought it was because he felt so responsible for the car accident that took Andy's life, and his guilt was causing his feelings to spiral out of control. Now, he wondered if there was a deeper connection, a blood connection that he could feel. Was that possible? Before having the knowledge that they indeed were related?

Sitting up on the side of his bed, he leaned over and opened the drawer of his night stand. He reached for the small metal chest that held the things he'd kept as a reminder of his months with Katie. Charlie had not allowed himself to open it in a long, long time.

Slowly he turned the clasp and opened the top, peeking inside as if he expected to be startled by something he'd forgotten was there. Without touching the papers or photos, he stared at the contents, knowing he was going to regret looking through the remnants of the happiest days of his life spent with the only woman he'd ever loved. Before he could pick up the first photo, someone knocked on his door and he knew it was her.

Rita had casually asked her dad who his fishing buddy was, and Paul had told her what little he knew about Charlie, which happened to include where he lived. Later, she left the house telling her family she was going to the store.

Charlie heard her knock a second time and knew he might as well answer the door. She probably wouldn't go away, or if she did, she probably would come back. He felt old. He hadn't seen Katie for at least nineteen years. He turned the doorknob and slowly opened the door. They stared at each other, neither saying anything for a few seconds. Then Charlie found his voice.

"Come in ... Rita. It is Rita, right?"

"Are you sure?" she asked him hesitantly.

"Sure if I know your name? Or if I want you to come in?" Charlie asked, with sarcasm he couldn't hide.

Rita, ignoring the sarcasm, stepped inside and was not surprised by the quality of his furnishings and the décor. She would've been surprised to see anything less. The house had a masculine feel to it, and anyone who entered would know that no woman occupied these premises.

Charlie closed the door and turned to face this woman he'd dreamed of over the years and thought he would never see again. Even though he knew she was real, he almost felt like it was another dream. She was nineteen years older and still beautiful.

"Well, I could ask you the same thing. Charlie or James?" Rita asked in return.

"Both would be correct. But somehow I don't think you can say the same. I think Katie may be an alias, although for the life of me I can't figure out why."

"I was young."

"That's your justification for giving me a fake name? What's your reason for running away? I looked for you in all the places I thought you might possibly be, and it was as if you'd vanished into thin air. Of course Katie Griffin only existed to you, me and a few other people. What were you doing and why were you lying to me?" Charlie demanded, becoming angrier as he questioned her.

"I left home and didn't want my parents to find me. I wanted to go to California and become an actress. Like I said, I was young and foolish and I never meant to hurt you. I thought it was exciting to be someone else, almost as if I was acting a part—certainly not being deceitful, which as an adult I began to realize was exactly what I'd been." Rita was trying hard to explain, but she knew her words sounded hollow.

"That doesn't explain why you left. I know I was older and settled, but I loved you and could've given you a good life."

"I knew how wealthy you were. I wasn't looking for someone to take care of me. I wanted to be famous and make my own money! I wanted to be rich and prominent in my own right."

All Charlie heard was actress, something about playing a part, being famous and hiding from her parents. It all sounded so sordid and wrong. Could a relationship under such false pretenses produce a beautiful person like Lizzie J.? He had to know—that was the first answer he wanted.

"Lizzie J. is my daughter, isn't she?" Charlie asked quietly, an echo of sadness overtaking the anger in his voice.

"Yes." That was Rita's only response as she held his gaze. She'd come home for help and to make amends with her daughter and parents. Never in her wildest imagination did she expect to be confronted by the father of her only child. But she was determined to correct *all* her mistakes, and ask forgiveness from *everyone* she'd hurt.

"Why didn't you come to me? I would have gladly taken her and you could have gone on with the life you wanted. You robbed me! Get out! Leave! I don't want to see you and I don't want to hear your explanations!"

"Please, can't we talk about this? I came home to ask my parents and my daughter to forgive me. I know I hurt you and I need your forgiveness, too," Rita pleaded.

"I don't know if I'll ever be able to do that. I told you to leave." Charlie wasn't yelling now, but his anger burned beneath the quietness of his voice.

"Well, I have questions too! I came back to Memphis the next year looking for you. All I could find out was that you'd sold the mill. No one would talk to me or give me any information. Why are you using the name Charlie, and how in the world did you wind up living here?" Now Rita was getting mad as well. She would take responsibility for what she'd done wrong, but Charlie, or James, or whatever his name was, wasn't completely innocent either!

Charlie glared at her. He wanted to push her out the door and back out of his life. He liked his life—no drama, no responsibilities, and no one to tell him what to do. He'd become complacent. Now in the course of one short day his world had been turned upside down. He'd found out he was a father, and with that knowledge came the realization that he would soon be a grandfather.

Rita glared back at him. She noticed he was fit and healthy looking. Nostalgia swept over her as she remembered the love they'd shared many years ago. She knew the chances of anyone ever believing she'd honestly loved him were slim, though.

"You didn't answer either of my questions. Why did you change your name to Charlie?" While glaring at each other, they both realized they needed answers. The anger in the room abated.

"I needed to escape the business world, make it harder for people to find me. After you left I started to ignore my business, and at the advice of good friends who cared about me, I sold it. So I started using my middle name Charles, and then after a while, I began to think Charlie Chandler sounded like a regular guy — and that's what I longed to be … a regular guy."

Rita thought about Clark and how he'd started to ignore their business when he started his affair. She sure wished he'd had good friends who could have stepped in and protected their investments.

"Why did you leave Memphis?"

"I was tired of living in the city, and one morning over a cup of coffee I read an article in the paper about Lake City. I was intrigued, so I drove here on a Sunday afternoon, and a few weeks later I moved here."

"How long have you lived here?"

"Six, maybe seven years. I don't pay much attention to time. What changed? Why do you suddenly want to come back and live here? Why now?" Charlie asked her.

"Well, it wasn't sudden. My husband, or rather ex-husband, walked out on me a couple of years ago and moved in with his much younger girlfriend. He didn't have friends looking out for his business like you did, and by the time I realized what was going on, it was too late. The business went under and I couldn't keep the house by myself. When you find yourself living in a furnished, seedy apartment in a not-so-good part of town, and you look in the mirror and see your youth is gone, you know it's time to realize your dream has turned into a nightmare."

Charlie felt a flash of sympathy for her but quickly squelched that emotion. He didn't trust her.

"That's quite a story," Charlie said.

"No harder to believe than yours," Rita shot back.

"Touché," Charlie said with a hint of a smile.

With their anger now set aside, uneasiness settled over them and they stayed quiet for what seemed an eternity.

Rita finally broke their awkward silence. "My dad told me you were the other driver in the accident back in August, and that's how you two became friends."

"Yes, that's true. I was the other driver. After the accident, I started going to church and one Sunday Lizzie J. followed me outside to talk to me. She wanted to tell me she didn't hold me responsible for the accident. Then I met your parents, and yes, we became friends."

"That must have been difficult."

"You have no idea the pain I've experienced since that fateful night. I didn't know Andy, but I've heard he was a fine young man. Lizzie J. loved him, and knowing that has made it even harder."

"The whole story seems almost unbelievable. Moving to Lake City, then being involved in an accident with a daughter you didn't even know you had? Are you sure you had no idea Lizzie J. is your daughter?"

"You have to remember, I didn't know where you were from and what your real name was. And … how could I know I was a father? Or that I had a daughter?" Charlie asked her quietly.

"What do we do now? She's always wanted to know who her father was. I never told her because I didn't think it was wise since I didn't know how to find you."

"Please don't say anything to her yet. I need time to think about this. It's not that I don't want to acknowledge her — I just need to be prepared if she doesn't accept me. That would break my heart again."

CHAPTER TWENTY-ONE

1971

JAKE WAS AWAKE early on Christmas morning, lying in bed, resisting the desire to go back to the woods. He loved the solitude, but memories always seemed to find him there and he didn't need that today. Even though he was a single man, he did have a Christmas tree. Of course it was decorated with John Deere ornaments, little bales of cotton and other things that looked somewhat masculine. He'd shopped diligently for these items — no fancy glass balls, silver and gold tinsel or dainty ornaments for his tree.

The thick oak mantel over his stone fireplace was decorated, but not with fake greenery. His was straight out of the woods, and the cedar aroma gave his house Christmas spirit. Lots of guys didn't care where they lived, and certainly didn't care about being responsible for their own house. But Jake loved his house and the land it rested on. And he enjoyed each brushstroke of paint he put on the walls. Even though Maggie Roberts still occupied most of his heart, this place had the rest of it.

Reluctantly, Jake got out of bed and went into the kitchen to start a pot of coffee before taking a shower. He had the whole day in front of him with no one to see or nowhere to go until time for dinner at his dad's.

Since his break-up with Maggie, his long hot showers had become a place for brooding. While the hot water cascaded over him, his thoughts turned to the lady, Caroline, who would also be at dinner. He smiled, thinking he had quite the ego to automatically assume Lillian's ulterior motive was to play matchmaker between them. He'd be embarrassed if anyone knew his thoughts. He remembered the look on his dad's face last night and wondered if he could be right.

Jake dreaded trying to make small talk with someone he didn't know. He'd tried to date other women and simply gave up. It was too much work, and he could never wait until the night was over and he could deposit them at their door.

He figured he would put in an appearance at dinner and leave as quickly as he could without being rude. He guessed in a way, by marriage, she was his step-cousin. Maybe it would be easier to make conversation if he kept that in mind. He sure hoped she wasn't looking to replace her husband.

After getting dressed, Jake went into the living room and turned on the Christmas tree lights. In the kitchen, he opened the curtains over the window and stood still for several minutes gazing at the fields around his house that were lying fallow until spring. This was the most difficult season for Jake. He loved the outdoors—especially spring when the birds were mating, the frogs were croaking and he could smell the fresh earth as he tilled the ground in preparation for planting. It would be several weeks before that would happen, though, so he slowly turned to the coffee pot, poured a cup, and went back to his recliner in the living room.

About mid-morning, Jake's doorbell rang. He certainly

wasn't expecting anyone and wondered who it could be on Christmas day. He opened the door to find Lizzie J., Trey, and little Maggie on his front porch holding gifts. Maggie was smiling, shyly. She was only two, and this was her first time to deliver a gift to someone. Trey had a gift for Jake, too.

"Hey, Merry Christmas! Come in!" Jake said and held the door open wide.

"Good morning, and Merry Christmas to you, too," Lizzie J. said and gave him a hug.

"Y'all didn't have to bring presents."

"Maggie wouldn't have it any other way. We had to get gifts for Uncle Jake."

"I wanted to, too, and you brought gifts to us last night, remember?" Trey said as he took off his jacket. Trey loved to visit Jake, especially during farming season. He loved spending time with Jake and his Grandpa Houston. Trey and Maggie both thought they were related to Jake, though Lizzie J. had tried over and over to explain that they were only friends. She'd finally given up and he became Uncle Jake.

"Well, thank you both," Jake said as he took the gifts from them.

"Open, open, huwwy," Maggie cried in her little girl voice, and the difficulty with her pronunciation made Jake chuckle.

"Okay, come over here on the couch and sit beside me, and I'll open this pretty package and see what's inside. Did you wrap it?"

"Yes," Maggie replied, her head bobbing up and down with great emphasis as she wiggled her way onto Jake's lap.

"I wrapped mine too," Trey said, wanting to sound important.

"Well, I would have expected you to, you're getting so big!"

Jake told him as he tousled his hair. Jake loved this little boy and never took their relationship for granted.

He opened Maggie's gift first—she insisted. With her mom's help, she'd chosen a thermos for Jake to take when he went hunting, fishing or working on the farm. Maggie clapped her little hands together when he opened it, and he praised her for the nice gift she'd given him.

Next was the gift from Trey. All on his own, he'd told his mom that Jake needed new bandanas. Jake tied them around his head in the heat of the summer to keep the sweat from running into his eyes. Trey told Lizzie J. that Uncle Jake's bandanas had holes in them and he needed new ones.

"Trey, did you choose these by yourself?"

"Yeah. Yours were looking awful. Now you can throw the old ones away!"

"Thank you. Next time you go out to the field with me, you can borrow one and we can each wear one."

"Great! That would be awesome," Trey said and gave Jake a look of adoration. "Maybe Aunt Maggie will come home in the summer since she couldn't be here today. Did you know she was snowed in at her house in New York City?"

Lizzie J. and Jake exchanged looks, but Jake didn't miss a beat and replied, "Yeah, maybe she will. I'm sorry you didn't get to spend Christmas with her."

"Yeah, me too. I wish she didn't live so far away."

Jake didn't respond. He lightly ruffled Trey's hair again and gave Lizzie J. a sad smile.

The visit didn't last long; the family had other stops to make. Jake hugged them all and thanked them for remembering him. When they were gone, his desire for a family was so overwhelming that he called his dad to see if he could arrive a little early for dinner. Suddenly, the house he loved so much seemed empty and lonely.

New York City was still covered in deep snow on Christmas morning. Since the sun was now shining, the runways at La Guardia were being cleared and some flights had already been allowed to take off. But Maggie had decided to cancel her flight to Arkansas. In the past twenty-four hours, she had made life-changing plans, beginning with her acceptance that she needed God in her life.

Her plan was two-fold. First, to finally acknowledge her musical talent was God-given and let Him lead her to a place of service. Maggie had proven her success by the world's standards; now she wanted to know what God wanted her to do with this gift.

Second, Maggie planned to grow in her faith and find out if she and Jake were meant to be together. She still loved him and knew he still loved her, but Jake's words about being sure you're with the right person kept running through her mind. She'd gone her own way with her music and never found true happiness and contentment; she certainly didn't want to make that mistake in a marriage relationship.

Knowing she needed to call her mom and Lizzie J. and break the news to them that she wouldn't be coming home anytime soon was upsetting. She didn't want to disappoint them, especially Trey and Maggie, but she knew her future depended on the decisions she would be making in the coming days. She didn't want outside influences, not even from the people who loved her. These decisions needed to be between her and God.

Maggie was twenty-six and a successful single woman living a privileged lifestyle. Even though she'd earned that lifestyle, she was aware few people get to travel while also experiencing the validation of their talent. For that she was truly grateful. And with her new faith and desire to serve God, she was also thankful to still be a virgin. Not by her choice, though, she thought—by Jake's commitment to God and his desire to follow God's commands. She wondered if Jake had waited, too.

These thoughts led her back in time to Lizzie J. and her mother. Maggie didn't want to be forty years old, divorced, and needing help from her mom. She wondered what blessings she'd missed out on in the past from her stubbornness and the appalling anger she'd had toward God. As Maggie studied her Bible in the coming days, she would learn about God's grace and be changed even more. Getting to know her Savior would also call to her memory the times she'd seen His intervention in people's lives, and she'd been totally unaware of it. One of those times was the birth of Trey and how that served as a healing between two people who truly needed each other.

CHAPTER TWENTY-TWO

Lake City, Arkansas
1964

AGGIE UNLOCKED THE front door, stepped inside and deposited her books on the table in the foyer. She knew she was alone in the house — an empty house felt, well ... empty. She went to her room to change clothes. The weather had turned warm while she was in school, and her sweater felt suffocating. She rummaged in her closet for something cooler that she'd not packed away at the end of summer the year before.

After finally getting dressed, but shunning shoes, Maggie padded barefoot into the kitchen to get a snack. The house felt warm and she pushed the drapes aside to open the sliding glass doors. She was startled to see her best friend curled up and fast asleep in the porch swing. It hurt Maggie's heart to look at her. Lizzie J. was close to her delivery date, and her little body was stretched to accommodate the baby growing inside of her.

Maggie stood immobile, brooding quietly for several minutes as she watched Lizzie J. sleep. She wondered what was in the future for Lizzie J., and more importantly, what lay ahead for the baby, now lying safe and secure in Lizzie J.'s womb. It was sad that Andy had died never knowing Lizzie J. was pregnant with their child. Maggie experienced a whole range of emotions when she thought Lizzie J. might have to give the baby up for adoption to some unknown couple. Disbelief was high on the list. Maggie was about to hear other news from her best friend that would fall into that same category.

Maggie quietly pushed open the glass door and stepped out onto the porch. Lizzie J. didn't move and Maggie wasn't sure what to do. She could tell she was sleeping soundly and didn't want to frighten her.

"Hey Lizzie J., it's me, Maggie," she said as she touched her gently.

Lizzie J. opened her eyes and a small smile spread across her face when she saw Maggie, her best friend, the one person in the whole world who understood her.

"Hey yourself, 'bout time you got home. I've been here so long I fell asleep. What time is it?"

"Almost three. How long have you been here?" Maggie asked.

"Most of the day, I guess," Lizzie J. replied as she slowly rose to a sitting position and yawned. Her stomach growled loudly.

"What was that?" Maggie asked. "You didn't eat lunch, did you?"

"No, I guess I missed lunch and I'm starved. I need to pee, too — hurry Maggie, open the door!"

"Okay, okay, now run — oh yeah, you can't," Maggie teased as she opened the door. Lizzie J. shot her a fake angry look and lumbered as fast as she could to the bathroom.

"Hurry back and let's get something to eat. You need to feed that baby, you know," Maggie yelled after her.

Maggie opened the refrigerator and took out all the makings for a sandwich. She found a bowl of leftover potato salad and set it on the counter. Lizzie J. returned to the kitchen and found a seat at the table. She was quietly watching when the memory of her morning and her conversation with her mom caused her to feel sick inside. Neither of them had said anything since coming in, and Maggie stole a glance at her friend.

"Lizzie J., what's wrong? Are you feeling sick? Are you in labor?" Maggie reached over and popped the bread up out of the toaster, laid down the tomato and knife, wiped her hands on a dishcloth and pulled a chair up close and sat down. "Are you okay? You look terrible. What's wrong?"

Concern and sympathy from Maggie caused Lizzie J. to lose control of all her emotions that had been building since her grandparents told her that her mother was coming for a visit. Lizzie J. put her head down, and the agony she'd been feeling all day came out in gasps as she cried and cried. Maggie tried to hug her and find out what was wrong, but Lizzie J. couldn't speak through her sobs. Maggie simply held her and let her cry.

Finally, Lizzie J. raised her tear-streaked face and said, "she's here — she came back and wants to live here again."

"Who's here? Who are you talking about?"

"My mom," Lizzie J. replied miserably.

"Your mom is here? Here in Lake City? When did she get here? What do you mean she wants to live here?"

"She came this morning. They didn't tell me she was coming until right before she arrived. I don't want her here. She's never cared about me before, so why now? Oh Maggie, everything is such a mess. How did all of this happen? I don't know where to go or what to do. I'm so afraid they will make me give my baby up for adoption. I'll run away before I do that. I promise you, Maggie, I will — I'll run away!"

"Shhh, don't say things like that. You won't have to run

away, and you won't have to give up your baby. I know that won't happen. We'll find a way for you to keep your baby. Andy would want you to. Maybe the Houstons will help."

"She's divorced. And she doesn't have any money," Lizzie J. said sadly.

"Your mom is *divorced*?"

"I overheard her talking to Nanny and Poppy. Clark left her for a younger woman, and they lost their business and their house. After the divorce, she was living in a bad part of town in a furnished apartment. Except for the clothes she brought, she sold everything else to be able to afford the trip out here. She tried to tell my grandparents that the reason she never took me home with her was because she saw how much they loved me and didn't feel it would be fair to take me away. Can you believe she would make up something like that? Now that she needs help, she comes here and acts like she cares about me! I couldn't listen to her any longer, so I left a note on the kitchen table that I was coming here and I haven't been back."

"Lizzie J., I'm so sorry. My mom has always said there was probably a reason that your mom left you with your nanny and poppy. Maybe what she told your grandparents is the truth. I know you've always wanted to be with your mom. Maybe this is a good thing for you."

"How can you say that? Surely you don't believe she can suddenly waltz into my life and become the kind of mom you've always had," Lizzie J. said, her misery evident in her words.

"Lizzie J., I know she can't change all the years she's been absent, but she can start changing today. Wouldn't that be better than if she was never a part of your life?"

"I don't trust her. She promised Poppy she would get a job and find a place to live as soon as she could. She always loved living in California, and she always wanted to be a famous actress. So now all of a sudden she wants to live in Lake City, Arkansas, again? I don't believe her."

"Well, time will tell. Now, dry your tears and let's eat. You need to stay strong for your baby."

"Thank you, Maggie. Since Andy died, I feel you're the only person in the world who understands me, and the only one I can trust. I get so mad at Nanny and Poppy. Why don't they understand how much I already love this baby?"

"I'm not sure. Maybe because you still seem like a child to your grandparents. Funny thing is most people their age were already married when they were our age!" Maggie said.

"You know, you're right! I remember Nanny said she was only sixteen and Poppy was nineteen when they got married. Maybe I need to remind them of that," Lizzie J. said, and smiled as though she'd found a way to get through to them and make them understand she was old enough to be a mother.

WITHIN A WEEK, Rita found a clerical position in Jonesboro. She had many long, serious, heartfelt conversations with her parents and felt confident she could restore their relationship with honesty and lots of hard work. She made no progress with Lizzie J., though. Her daughter was barely civil to her, and Rita sadly began to see all she'd missed during the years away. She was determined to reach her daughter, even if it took another eighteen years.

Charlie Chandler was another matter. Rita hadn't seen him since the day she'd gone to his house. Gratefully, with her new job, she was away all day and tired when she returned home. Night time, however, brought memories to the surface she'd not thought about in many years. She was still amazed that he lived in Lake City. What were the chances that out of all the places he could have chosen to live a different life he wound up in this little farming town nestled along the St. Francis River? Was that fate? Or divine intervention? She didn't know.

Sleeping late on the first weekend of her new job was Rita's plan. She knew, though, the best laid plans can go horribly awry. Everyone in the house was up at six. Lizzie J. was in labor! She'd awakened Nanny, and while standing next to her grandparents' bed, her water broke and the warm fluid that had cushioned her baby began trickling down her legs and dripping onto the floor.

"Nanny, I've been having contractions for awhile, and my water broke. I think I'm in labor! We need to go to the hospital. Can you call Maggie? I want her to be there," Lizzie J. said as she caught her breath between contractions. Lizzie J. was worried. She knew it was too early to have this baby; she was still two weeks away from her delivery date. Her doctor had told her that first babies take a long time and the labor is usually long. If this was only the beginning, she thought, it was going to be a long day.

"Lizzie J., it's too early—we can call her later," Nanny said as she jumped up from her bed. She hurriedly threw on some clothes and began scurrying around trying to be sure they had everything they would need. She was flustered; her baby was having a baby. She wondered how this could happen again, as she remembered the day Lizzie J. was born.

"Mom, if Lizzie J. wants Maggie with her and Maggie wants to be there, I think we should call her. How about I call her and let her know, okay?" Rita asked gently. She'd heard all the commotion, gotten out of bed and was standing in the doorway listening to their conversation.

Lizzie J. could feel the resentment rising in her chest. She didn't want her mom to help, didn't want her to go to the hospital with them, and didn't want her in her life. She wanted her to go away! Rita knew how her daughter felt about her. She had naively thought that after a few days Lizzie J. would be more receptive to her, but if anything, Rita felt more resentment from her daughter with each passing day. She would not give up! Since she'd moved back here to a simpler way of life, she had discovered it felt good and right.

"It's okay, you don't have to call her. Nanny can call her later," Lizzie J. said, dismissing the help her mom offered.

Rita didn't reply.

Maggie was waiting at the hospital when they arrived. Lizzie J. saw her standing by the front door. "Nanny, did you call Maggie?"

"No. Rita, did you call her?" Madeline asked.

"Yes, Lizzie J., I knew it was important to you and I wanted her to be here too."

Lizzie J. didn't reply. Madeline hurried inside and asked if someone could bring a wheelchair out to get Lizzie J. This might be a first baby, but her contractions were intense and coming close together. When they got her to the maternity floor and examined her progress, they found she'd already dilated to seven centimeters. The nurses calmly went through their normal routine, while Madeline, Rita and Maggie paced the hallway and worried.

Finally, they allowed the women to go into the labor room with Lizzie J., but after only a few minutes, Madeline became faint and had to leave. So Lizzie J. was left with her mom, who she always felt had abandoned her, and her best friend, who she trusted more than anyone else.

Maggie had never witnessed the birth of a baby. Over the past few months, she'd had somewhat of an education as she watched Lizzie J.'s belly burgeoning with the new life growing inside her. Now she would see the results of all those months of pregnancy.

"Ohhh, it hurts so much, I can't do this!" Lizzie J. cried.

"I know it hurts. It won't be much longer, and it's the only way to get this baby into the world," Rita told her daughter.

Her contractions were close together, and the pain intensified, causing Lizzie J. to cry out and moan. Maggie wasn't much help. She wanted to be, but she was uncomfortable in this situation and actually felt nauseous. She stayed in the room, unable to offer Lizzie J. any comfort. Since Madeline was not there either, the comforting and reassurances had to come from Rita.

The nurse would come and go, checking on Lizzie J.'s progress and vital signs. Rita never left her daughter's side. She crooned soft encouraging words and cooled Lizzie J.'s brow with a wet cloth. Since she'd been absent from her daughter's life, it occurred to Rita that any time Lizzie J. had been sick, her grandmother, Madeline, had taken care of her. That thought made her physically sick, and she had to push those images from her mind to stem the tears she felt building. She wanted to be strong for Lizzie J. — she would not think about that now.

Now and then, Maggie left the room and reported to Lizzie J.'s grandparents, who sat in the waiting room. She wanted to be strong for her best friend, but she felt relieved to be away from the moaning and struggle. She was more convinced than ever that she was not ready to be married, and she definitely wasn't ready to have a child.

Maggie stood for a long while at the windows, looking out on the beautiful sunny day, reluctant to go back to the labor room. Then she looked around the waiting room, noticing the plastic chairs, old magazines, and empty coffee cups that littered the tables, and wondered about the others waiting, too. Now and then, an expectant dad would come out and update the waiting family members, excitement and joy on all their faces. Watching the others somehow made Maggie sadder, and she decided being with Lizzie J. was better than this, so she went back in, promising herself she would be strong.

"Hey, I'm back. Your grandparents are patiently waiting. How are things in here?" Maggie asked.

"Her cervix is almost completely dilated. When that happens she can start to push. Hopefully, it won't be too much longer," Rita explained.

Lizzie J. moaned as another contraction began. Before it was over she was grunting, and Maggie closed her eyes, willing herself to be strong and remain in the room.

"How much longer? I feel like I need to push. Please get the nurse to come back in," Lizzie J. begged.

After two more strong contractions, the nurse came in and was surprised that Lizzie J. was ready to push this baby out into the world. Soon the room was full as the doctor and two more nurses arrived. A cart was brought into the room to hold the baby, and the pediatric nurse began readying the items necessary for all the things she would need to be sure this baby was healthy. "Lizzie J., you're ready to push. We'll count to ten when you begin, but don't stop pushing until we say ten, okay?"

Maggie began to feel excitement building in the room and

knew something miraculous was about to happen. She was allowed to stand on one side of Lizzie J., at the head of the bed, with Rita on the other side.

After thirty minutes of watching Lizzie J. push, cry, sweat, groan, and make other sounds she didn't know a human could make, Maggie felt no more excitement. She was shocked at the number of people gathered around watching for this baby to make an entrance, with Lizzie J.'s legs spread wide to make room. Maggie had never given much thought to the birth process or how many people would be needed. She seemed to be the only one in the room uncomfortable with the situation; even Lizzie J. seemed uncaring.

"Keep pushing, Lizzie J. We can see the baby's head, with lots of black hair," the nurse announced.

"Ohhhh, I can't push. I'm too tired!!!!"

"Yes you can! Now push—one, two, three, four, five, six, seven, eight, nine, ten. Okay, now breathe. Here comes another strong contraction. Push Lizzie J., keep pushing—the baby is almost here! The baby's head is out; one more push to get the shoulders and it will all be over. Push Lizzie J.!!"

Lizzie J. raised her head and shoulders from the bed, drew her knees high, gave a hard push, and the baby slipped from her body into the bright lights of the delivery room—a tiny, perfect boy.

Andrew Alexander Houston III entered this world as a healthy six-pound baby with a head full of raven black hair. His cries were strong and robust. As he made his presence known, his mother, grandmother, and adopted aunt all wept tears of joy and relief.

After her son was checked out by the nurses and swaddled in a warm blanket, Lizzie J. was finally allowed to hold him.

She shed tears of joy, grateful that he was healthy, but also tears of grief, for this child would never know his father. She vowed to her son that she would talk about Andy, share photos, and try her best to introduce him to his father who had passed into eternity unaware of his existence. This day was bittersweet.

Later in the evening, when Lizzie J. was settled into her room, the enormity of her situation was all she could think about. Even though her grandparents had held the baby, she was still afraid of what they might suggest or who they might have waiting to take him away. Maggie was ready to tell Lizzie J. goodbye and go home. It had been a long day and she was ready to get some rest. She knew Lizzie J. needed rest, too.

"Maggie, thank you so much for being here today. It was so great to have you in the room with me when little Andy took his first breath."

Maggie started to reply when she noticed tears running down Lizzie J.'s face.

"Lizzie J., what's wrong? Why are you crying?" Maggie asked.

"Oh, Maggie, I'm so afraid they'll take him away. What if they have a couple waiting to come and get him?"

"Lizzie J., I don't think they can do that. I'm almost certain you would have to sign papers allowing that. Besides, now that your mom is here, you have extra help."

"I can't depend on her."

"She was here today and never left your side. You never needed her before; you always had your Nanny and Poppy, and she knew that. Give her a chance. If you're right, and she lets you down, then you can tell me 'I told you so,' but she deserves a chance."

"I don't think she deserves anything! She left me with my grandparents when I was a baby. When I look at my baby, I can't imagine leaving him with anyone."

"Be careful not to judge her actions when you weren't in her situation. Sometimes when we have all the details we understand things a little better. Some mothers do give their babies up for adoption. They love them so much, and they want their babies to be taken care of if they can't do it. It takes a lot of love to do that. Maybe your mother loved you more than you can imagine."

"I doubt that, and honestly, I don't want to talk about it."

"Okay, I'm sorry. We won't talk about that now. Your baby is beautiful, Lizzie J., and I'm so happy you have him to love. You'll always have a part of Andy." Maggie hugged her best friend and left the room, suddenly feeling like she'd somehow lost something special. She'd watched her best friend give birth to a perfect, little person who would need his mother more than Maggie had ever needed her. Maggie knew the birth of this baby had moved her to second place in Lizzie J.'s life.

Out in the hallway, as Maggie was saying goodbye, she asked Rita if she could talk to her for a minute. Maggie told her that Lizzie J. was afraid she would be forced to give her baby up. Rita assured Maggie that wouldn't happen, and she would reassure Lizzie J. about that too.

Lizzie J.'s fears were soon put to rest. The love she had for this baby that she'd carried these many months spread to the rest of the family. As soon as they gazed at this precious baby boy, they rallied around him and his mother and closed ranks. There would be no adoption. She would keep her baby.

RITA KEPT HER promise to her parents. She worked hard on all areas of her life and saved every dime she could from her new job. She was a huge help to her daughter since the birth of little Andy. And now, the first of May, not yet two months since her arrival, she was moving into an apartment in Jonesboro. It was affordable, not fancy, in a safe part of the city. Rita wanted Lizzie J. to move with her and go to night classes at Arkansas State while she kept the baby. Lizzie J. refused her mom's offer of help, so Rita decided to go forward with her move and not be a burden to her parents any longer. For now, Rita would live there alone, and Lizzie J. and little Andy would remain with Nanny and Poppy.

Lizzie J. and Maggie were in Lizzie J.'s bedroom trying on their caps and gowns for their high school graduation. Lizzie J. had worked hard to earn the credits she needed to graduate with her class, and they were both a little amazed that their school years were coming to a close. Neither had mentioned Andy, but his presence seemed to be everywhere. He should be graduating, too. It was as if they had silently made a pact to not speak about it, and hopefully their silence on the subject might make it easier.

The bedroom Lizzie J. had grown up in had been many things: a nursery when she was a baby, a little girl's room all pink and purple, a teenager's room with pictures of the current heart-throbs cut out of magazines and taped to her walls. All those things had passed. It was now a bedroom for her and little Andy, crowded with his crib and baby dresser. The perfume on her dresser gave way to baby powder, baby lotion and other things a baby needs. Lizzie J. would put on her cap and gown and walk across the stage at graduation and accept her hard-earned diploma. On the outside she would look like all the other graduates, but inside she was a different person. She'd grown up in the past year, and what she had wanted would take second place to what she must do.

MAGGIE AND JAKE were still together. Their relationship had remained strained since the beginning of the year when they had their conversation about where she would go to school. Jake knew he loved Maggie, but he also knew this year would bring a separation with many miles between them, and he wondered if their relationship would survive. Maggie knew she loved Jake, but she didn't feel the same anxiety about where they were headed.

J.D. was well aware of the problems between Maggie and Jake. He knew Jake was dreading the summer, knowing that Maggie would be moving to New York City a few weeks before he had to return to college. Dating had been sporadic for J.D., and he never went out with the same girl more than twice. They both thought that growing up seemed to be way more complicated than either of them had ever imagined.

On Mother's Day, Jake and J.D. stayed in Lake City for the weekend. J.D.'s parents were visiting, and at the invitation of Jake's parents were coming to church. Mother's Day was a big day at the church with recognition of all the mothers in attendance and later a potluck dinner.

Later, J.D. would be leaving with his parents to go home to Marianna for the summer. Jake had already moved his clothes into his dad's house and would be working for Mr. Houston. J.D. and Jake had finished their first year of college and knew they would miss each other. They'd both changed and matured in a lot of ways.

J.D. and his parents arrived at the church a little late, found seats close to the back, and quietly sat down during the announcements. All the mothers were wearing corsages, and since it was Mother's Day, there wasn't an empty seat in the church. It was another holiday that brought people who don't regularly attend and drew lots of visitors from out of town like J.D. and his parents. After the announcements, the pastor began to recognize the mothers, asking them all to stand. He identified the oldest mother there and presented her with a bouquet of flowers. Then, the youngest mother was recognized with flowers too...Lizzie J.

J.D. knew, of course, about the baby, but Andy's death had somehow doused his feelings for Lizzie J. He was relieved that he no longer thought of her every moment and surprised his feelings had changed so suddenly and drastically.

He watched as they brought her a bouquet of flowers and felt the blood rising to his face and sweat breaking out on his forehead. Suddenly, the room felt suffocating, and his heart seemed to be beating out of his chest. J.D. had not seen her since Andy's funeral. He'd never seen her pregnant, and even though he knew she was a mother now, she looked the same. Then as he watched her, he realized she didn't look the same. She was more beautiful and he wondered how that could be possible. There was a glow she'd not had before, a look of pure contentment on her face. How was this possible considering all she'd been through in the past year?

J.D. felt trapped. He wished he'd not come today. He was

completely surprised that seeing her across the room could cause such strong feelings that he'd not experienced in a long time. Now he would have to talk to her at the dinner. Where had these thoughts and feelings been all year? Had he subconsciously suppressed them? One thing he knew for sure — she would never know how he felt.

Later in the fellowship hall, he'd been successful in avoiding her. She'd been taking care of her baby, but then J.D. noticed someone leaving the room with him, so Lizzie J. was free to visit. Suddenly, she was coming his way and he had nowhere to go.

"Hey, Jake. Hi J.D. How are you two?" Lizzie J. asked as she pulled up an empty chair and sat down as they finished dessert.

"Good, how are you?" Jake asked. J.D. nodded hello.

"I'm fine. Looking forward to graduation day."

"How's little Andy? I haven't seen him since the day he was born. I bet he's getting big. Where is he?" Jake asked, looking around the room and expecting to see someone holding him.

"My mom took him home. He needed a nap and he sleeps better in his crib. We started calling him Trey, you know, since he was the third in line to have his name. The name seemed to fit."

"Hey, I like that — makes me remember our conversation about nicknames. That little man fits right in. Don't you agree J.D.?"

"Yeah, I like that," J.D. replied, thinking, she's even more beautiful than I remembered. Don't open your mouth; you are bound to say something stupid. She cannot know how you feel!

"Do you have a picture of him?" Jake asked.

"Well of course — I am a mom you know. All good moms

have lots and lots of pictures," Lizzie J. replied, as she looked in her purse for her little album of photos.

"She's a good mom, too. I watch her all the time," Maggie replied as she joined the conversation.

"Here's the most recent one." Lizzie J. handed over the picture of her and Trey.

"He is big! What are you feeding him?"

"He is healthy looking, isn't he?"

J.D. was eating his dessert and trying his best to avoid looking at the picture, but Jake wouldn't leave him alone.

"Look at this little guy, J.D. I do believe he will make a good farmer some day. Don't you?"

J.D. took the photo, looked at it and handed it back. He noticed how much the baby looked like his mother, with raven black hair and blue eyes. He tried to see some resemblance to Andy, but right now all he could see was Lizzie J.

"He might be a farmer—you never know," J.D. replied with the only words he could think to say. He was thinking about the first time he'd met Lizzie J. He had wondered, that first day, if he could have a chance with her if Andy wasn't in the picture. Now Andy wasn't here, but knowing Lizzie J. had given birth to his child made it seem as though he was, still making her off limits.

CHAPTER TWENTY-THREE

1971

I T WAS CLOSE to noon on Christmas day and Jake had just finished speaking on the phone with his dad. Jake felt melancholy, ready for this joyous season to come to an end. He was feeling sorry for himself and knew that was immature but couldn't seem to help it today. The day had actually started out okay until the visit from Lizzie J. and the kids left him feeling alone.

Thinking back to the evening before, he wondered if it would have made any difference had Maggie answered her phone when he called. He wondered why she hadn't. Where in the world could she have been if she was snowed in? Maybe she was with that guy he saw her with and didn't want to answer her phone. With that thought, his melancholy mood changed to dark and somber.

Would he never get this woman out of his system?

Getting out of his recliner, he took his anger out on the foot rest as he slammed it back to the chair. Then he stood there feeling like a five-year-old throwing a tantrum.

Cara, Mark, and their three little girls would be arriving at his dad's soon, and the thought of his nieces made him smile.

He put on a jacket and loaded all the gifts in his truck. Jake felt bad that he didn't have gifts for the family he'd met last night. Had he known about them, he would have. He was still unsure why he'd not been told earlier about this lady and her two children who were suddenly making Lake City their home. Anyway, he was glad Cara and Mark would be there to help the conversation along.

His dad's house seemed full with the extra family. Five little people made for a noisy time, but it was a good time, Jake thought. This scene before him was exactly what he wanted. The Christmas tree blazed with lights, the fire roared in the fireplace, the smell of spices emanated throughout the house, and loud squeals and giggles came from the children.

"Hey you, come give me a hug," Cara said as soon as Jake could deposit his gifts under the tree.

"You look beautiful, as always," Jake told his sister as he gave her a huge bear hug.

"Aw, I bet you say that to all the girls," Cara said and laughed.

"Well, I do if their names are Lisa, Jennie and Susan!" Jake said loudly, as all three nieces hugged his legs and nearly knocked him over. They adored their Uncle Jake!

"Man, it's good to see you. It's been way too long — you need to make a weekend trip to Marianna," Mark told Jake as he gave him a hug.

Jake picked up his two youngest nieces, backed up to the sofa, sat down, and Lisa, the oldest, snuggled up next to him since there was no room on his lap. Jake was thankful the somber day had turned to one of joy. He missed Cara and Mark and loved their family. As usual, when he was around them, he promised himself he would visit them more often.

Jake then noticed Caroline and her children watching the whole exchange. He sat his two nieces down, promising to come back, and went forward to say hello.

"Hi Caroline, Merry Christmas," Jake said. "Hi Greg, hi Kristen, Merry Christmas to you, too! Was Santa good to you this morning?"

Neither one answered him, but they did nod their head yes, and Kristen grabbed hold of her mother's leg, looking up at Jake fearfully.

"I'm afraid Santa was a little too good this morning. Merry Christmas, Jake. It's good to see you again," Caroline responded sweetly.

"Come join us," Jake invited. "I'm sure you've already met my sister and her husband."

"Yes, Cara and I found out we have a lot of things in common. Of course, when you have children it's usually easy to find common interests."

"Well, I wouldn't know about that," Jake said and laughed. "The children in my life belong to others so I can give them back at the end of the day."

"Oh, do you have other nieces and nephews who live here?" Caroline asked.

"Friends of mine have two children, Trey and Maggie, and they think I'm their uncle, though we aren't related. It's a long story, and one I'm sure you'll hear if you live here very long."

"Since Cara doesn't live here, you must be grateful for your friends and their children," Caroline replied. She wondered about this handsome single guy. There had to be more to the story than she knew. He seemed to be so nice and she found him very interesting. All she'd heard about him so far was that he was a farmer, lived alone, and had never married. Caroline had never heard about Maggie…yet.

"I am grateful. We've been friends a long time," was Jake's only reply.

Caroline could sense that the conversation about his friends was over, so she didn't ask any questions. She did make a mental note to ask Lillian about everything she'd heard today.

"Caroline, do you work?" Cara asked.

"I do. I'm a paralegal at a law firm in Nashville. After my husband died, I moved back to Nashville to be close to my sister and her family. A year after I moved there, her husband got a promotion and they were transferred to Kentucky. Aunt Lillian invited us to come here for Christmas."

"That sounds like interesting work. Are you planning to look for a job here?" Cara asked. She'd already been informed that Caroline and her children were moving to be close to Lillian.

"Yes, but we'll be going back to Nashville tomorrow. I have to give a two-week notice at my job. Until I find a job and a place to live, Aunt Lillian has graciously offered to let us stay here. Hopefully, it won't be for long."

"I'm sure Lillian and Dad will enjoy your company. They're always trying to talk Mark and me into moving here. We love our home in Marianna, though, and it isn't that far from here. Is it Jake?" Cara asked him, with emphasis.

"No, it's not, and yes, I promise to try to visit more. That jab was meant for me. They obviously don't realize how busy I am," Jake said.

"Yeah, sure, we know how busy you are this time of year. Let me see — crops are laid by, equipment has been cleaned and serviced, and the coffee shop out on the highway is running efficiently every day when you check on it with all your farmer friends. That's what keeps you busy right now!"

"Okay, okay, now stop. You're embarrassing me in front of Caroline. She's going to think I'm the worst brother there is. Cut me some slack, will you?" Jake teased back.

Caroline enjoyed the banter between the siblings, and it made her miss her sister. Her brother-in-law could get transferred again, and she couldn't keep following them. Since her parents were deceased, Aunt Lillian seemed to be the perfect choice, unlikely to ever move. When Lillian extended the invitation, Caroline decided to move here. And now she'd met Jake. He was easy on the eyes. That thought surprised her. She'd not met anyone she was even remotely interested in since the tragic death of her husband. But this guy seemed different, and she couldn't wait to get to know him better.

Jake stayed later that evening than he'd planned. Though the Christmas tree was barren of gifts underneath, the lights shone brightly, the fire blazed, and the Christmas spirit lingered.

Cara and her family left for home with hugs all around and a promise from Jake to visit soon. Caroline went upstairs to put her children to bed. When she came back down, the four adults stayed for another couple of hours conversing, which gave Jake and his dad an opportunity to get to know her.

As much as Caroline enjoyed the conversation, she was anxious to get her aunt alone to ask all the questions running through her mind about this handsome, rugged guy who had suddenly appeared in her lonely life. Her opportunity came the next morning. Sal returned to work and Caroline didn't plan to leave until noon. After breakfast, while she and Lillian were finishing their coffee, she broached the subject.

"Thank you for inviting us to spend Christmas with your

family. Yesterday was wonderful and we enjoyed being here. I'm happy to finally meet Sal's children," Caroline said.

"Well, you've been busy living your own life all these years. They are both kind and generous people."

"I understood from some of the conversation yesterday that Cara has never lived here. Is that right?"

"Yes, she still lives in the home where Sal and his wife raised their family. Their mother died when Cara was seventeen and Jake was only twelve. Sal moved here and went to work at the bank when Jake was in the middle of his junior year of high school."

"That must have been hard, to move from the only place you've ever lived when you're only sixteen," Caroline said, thoughtfully.

"I'm sure it was, but Jake is a very strong guy, physically, mentally and spiritually as well."

"What is the story about his friends who have two children that call him Uncle Jake? He never explained."

"Oh, that would be Lizzie J. Lizzie J. and a boy named Andy Houston had been boyfriend and girlfriend since third grade. Maggie Roberts was Lizzie J.'s best friend, and when Jake moved here, he and Maggie started dating. Jake was a year older than the others, but he and Andy became close friends very quickly. The four teenagers went everywhere together. The year Jake started college, and right before the others started their senior year, Andy was killed in a car accident."

"That's terrible. What happened?" Her interest piqued, Caroline wanted details.

"Andy, Lizzie J. and Maggie were driving home from Jonesboro and got caught in a terrible thunderstorm. They were involved in a head-on collision with another vehicle. All three were thrown from the truck, but Andy was the most critical. He had severe head trauma and never woke from a coma. He died about two weeks after the accident."

"That is so sad. So Lizzie J. got married?"

"She is now, but Trey, her oldest, is actually Andy's son. When he died, neither of them knew she was pregnant. It was a sad time for everyone involved. But she's married now, and they have a little girl named after Maggie Roberts, who is still her best friend."

"That is quite a story. So where is this best friend Maggie? Is she married? Does she still live here too?"

"Well, that's quite a story, too, and a very complicated one."

"Do tell — I'm dying to know."

"She lives in New York City and is quite famous."

"For what? Is she an actress? This is getting better and better."

"She's a classical pianist and plays concerts all over the world. You've never heard of Margaret Mae Roberts?" Lillian asked.

"So you're telling me that Margaret Mae Roberts is Maggie Roberts from Lake City, Arkansas, and Jake used to date her?" Caroline asked in amazement. Nearly everyone had heard of her, even if not a fan of that genre of music. Caroline was intrigued even more with Jake Martin.

"Yes, she is. She was born and raised here. Her mother still lives here, but Maggie's dad is deceased."

"So Margaret, I mean Maggie, never married? Are she and Jake still an item? Is that why he has never married?"

"Honestly, for the last couple of years we've all been confused about their situation. She went to the Manhattan School of Music during her college years and began her career immediately afterwards. Jake graduated from Arkansas State and started his farming career. We know that he traveled to New York about a year ago, and since his return, he's refused to talk about her and doesn't even want to hear her name mentioned. Sal and I have tried to stay out of it, so we don't know what happened or what is going on between them now."

"Sounds like soap opera drama. That is one of the craziest stories I've ever heard. So they've been involved, or not involved, since high school, and neither one has ever married?"

"No. I understand from sources here in town that about two years ago she bought a very expensive apartment in Manhattan. And when Jake could afford it, he bought the property he lives on. There was an old farmhouse that he intended to tear down to build a new house, but instead, he remodeled it and it's quite beautiful."

"Since he doesn't want to talk about her, or even hear her name, makes me think he still loves her. What do you think?" Caroline asked.

"Who knows? Guys keep their feelings inside and they don't like to talk about it. My guess is he's tired of waiting on her. She was always promising him things would change and she'd be ready to get married, but she kept postponing it. I think he's probably given up. I see the way he watches Cara and Mark with their family, and Lizzie J. with her children, and I know Jake wants that for himself."

"I can't imagine the turmoil he must be going through. I know people feel sorry for me because Mike died in the war, but at least I know he loved me and was devoted to me and the children. If he was still alive, he would still be my husband. Must be awful to be in love with someone who is alive and well, but you can't have them," Caroline said softly.

"I know Jake believes God has someone special for him. He's always believed it was Maggie, but I know if Jake is not sure about Maggie, he would turn away from that relationship. Maybe that has happened."

"What does she look like?"

"She's about five-seven, with long blonde hair and green eyes. She's very attractive. I have some photos taken through the years. Do you want to see them?"

"Sure."

Lillian went to the bookshelf in the living room and brought out a photo album she'd started when she married Sal. Caroline looked at every photo on every page, beginning with Jake's senior year in high school. Maggie was beautiful, and as she'd matured, Caroline could see she was also elegant and looked almost regal. Jake had always been handsome, and he'd matured into a rugged-looking guy, probably from working outside most of the year.

They might not be together now, she thought, but she could tell they were in love. She could see it in every photograph. She did notice, though, that Christmas two years ago was the last time there were pictures of the two of them. Any woman who set her sights on Jake would have to tread very carefully. And that includes me, she thought. It would be very easy to fall in love with a man like Jake Martin.

CHAPTER TWENTY-FOUR

Lake City, Arkansas
1964

*T*HE SUMMER AFTER Maggie and Lizzie J. graduated from high school brought many changes again. Maggie and her parents went to New York twice to find a place for Maggie to live while in school, while Jake worked long hours on Mr. Houston's farm. Being a mom made Lizzie J. busier than she'd ever imagined, and sometimes she felt so alone, especially when Trey didn't sleep well at night. She rocked her fussy baby in the dark hours while others slept peacefully.

Maggie didn't realize how hard it would be to say goodbye to everyone and everything she'd known her whole life. As the days wound down to her departure from Lake City to a big city full of complete strangers, she began to question her decision.

Maggie had supported Lizzie J. throughout her pregnancy; now, Lizzie J. gave Maggie the courage to put her fears aside and move forward to make her dream a reality. The best friends spent many days together that summer, knowing that the birth of Trey had changed them and this separation would bring an even bigger change, taking them down very different avenues in life. They made a pact to stay best friends, no matter where they went or who they were with.

Jake worked hard that summer. Every field he plowed and every row he traveled down reminded him they would soon be separated by many miles. The road from Arkansas to New York seemed so long that Maggie might never find her way home. During those times alone on the farm, Jake had no idea about the twists and turns and crazy detours their relationship would undergo in the coming years.

Though Lizzie J. had encouraged Maggie to pursue her dream, and had given her the courage to look forward and not back at the past, Maggie was still unprepared for the difficulty she experienced saying goodbye.

The trailer was packed and hooked to the back of the car. Jake and Maggie had spent time together the night before, but he'd come to her house that morning, along with Lizzie J., to say goodbye.

"You have my address—I will expect pictures of Trey to arrive at least once a week," Maggie said to Lizzie J. "Let me hold him one more time."

"I'll do my best, but being in night school will be difficult. Call me when you can. Late at night will probably be best. I'll miss you Maggie Mae Roberts," Lizzie J. said as she handed her baby over to Maggie. She couldn't stop the tears that rolled down her face. They'd been inseparable since kindergarten. She wondered how they would ever survive without each other.

Maggie held Trey close. She loved his baby smell. And though she wasn't ready for babies of her own, she knew that someday she wanted to experience the joy of children. After kissing his fat cheeks and nuzzling him, she handed him back to his mother, and now Maggie's tears were coming fast, too.

"I love you, Lizzie J.," Maggie said, as she hugged her.

Then she turned to Jake. Maggie's parents and Lizzie J. walked away, giving them a little privacy.

"Jake, I know we've talked about this before, but I have to say it again. I feel I'm supposed to take this opportunity, that it's a once-in-a-lifetime chance."

"Yes, and I've told you before that I understand and support you. I will miss you *so* much. *Please* write to me and call me when you can."

"I will. Jake, I'm so scared. Even though I want to do this, I won't know anyone and I'll be all alone."

"You'll meet people, and you won't have any trouble making new friends."

Jake put his arms around her and they held onto each other, reluctant to let go. Finally, Jake pulled back, brushed her tears away, cupped her face between his hands and gently kissed her. He'd promised himself he wouldn't cry like a baby, but as hard as he thought this would be, he underestimated the intensity of his emotions now that the time had come to say goodbye. Maggie saw his tears and fought the desire to change her mind and stay. Both felt they were being torn apart. With another kiss, they slowly pulled away from each other, a silent longing in their eyes.

Maggie and her parents got in the car and pulled out of the driveway. Maggie sat on her knees in the back seat looking back as long as she could. Lizzie J., holding Trey in her arms, and Jake beside her stood watching as the car rounded the corner, gone from their sight. They looked at each other and marveled that now they were both alone. Lizzie J. was without Andy, forever, and Jake was without Maggie for who knew how long.

LIZZIE J. RETURNED home. She had to pack for the move to Jonesboro; she'd finally accepted her mom's offer to live with her. Lizzie J. knew she needed to go to school and she needed her mom's help. Rita had been trustworthy since she'd moved back. Her focus had changed; she was no longer wrapped up in herself and had found out that focusing on other people actually made her happy. She was amazed and happy when Lizzie J. told her she wanted to come and live with her.

Even though Lizzie J. was moving only fifteen miles away, it was still difficult to leave her bedroom in her grandparents' home. But she needed an education and help with Trey.

Jake and J.D. found an apartment for their second year of college. It wasn't much more expensive than living in the dorm, and neither of them was interested in the social scene — they were there to get their degrees and move on with their lives. Ironically, the apartment they found was only a few blocks away from Rita's.

MAGGIE HAD NO idea how hard it would be to say goodbye to her mom and dad, watch them drive away and leave her all alone. Her parents remained strong until they were out of sight, and then they broke down and cried. Leaving their only child in New York City at the tender age of eighteen had never been on their agenda.

The first month was painful for Maggie. She missed her home, her parents, Jake, Lizzie J. and even her piano teacher.

New York City was exciting at first; then it was loud, boisterous, and irritating. Maggie longed to go for a ride with Jake in his Chevy on the country roads on the prairie, south of town. She never wanted to pick cotton again, but she couldn't stop wondering if there were bolls on the stalks yet and how soon the cotton gins could be heard through her open bedroom window at night. Everyone here locked their doors, their cars and anything else they held valuable. There were too many people, and they talked funny. She felt as though she'd moved to a foreign country.

Maggie had to register for the times she wanted to use one of the pianos in the practice hall. If there was an empty hour, she took it. Her practice time was the only thing that felt familiar. By the first of October, she'd gotten into a routine. She worked so hard she couldn't wait to lay her head on her pillow and sleep. Sleep, take classes, practice and eat was about all she did. At least every hour was full, which kept the loneliness and homesickness at bay.

CHAPTER TWENTY-FIVE

Jonesboro, Arkansas
1964

HE TWO-BEDROOM apartment where Rita and Lizzie J. lived was clean and sparsely furnished. It was also very small. Since moving here, Lizzie J. knew she had made the right decision. Her mom worked during the day and Lizzie J. had the apartment all to herself. She had a routine with Trey that allowed her to keep up with her classes, and she was grateful he'd not been sick and took good naps.

As soon as Rita walked in after work, Lizzie J. walked out. They were on a tight schedule and there was no room for error, or Lizzie J. would be late for class.

Lizzie J. loved college classes, and right now her plan was to become a teacher. By the time she graduated, Trey would be in pre-school. When he started kindergarten, they would have the same schedule and she could be home with him in the summer. It seemed to be a perfect solution to single parenting. To graduate that quickly, though, she had class every night of the week.

One day she saw Jake when they ran into each other at the corner grocery store. Jake was busy too, she found out. He was taking a full load of classes and working on the farm on the weekends for Mr. Houston. Since both were in a hurry, their conversation, mostly about Maggie, was brief. They did exchange phone numbers and promised each other they would get together soon.

The next week, as Lizzie J. was waiting on her mom to come through the door so she could leave for class, the phone rang.

"Hello," Lizzie J. answered.

"Lizzie J., it's me, Mom. I'm going to be late. I'm sorry."

"What happened? Where are you?"

"My car broke down, so I walked to the closest gas station. I'm waiting for the tow truck."

"I can't miss class—we're having a test! How long will you be?"

"Lizzie J. I have no idea. I'm so sorry. Hey, I have to go—the tow truck is here."

The line went dead and Lizzie J. was left holding the receiver, wondering what in the world she would do. She knew if she called Nanny, she would come, but Lizzie J. would still be late, very late. Suddenly, she remembered Jake lived very close and she had his phone number. As she dialed, she prayed he would be home and could help.

"Hello."

"Jake?" Lizzie J. asked.

"No, this is J.D. Jake isn't here right now. Can I take a message?"

"Oh, hi J.D. This is Lizzie J.," she replied. He'd already recognized her voice.

"Hi Lizzie J., how are you?" J.D. asked, trying to prolong the conversation. How convenient that Jake wasn't here, he thought.

"I'm doing well. I called to see if Jake could do me a favor. Will he be back soon?"

"No, he went out to the farm. His classes on Tuesday are over early, so he went to work. They started picking cotton this week, and Mr. Houston needs him whenever Jake has some free time. Is there anything I can help you with?" J.D. asked hopefully.

"I need help. My mom's car broke down and I'm going to be late or miss my class, and we're having a test."

"Do you want me to go help her?"

"No, a tow truck was coming to take her car to have it checked out. I hate to ask you this. Have you ever babysat before?" Lizzie J. asked hesitantly.

"You need a babysitter?"

"Yes, and I also need to borrow your car. I know that's asking a lot, and hopefully it won't be for long. Mom should be here as soon as she can get the car situation taken care of. Trey is a good baby," Lizzie J. said encouragingly.

"Sure, I'll be happy to. Please be sure he has on a clean diaper by the time I get there," J.D. said and laughed.

"Oh, thank you so much. You'll be a life saver, or at least a class saver! We're in apartment 32 at the Oaks. We're only a couple of blocks from you. Can you leave now? I'm already running late."

"I'll be right there." J.D. hung up the receiver and thought this had to be the luckiest day of his life.

It seemed to Lizzie J. only moments had passed before the doorbell rang. She wondered how in the world he'd gotten there so fast.

"Hey, come in," Lizzie J. said when she opened the door.

"Hi. It's good to see you. What do you want me to do?" J.D. asked.

Trey was in a playpen with toys scattered all around. Fortunately, he wasn't afraid of strangers and smiled at J.D. when he approached.

"Hey, big guy, how are you?" J.D. asked him softly, not wanting to frighten him.

"He does have on a clean diaper, and hopefully he won't have a dirty one before my mom comes. If he does, here's everything you'll need to change him. There are bottles in the refrigerator, but he should be fine — it hasn't been long since I fed him. Are you sure you are okay doing this?"

"I've been around babies before. Go on to your class. I promise he'll be fine — I've got this. Here are the keys to my car. It's the blue one parked in your mom's spot. Now go."

"Thank you so much, J.D. I won't forget this!"

When Lizzie J. was gone, J.D. thought about how he happened to be here in her apartment taking care of her and Andy's baby boy. Life sure can throw some curve balls, he thought as he looked at Trey. He'd seen him on Mother's Day at the church when he was only two months old. Now, his personality was emerging, and he could get to know him. J.D. still couldn't see anything about him that reminded him of Andy. That was probably because he had Lizzie J.'s black hair and blue eyes. Or maybe, J.D. thought, he wanted to think of this baby as belonging only to Lizzie J.

Trey looked as though he was about to cry. J.D. went to the playpen and picked him up. He was a fat baby with rolls on his chubby arms and legs. He was a beautiful baby, J.D. thought, and how could he not be with a mom who looked like Lizzie J.?

J.D. had been there only about an hour when the front door opened. He'd not been introduced to Rita, and she was startled when she walked in and saw him holding Trey.

"Hello. Who are you? Where's Lizzie J.?" she asked immediately.

"Hi, I'm a friend of Jake. My name is J.D. Hope I didn't scare you. Lizzie J. called to see if Jake could help her out, but he wasn't there, so I offered," J.D. replied.

"Oh, that was so nice. I'm Rita, Lizzie J.'s mom. It's nice to meet you," Rita said as she took off her jacket and hung it in the coat closet.

"It's nice to meet you, too. I was glad to help. She drove my car to class. Is it okay if I wait here until she gets back? Trey and I have been getting along great, haven't we Trey?"

Trey smiled at him and laid his head on J.D.'s shoulder.

"Sure. Do you mind watching him for a few more minutes while I go change clothes? It's been a stressful day."

"No, I don't mind at all. Go right ahead."

J.D. had heard some information about Lizzie J.'s mom from Maggie and Jake. He'd had a visual image of her that was far removed from how she actually looked. She appeared younger than she was. Her hair was the same raven black color as Lizzie J.'s, and she had beautiful brown eyes. She looked more like Lizzie J.'s older sister than her mom.

"I'm back. Again, thank you so much for coming to our rescue. We are always on a tight schedule, since we only have one car and I'm the only babysitter," Rita explained.

"It was no problem. I was glad I was home and could come on such short notice."

"So how long have you known Lizzie J.? I haven't heard her mention you before."

"Almost two years. I met her through Jake. I'm from Marianna, where Jake lived before he moved to Lake City." Great, he thought, I've never been mentioned. I guess that tells me she doesn't know I exist.

"So you and Jake share an apartment close to here?"

"Yes ma'am, about two blocks away in the next apartment complex."

"Are you a full-time student?"

"Yes, I am."

"So, J.D., what do you want to be when you grow up?" Rita asked and smiled at him.

"I'm planning to go to law school after graduation. I've always wanted to be an attorney. If that doesn't work out, I wouldn't mind being a history teacher," J.D. told her, wondering why she was so interested in him and his future plans.

"The difference in salary between an attorney and a teacher is quite a lot."

"Like a lot of professions, it can be a success or a struggle."

"Well, J.D., not only do you seem to be a good babysitter, you also seem to know where you're headed. How about joining Lizzie J. and me for dinner? Sort of payback for babysitting."

"Are you sure? I don't want to impose," J.D. replied, thinking yes, of course I want to stay!

"That's the least we can do. I know Lizzie J. needed to be in class to take a test tonight."

"I can't say no to that invitation, I'd be happy to stay. Why don't I play with Trey while you prepare dinner? I think we're becoming great friends."

"Trey doesn't see many men. He sees my dad about once a week; the rest of the time he is surrounded by women. He's probably excited to be with a guy. They learn that early, I think."

LIZZIE J. HAD TROUBLE concentrating on her test. She'd never left Trey with anyone other than her mom and her nanny. Certainly never a guy! What was she thinking? What if something happened to her baby? J.D. had seemed confident, so she tried to stop worrying. She'd only been around J.D. a few times in the past couple of years. He'd changed, matured, and gained a little weight. She remembered him as tall and skinny, though he hadn't seemed that way today.

She finally finished her test. When she got to her next class, there was a note on the door that the professor was ill and class had been cancelled. Freedom....

The aroma of food cooking was the first thing she smelled when she opened the front door. J.D. and Trey were in the living room, and as she got closer, a different odor hit her and immediately she knew what it was. J.D. was holding a diaper and had a look of relief on his face when he saw her.

"Hey, how did it go?" Lizzie J. asked innocently.

"Great, until a few minutes ago."

"Were you about to change his diaper?"

"Sure. Your mom is cooking. You don't think I can?"

"You sure looked happy to see me when I opened the door!"

"Oh, you noticed that, huh?" J.D. asked sheepishly.

"Here, let me have him. I might need you to babysit again, so I don't want to scare you off!" Lizzie J. changed Trey's diaper while J.D. watched.

"So, that's how you do it," J.D. said and laughed.

"I thought you'd done this before," Lizzie J. said with a look of surprise on her face.

"In my defense, I never said I'd changed a diaper. I said I'd been around babies before."

"Thank you. And thank you for letting me drive your car," Lizzie J. said softly.

"How was your test?"

"I think I did okay. I was a little concerned about Trey, but tried not to worry. My second class was cancelled. That's why I'm home early."

"Your mom invited me to stay for dinner."

"Really?"

"You don't mind, do you? She said it was payback for baby-sitting. I think she was startled to see me. We'd never met until tonight. She seems nice, and friendly."

"She is," was Lizzie J.'s only reply.

Later, after dinner, J.D. said his goodbyes. Lizzie J. insisted on cleaning the kitchen since her mom had cooked. After she was finished, she brewed two cups of tea and joined her mom in the living room.

"J.D. seems like a nice young man. You've never mentioned him," Rita said.

"He lived in Marianna until he moved to Jonesboro to go to college. I guess he felt like a fifth wheel whenever he was with the four of us. He came to Andy's funeral, and I saw him back in May at the church on Mother's Day, but that's about it. I don't know him very well, but J.D. and Jake have been friends their whole lives."

"He's very handsome, don't you think?" Rita asked.

"Yeah, I guess. I've never thought about him that way. I did notice tonight that he's put on some weight. He was skinny in high school. I know he played basketball—actually I think he was their star player. Maybe all that running kept him skinny."

"Does he have a girlfriend?" Rita asked.

"I don't know, maybe. Like I said, I don't know him very well. Why do you want to know?"

"No reason, just curious. Most guys who look like him have a girlfriend or two, or three," Rita said and laughed.

"You aren't trying to play matchmaker are you?" Lizzie J. asked, suddenly suspicious of her mom's questions.

"Well, you have to admit he was good with Trey. He's handsome, he's getting an education and he likes you."

"What do you mean?"

"He dropped everything, came to babysit, loaned you a car, stayed for dinner and hung on every word you said. Open your eyes, Lizzie J. He's attracted to you," Rita explained and smiled broadly.

"He doesn't even know me. Your imagination has gone wild. He's a very nice guy who wanted to help because Jake wasn't there. That's all there was to it!"

"Okay, whatever you say."

CHAPTER TWENTY-SIX

Lake City, Arkansas
1964

MAGGIE WAS HEADED home for Christmas break. She'd completed her first semester of school, dealt with a lot of homesickness, met a few people she thought she could be friends with, and she could finally get around in the city without getting completely lost.

Lizzie J. had kept her up to date on Trey, sending photos often, though not every week as Maggie had requested. In her letters, she mentioned J.D. more and more as time went by. Maggie never asked her about it, but she was anxious to see for herself what was going on.

Since her flight landed in Memphis late that evening, she wouldn't see Lizzie J. until the next day. Jake was picking her up and she couldn't wait to see him. When she spotted him standing by the baggage area, her heart began to beat so fast she could hardly breathe. He was ruggedly handsome, she thought, even more than when she'd left in the summer. He'd not seen her yet, so she stood still for a minute watching him. She also noticed other women looking at him, a striking figure of a man who stood out in a crowd. He looked her way, and the look on his face told her everything she needed to know. He still loved her. Their strained relationship, before she left back in August, seemed to have mended.

She ran to him and he scooped her up in a big hug. He couldn't stop looking at her. He'd missed her more than he'd thought. They had three weeks to be together and then she would be gone again, but he wouldn't think about that right now. She was here.

"Aw, Maggie Mae, I've missed you so much!"

"I've missed you, too, and everyone else," Maggie told him as she pulled back from his embrace to look at him. His eyes seemed even darker than she'd remembered. She always felt she could see his soul when she looked into his eyes. I love him so much, how will I ever be able to leave in three short weeks, she thought.

"We need to get on the road. I had to almost beg your parents to let me come pick you up. They can't wait to see you."

"Let's go. I can't wait to be at home, see everyone, and sleep in my own bed."

The ride back to Lake City seemed quick since they had so much to say. It had been almost four months since Maggie's move to New York, but it seemed much longer to both of them.

Maggie was filled with wonder as she looked out the window at the passing countryside, each mile taking her closer to home. The moon was full and luminous in the winter sky and the stars were bright and shimmering away from the lights of the city. Without the tall buildings, the sky seemed magnificent and never-ending. Struck by the many differences between north and south, she realized why New York City had felt like a foreign country. Everyone there seemed to be in a hurry, passing you on the street and never looking at you. She missed the friendliness of southerners who waved at every car they passed whether they knew the people or not. She missed the small town and farms, the front porches, mason jars full of sweet tea, neighbors who dropped by to say hello, barking dogs, and the list went on and on. She was taken completely aback at these revelations over the past few months. Maggie didn't know how much she loved her home until she was gone from it. However, she still felt privileged to live in New York and study from the best in the field of music. She planned to finish her education then return home, but that day seemed so far away.

The next morning Maggie woke to the smell of bacon frying and coffee brewing. Jake had stayed late the night before, and along with Maggie's parents, they'd talked well into the early morning hours. She rolled over and looked at her clock and marveled to see nine a.m. It had been a long time since she enjoyed the luxury of sleeping in. It took a few seconds after she opened her eyes to remember she was only visiting. A little touch of panic ran through her as she thought about how quickly the days would pass before she had to leave.

Maggie heard the doorbell ring and wondered who could be coming at this hour of the morning. She didn't know her mom had invited Lizzie J. and Jake to breakfast, and her mom didn't know the two of them were bringing J.D. Maggie heard voices, and listening intently, she realized it was Lizzie J. Before she could get up, her door flew open and Lizzie J. ran over and pounced on Maggie's bed like she had so many times through the years. They squealed with delight as they hugged, cried and laughed!

Lizzie J. stayed by Maggie's side while she dressed for breakfast.

"Where's Trey?" Maggie asked.

"I dropped him off at Nanny and Poppy's. We'll go back and get him after breakfast. I wanted to visit with you, and if he gets fussy he can be very demanding!"

"Aw, I bet you make up stuff about that sweet baby all the time!"

"Well, while you're home I'll let you babysit and you can see for yourself. Or ask J.D. — he'll tell you how fussy Trey can be."

There it was! Already, Lizzie J. mentioned J.D. Maggie could hear something special in Lizzie J.'s voice when she said his name. Interesting....

"So J.D. has been babysitting?" Maggie asked.

"He's been a lifesaver, quite a few times. He's such a good babysitter and Trey loves him. When J.D. is around I become non-existent to my own son," Lizzie J. said, but laughed good-naturedly.

"Who's with Jake? I hear two male voices."

"Oh, we brought J.D. Is that okay?"

"Sure, absolutely, it's fine. Let's go eat. I'm starved."

During breakfast Maggie kept watching the interaction between Lizzie J. and J.D. When she'd left four months ago Lizzie J. was still grieving the loss of Andy. Lizzie J. looked so happy this morning and she seemed to hang on every word J.D. said. Maggie looked at Jake, and her mom and dad, and wondered if she was the only one who noticed the attraction that was obviously mutual, judging by the way J.D. looked at Lizzie J. She wondered how things could change so drastically in such a short period of time.

Suddenly, she was worried about losing Jake! She'd never, ever thought he might find someone else to care about, but now since she was absent from his life she wondered if that could happen. She'd always heard "absence makes the heart grow fonder," but she'd also heard "out of sight, out of mind." Sitting there enjoying breakfast with all the people she loved most in the world, she began to wonder which one would apply to her and Jake. They both had a lot of classes in the next three years. Why did everything seem so complicated? Would their love survive?

ON MANY NIGHTS during the past four months, Charlie had come to Rita's apartment while Lizzie J. was in class. He had no idea how much he could love someone until he fell in love with his grandson. Rita and Charlie talked about what life could have been for them if they hadn't made mistakes so many years ago. But since they couldn't change the past, they decided to enjoy the present and their new love, their grandson.

They discussed how to tell everyone that Charlie was Lizzie J.'s father, but every idea seemed daunting. However, they didn't have to devise a plan, as a scenario they'd never thought of erased all their fears and anxiety. All it took was the love of a nine-month-old baby!

Lizzie J. had noticed her mom and Charlie in conversation together, standing apart from others, after church a few times. She'd not thought anything about it until the Sunday she witnessed her mom holding Trey as he reached out for the man. Her mom tried to restrain him but finally handed him over to Charlie. Then Lizzie J. saw her son do the strangest thing. He calmed down and laid his head on Charlie's shoulder, satisfied. The scene looked surreal.

Realization began to seep into her brain. Mysterious Charlie Chandler had the most beautiful blue eyes. She'd noticed that about him before, but many people have blue eyes, she'd thought at the time. Now she realized those blues eyes looked exactly like her blue eyes...and Trey's. She'd also noticed a familiarity between them when watching her mom talk to Charlie on other occasions. But she'd dismissed it without much thought.

Lizzie J. broke away from her conversation and walked over to them. She spoke to Trey, and he ignored her.

"You must have some kind of magic spell over Trey," Lizzie J. said. She noticed her mom and Charlie both looked uncomfortable when she approached, almost as if they'd been caught doing something wrong.

"I think he likes men," Rita replied quickly.

"Really? Which men would that be?"

"Well, he's around J.D. all the time, and you know he loves him," Rita explained.

"He's a fine-looking baby, Lizzie J. I know you must be so proud of him," Charlie said to her, suddenly feeling ill at ease. Neither Charlie nor Rita had ever thought about Trey getting older and giving away their secret.

"Thank you, and yes, I'm very proud of him. He's a very good baby. He sure seems to like you...a lot!"

"Well, he likes J.D. a lot," Rita defended.

"He knows J.D.!" Lizzie J. replied. Then she was stunned as Charlie tried to give her son to her and Trey cried and reached back for him. Lizzie J. wondered what was going on as she took Trey, said goodbye and went to the car to wait for her mom to join them. Trey was still hiccupping from his crying and Lizzie J. knew he was truly upset at leaving.

Her mom opened the car door and slipped into the driver's seat. She started the car, and instead of heading out to the highway, she went toward the south end of town.

"Where are we going?"

"You'll see," Rita replied.

"Mom, what's going on?" Lizzie J. asked. Deep in her soul, she knew.

"We're going to Charlie's house. He's right behind us and we want to explain how he knows Trey so well."

Lizzie J. was in turmoil. She knew she was about to find out Charlie Chandler was her biological father. All these years she'd begged her mom to tell her. She'd wanted a dad so badly. She'd also wanted her mom to take her to California, but that had never happened. In her wildest dreams, she'd never imagined she would end up with both of her parents living here. However, she knew that was exactly what was happening.

As Lizzie J. listened to the story of how her mom had lied, how her dad hadn't known the truth, and why they'd acted the way they both had through the years, all she could think was how blessed she was to finally know. Instead of feeling blessed, some people might have been angry because of all the lost years. Lizzie J., though, had lost the love of her life in a tragic accident at a young age and learned that life is fleeting. She would not hold a grudge against these two people who had given her life. Maybe they'd not given her life under ideal circumstances, but they'd given her life.

Rita and Charlie went to see Rita's parents, and for the first time they heard the true story about how Lizzie J. was conceived. They were as shocked as Lizzie J. had been to hear how Charlie Chandler had chosen Lake City to be his home from the article he'd read in a newspaper.

As the news circulated through the small town, it lay to rest all the gossip that had surrounded Rita, her daughter, her parents, where Rita had been, who the father was, and why she'd left her only child. Lake City would have to find other people to wonder about now that they all knew the truth about Rita, Charlie Chandler and Lizzie J. And hearing that Charlie was a wealthy man was almost unbelievable to everyone. There were several people who believed he'd made up that part of his life, but others who knew the Raines family knew they would know the truth. Those who believed it was true surmised that it had to be the reason Charlie had always remained somewhat of a mystery, by his own choosing.

In the following days, Lizzie J. thought more and more about how her life had changed in the past eighteen months. Losing Andy had been tragic, and without him by her side she'd had to tell everyone she was pregnant. She'd felt vulnerable, ashamed and exposed during those dark days. Having to drop out of school and finish her senior year studying at home had left her feeling excluded. Now, here she was with a beautiful baby, a mom and a dad, and attending college and planning for the future. Granted, it wasn't the future she'd envisioned since she was a little girl, but she'd learned along the way...life was only perfect in the movies.

Lizzie J. gave Maggie all the details about how she'd learned who her father was. She was so happy to have Maggie to talk to, and they spent as much time together as possible during Christmas break. Maggie visited Lizzie J. at the apartment, and while Trey took a nap they had time to be serious.

"So have you called Mr. Chandler dad yet?" Maggie asked.

"No, that's weird! To know how many times I saw him in

town and how many times he came to the house to go fishing with Poppy kinda creeps me out," Lizzie J. said.

"Has he said anything about the accident since you found out the truth?"

"No, I don't think there is any reason to talk about it. He was on the road that night, same as us. I certainly don't hold him responsible. It's crazy, though, that he is the one who hit us that night. The whole story about him and my mom is crazy."

"Do you think he's telling the truth about having so much money?"

"My mom knows it's true, remember? When she met him, he still owned the mill in Memphis. At least we know she wasn't seeing him for his money or she would've never left," Lizzie J. said.

"Do you think they still love each other?"

"Oh, gosh, I don't know. I haven't even thought about that. It's been so long since they knew each other. That would be even crazier, wouldn't it?" Lizzie J. asked in amazement.

"Well, you never know — stranger things have happened, like you and J.D., for example."

"What do you mean?" Lizzie J. asked innocently.

"Come on, Lizzie J., it's me, Maggie. Remember I know you better than anyone. You like him, don't you?"

"You know I do like him, but it's a completely different feeling than the way I felt about Andy. Can you love two people the same, but differently?"

"I don't know. Remember, Jake is the only guy I've ever loved. So I'm no help. What do you like about him?" Maggie asked.

"He's so gentle. He's a big guy physically, but he speaks softly and he's so great with Trey. And he cares about me. Even though he's never told me he's interested in me romantically, he does everything he can to make my life easier. He's very intelligent and has helped me with some of my classes, too. I find myself wondering what I would do without him in my life."

"Hmmm, sounds like he has a plan."

"What do you mean? What kind of plan?"

"Oh, maybe a plan like, I will be so helpful she won't be able to live without me type of plan," Maggie said and laughed.

"Why would he do that?"

"Lizzie J., he loves you!"

"No he doesn't. He's trying to be nice!"

"Wow, how old are you? Eight?" Maggie asked, and laughed again.

"If he cared about me why wouldn't he tell me?"

"Maybe because the guy you loved since third grade died less than two years ago and you needed time to heal."

Lizzie J. was quiet, taking in Maggie's words. Did she still love Andy? Yes, she thought, absolutely! Would she always love Andy? Yes, absolutely! Would she heal? Yes, she would. How long would it take? She didn't know.

"I don't know — are you sure?"

"Lizzie J., he's handsome, he's nice and he could probably date anyone he wished. Instead, he's spending time babysitting, helping you study and anything else you need. Now, tell me, why do you think he would do that? I don't know any guy who is that nice!" Maggie scoffed.

"Yes you do! Jake is that nice! He's waiting on you, isn't he?"

"Our situation is a little different, don't you think?" Maggie asked.

"I know he loves you, and he misses you so much. Remember, Maggie, he's handsome, one of the best-looking guys I've ever met, and other girls see that. Be sure you come home every chance you get, and you need to write him more often," Lizzie J. warned.

"Do you know something I don't know? Is he seeing someone?" Maggie asked with the sound of fear in her voice.

"No, I don't. I do know that a relationship is hard to maintain when you are so far apart. I don't want to see you get hurt."

"Now you have me worried. Should I be?"

"I don't mean to worry you, just trying to give you advice. You've been giving me advice for the past thirty minutes, thought I'd help you out too," Lizzie J. said and laughed, trying to lighten their mood.

CHAPTER TWENTY-SEVEN

New York City
1971

MAGGIE STOOD AT the front window watching her neighbors shoveling the heavy snow away from and off of their cars. The sun was blinding as it reflected off the pristine, snow-covered surfaces. It was still bitterly cold, and even the bright sunlight couldn't penetrate the frozen landscape. This scene from her window would, no doubt, be there for many days.

She turned away and looked at the decorations she'd brought out the night before. Maggie was twenty-six and this was the first Christmas in her young life she would spend completely alone. What would she do?

She had many things to think about and many decisions to make. Things that had occurred in her past she suddenly felt needed to be rectified immediately. She also felt a sense of urgency about her future. This was a new emotion for Maggie. Thinking back to her conversation with Lizzie J. the first Christmas after moving to New York City, she realized she'd always procrastinated when making important decisions.

Maggie wasn't yet ready to share the fact she'd come to

understand God's love for her after all these years. Why she felt that way she wasn't sure. She was excited to finally have faith that God was real and to understand He had provided Jesus as a way to salvation. She knew, somehow, God had a better way for her to share this change in her life other than a long distance phone call. So, for the first time in her life she would wait...on God

She glanced over to the piano and thought about the Christmas Eve service where she'd played in church for the first time in her life. The thought gave her satisfaction. Maggie picked up her Bible lying on the table beside her chair and turned to Jeremiah 29:11, underlined in red: "'For I know the plans I have for you,' declares the Lord, 'plans to prosper you and not to harm you, plans to give you hope and a future.'" She'd read that verse many times in the past few months since she'd gone to the bookstore and purchased her Bible. Now she looked closely at the following verses: *You will call to me and come and pray to me, and I will listen to you. You will seek me and find me when you search for me with all your heart.* She thought about seeking God with her whole heart and what that truly meant.

Maggie's heart had been given to her music and to Jake for so many years, she wasn't sure if there was room for God. She'd been so sure about what she wanted out of life, and it worried her to give up control. But somehow seeking God with her whole heart was tied to God's plans for her future. That made her think of another favorite, Matthew 6:25–34, about worrying. She had found it astonishing that Jesus said she wasn't to worry about anything—if she sought the kingdom of God first, then all the things she needed would be added. Not necessarily the things she wanted. That passage was telling her not to worry about the future but to take care of today. So, that Christmas day Maggie began to study God's word anew, with her whole heart, and to pray in earnest for direction in her music and her personal life.

The changes began almost immediately. A few days after Christmas, she received a call from another church in her neighborhood asking if she would be interested in playing for their church services. Surprised they would dare to ask her to volunteer — she was, after all, a world-renowned pianist — she prayed and told God surely she wasn't expected to do that. He revealed to her that she certainly was!

Maggie began attending church every Sunday, playing the piano and giving the congregation a taste of what it must sound like in Heaven. She became so involved that when she had a concert on Saturday night, she would fly back on the red-eye and attend church with no sleep.

The sermons Maggie heard during those church services taught her about forgiving, practicing selflessness instead of selfishness, loving without expecting something in return, sharing with others (which she'd seldom had to do before), and being grateful. Maggie searched the scriptures that pertained to the subject of the sermon, and her Bible began to show how much she used it. She knew she was changing. God constantly spoke into her life through the sermons, her private studies, and especially through her music.

Using her music gave Maggie a chance to learn about serving without compensation and without expecting any recognition. She formed a new appreciation for all the people who served at the church she attended in Lake City. Her involvement made her realize it took many people to have the doors open on Sunday.

Maggie enjoyed playing her music in church more than she'd ever enjoyed playing her concerts. The compensation wasn't money but blessings. She'd heard that term her whole life—she just never understood it. She began to experience the joy of doing for others. She also began to realize how much she'd been loved and cared for by her parents and friends. She'd been a slave to her career, and being so engrossed in her pursuit of fame and fortune had robbed her of time with family. Maggie thought back to her daddy's funeral…painful memories.

Lake City, Arkansas
1970

EARLY ON THE MORNING of January 2nd, 1970, Maggie was once again at the airport. Just the day before she'd returned from Arkansas where she'd spent a wonderful Christmas season with her family and friends. Now she was numb with pain. Only a little more than twenty-four hours ago she hugged him good-bye. Now she realized he held her a little longer than usual. She was anxious to get back to the city, to her life here, so she pulled away instead of holding onto him. That was it…their last hug…their last words…and their last good-bye. Maggie hadn't even had time to unpack when she got the call that changed everything…everything.

When she arrived at her gate she looked around for an empty seat far away from the other passengers. People were talking and laughing and it all sounded chaotic and somehow wrong. Her daddy, Oliver Roberts, no longer occupied this world. He would never kiss his wife again, or sell hardware, or go fishing. He also would never call Maggie again, asking her when she was coming home for a visit, because he would never take another breath. He collapsed from a fatal heart attack not long after they'd said good-bye the day before. He died a tragic death with no warning, no sickness. Jake had called her and given her the devastating news. She knew he didn't want to tell her, knowing she was all alone, but it had to be done.

In a few hours she would walk into her childhood home and he wouldn't be there. She wanted to run outside, shake her fist at the sky, at God. This was His fault! Maggie was coming undone inside. Her anger was coming back to the surface, the same anger she'd experienced with the death of Andy.

After the phone call from Jake, Maggie cried throughout the long night. Sleep eluded her, and she was glad. She had a habit of dreaming and those dreams confused her, causing her to question the life she was living. Now, all she could feel was grief, emptiness, disbelief and dread. So she shut down emotionally. She decided not to feel, not to think, to go through the motions of the next few dreaded days and return to her predictable life in the city. She was in control of her life here, and that would be her focus until she could return.

The day was dreary, and when the plane hit the runway in Memphis, the slight drizzle that was falling earlier had changed to a steady downpour. Her tears seemed to have dried up, and she felt as though the sky was crying on her behalf. If she could cry, she thought, her tears would put the sky to shame. As she walked to the baggage area, she steeled herself for what was to come. Jake would be there to take her home.

Jake saw her first and could tell she'd been crying. Her eyes were red-rimmed, swollen and puffy, and she looked lost. They'd celebrated Christmas together and he'd tried not to bring up the subject of when, if ever, she would move home. Only God knew how much Jake loved Maggie, and only God knew why he'd never given up. However, when she left the day before, he was frustrated with her decision to hurry back to the city and her life there. Jake knew she could have stayed longer. She didn't want to. He wasn't thinking about that now, though. He loved her and watching her broke his heart. He knew what she was feeling. He'd been there. He'd said good-bye to his mom many years ago so he knew what the days, weeks, months and yes, even years, held for Maggie.

She gave a weak wave when she saw him. He walked toward her and opened his arms. He held her, expecting her to cry. She didn't. He whispered to her how sorry he was, and she drew back from his embrace. That was all.

"Thanks for coming. Can you get my bag? It's the red one with the white ribbon on the handle," Maggie said stoically.

"Sure, wait right here," Jake said gently, and went to get it for her. He was concerned. Maggie seemed disconnected and distant. Jake knew the grieving process and that it was a very necessary part of healing when you lose someone you love.

There was little conversation between them on the ride back to Lake City. Maggie asked very few questions, while most of the time staring out her window, turned away from Jake, withdrawing into a shell that would house her grief for the next week.

Maggie was shocked when she saw all of the cars parked outside of her parents' home. So many people. Her daddy was well-known in this small town. He'd been the hardware man for many years and knew everyone on a first-name basis. She'd never thought about the fact that his death would affect so many people — not only her family, but friends and customers.

"Are you ready to go in and see your mom?"

"In a minute. Do you mind?" Maggie asked in a whisper.

"Of course not, take your time. I know this is hard, Maggie. You don't know how much I wish I could change this for you," Jake said softly and reached out to touch her. He touched her cheek and moved her hair away from her face. She continued to stare straight ahead.

"Jake, I don't know if I can do this."

"You can, I know you can. Your mom needs you, Maggie," Jake encouraged.

They were parked a few houses away due to the other cars lining both sides of the street. Maggie saw the oak tree and the swing her dad had hung for her when she was a little girl. She knew the rope was new. He changed it frequently and encouraged any of the neighborhood kids to try it out, which they often did. Don't think, don't look, don't feel, do what you have to do and get back to work. Everything will be back to normal once this is over.

"I'm ready," Maggie said.

Jake suggested they go around the house and in through the back door. Maggie agreed and appreciated his thoughtfulness. Hopefully she could find her mom without having to speak to a lot of people. As soon as they entered the kitchen, Maggie saw her mom sitting at the table with her sister, Maggie's Aunt Bridget, having a cup of coffee. When they heard the door open, both women looked up at Maggie and Jake. It took only a moment for Maggie to see how incredibly sad her mom was, and she had to fight the temptation to turn around and run through the door, back outside where other people's lives were still the same. Don't think, don't look, and don't feel ... her new mantra.

"Maggie." Her name was all her mom said as she came around the table.

"Mom," Maggie replied, and all her resolve to not think, not look, and not feel disintegrated into unbearable grief when she felt her momma's arms around her. Even if Maggie had not known her daddy had died, she would have known something was amiss. She'd not moved past the kitchen, but his presence was gone, his essence missing from the heartbeat of their home. Maggie could almost feel the house groaning for its master.

Maggie and her mom stayed up late talking into the early morning hours. Maggie was amazed at the things her mom said. Obviously her parents had discussed the fact that one of them could be left behind, to live out his or her remaining days alone. She was shocked to learn her parents had grave sites in Jonesboro and a funeral plan with a local funeral home. Everything had been planned and was ready.

At the funeral, though her heart was hardened, Maggie tried to listen and find solace in the pastor's words. She didn't want to be sitting in this church, looking at the casket that held her daddy's cold body. She didn't want to hear her mom cry and see how alone she was.

Food had been brought by many people, and the women from the church and a few neighbors gathered at the house to serve the family when they returned from the cemetery. Everyone told her the service was beautiful.

Then the evening was finally over. Everyone went home, back to their own lives, leaving Maggie and her mom with a few close family members. And tomorrow they would leave too. Maggie would be left with her mom and she didn't know if she could bear it.

Maggie remained in the living room long after everyone

else had gone to bed. She began to process the service and thought back over what the minister had said. She was surprised at some of the music her dad had chosen. The minister explained that *I Surrender All* was the invitation song given at the service the day that Oliver Roberts gave his heart and life to Christ. Listening to the words of the song gave her the same feeling she had whenever Jake talked to her about God. She didn't want to hear it.

Maggie found a pillow and blankets in the linen closet and curled up on the couch. Though she was exhausted, sleep didn't come right away. The word surrender kept running through her mind. She didn't like that word. Surrendering felt like giving up. Or giving in. Why did her daddy choose that song? She heard the explanation given by the minister; however, something kept gnawing at her, a deeper meaning perhaps. Sleep finally came, and Maggie's questions about surrender were gone, at least for now.

The next day brought the reality of change for Annie Roberts. The first few days after the death of a loved one is filled with people surrounding the bereaved with their presence, bringing food and companionship as plans are made for a funeral and laying to rest the earthly body of the one who passed into eternity. After that is finished, all the friends and family members return to their everyday lives and the loved ones left behind are alone. With reality....

Annie and Oliver had been married for thirty-six years. He'd recently celebrated his fifty-eighth birthday and looked healthy. He was not overweight, didn't smoke and never seemed stressed. His sudden demise was a shock to everyone.

After sharing lunch and a brief last visit, Annie said a tearful good-bye to her sister Bridget. She was left alone in the house with Maggie, who would be returning to New York soon. Annie had always been a strong woman and thought she was independent, but today she felt anything but that. Everywhere she looked she saw something of Oliver's. His clothes hung in their closet, his shoes were lined up neatly on the floor, his ties hung in perfect order on the rack on the back of the door, and when she went into the bathroom and saw his razor, that was the catalyst that opened a flood of tears.

Maggie found her mom holding her daddy's razor and sobbing. Maggie thought her heart would break. She was grieving the loss of her daddy, and now she was expected to help her mom. So she held back her own tears while she wrapped her arms around her mom and held her tight. Maggie insisted her mom lie down to rest for awhile and soon Annie fell asleep.

Maggie sat in the chair in her parents' bedroom clutching her daddy's wallet as she let her tears rain down. She was tired, too, and soon her eyes closed and she slept in the chair, the wallet falling onto her lap as her body relaxed and her grip loosened. When Maggie finally came awake, dusk had arrived and the room was bathed in soft, early evening shadows.

Annie and Maggie had a quiet dinner together from all the leftover food. Both women picked at their dinner, neither one having much of an appetite. Once again they stayed up late, talking into the night, a different bond borne of grief.

The next day Maggie went with her mom to the hardware store. They didn't have a store manager — Oliver had done that, and Annie was the bookkeeper. They had two full-time employees, but neither of them had the expertise to run the whole operation. After only a few minutes at her desk, Annie was in tears again. Everything in the store represented the hard work Oliver had done to build this business. Annie knew she couldn't do this without him or someone who could manage it for her.

Maggie sat down across from her mom and started asking the hard questions. Did her dad have life insurance? Did she want to keep the store and find a manager? Did she want to sell the store? Annie went to the filing cabinet and brought a file over to the desk. There she found their wills and life insurance policies. Maggie was stunned. There was a $250,000 life insurance policy on her daddy, with her mother as the beneficiary. He'd had the policy since Maggie was a little girl. He had wanted Annie to be able to stay home and raise Maggie if something happened to him.

Oliver Roberts had been frugal. He had worked hard and been careful about debt. As a result, Annie would never have to work again unless she wanted to. She was solvent. Everything they owned was theirs — no liens or mortgages. What a gift, Maggie thought. With a good financial advisor, her mom would never have to be concerned about money. But Maggie knew her mom would trade every material possession and every dime she had to have her beloved husband back.

Jake saw Maggie briefly every day after the funeral. He was considerate of the time he knew Annie needed with her daughter. He was also hoping this event might cause Maggie to consider moving home. Jake called to invite Maggie and Annie out to dinner, thinking a change would do them both good. Annie declined but insisted Maggie should go. She assured her daughter she would be fine, and she had to start learning to be alone at some point, so Maggie agreed to go.

As soon as Maggie got in the car with Jake, she felt the weight of sadness subside. She wanted to return to New York.

She'd been away from her music, and with a concert scheduled soon she needed to practice and be prepared.

"How are you?" Jake asked.

"Okay, I guess. It feels good to be away from the house."

"How's your mom doing?"

"Sometimes she seems okay, and at other times she cries and cries. I think she'll have to sell the store. Every time she tries to work she starts crying, then comes home and goes to bed. She doesn't need it. Daddy left her in good financial shape. She won't ever have to work unless she wants to."

"Well, that's good."

"Yes, I was surprised that they were so prepared for something like this."

"Do you think your mom will be okay alone?" Jake asked her.

Maggie kept her gaze straight ahead, knowing her answer was not what Jake wanted to hear. "I hope so. I need to get back to the city."

Jake glanced at her and wondered how she could even think about that right now. "Maybe you should consider staying another week or two."

"Jake, I can't."

"Can't, Maggie, or won't? Which is it?" A hint of anger came through in his question. Jake was trying hard to maintain his composure, but all the years of hearing her excuses had worn thin, and realizing that Maggie would never see someone else's need as greater than her own made him angry. And it was her own mother who needed her!

"Jake, you know I have a concert scheduled. I really can't stay longer."

"Maggie, you can do anything you want to do. No one is

252

forcing you. What will it take for you to think something or someone is more important than your career? I don't get it!"

"Don't yell at me! What do you mean? It's my career! It's how I support myself! Tickets are sold and people are expecting me to give them a concert!"

"I am so sick of hearing about your precious career! You actually think that is more important than the well-being of your own mother?" Jake yelled.

"Excuse me? Don't bring my mother into this. You've never understood—you've never supported me!"

"Are you kidding me? What world are you living in? I forgave you for not being truthful about where you were going to school. You promised you would move home when you graduated. That's been more than two years, Maggie, two years! And you accuse me of not supporting you? You are unbelievable, you know that?" The pent-up frustration and anger Jake had suppressed for so long had come to the surface.

"I was coming home, but I couldn't turn down the opportunity that was offered to me! Jake, I've made more money in the last two years in the city than I could make in a lifetime teaching music. How can you expect me to give that up?"

"Money? Is that what this is all about? I guess I never gave up hoping that somehow I would someday be more important than your music! Wow, Maggie, you'll never change! I've been competing for your love and attention for way too many years! Now I'm competing with money?"

"It's not a competition, Jake!"

"Oh yeah? Your parents have competed for your attention for the last six years. How many times did your dad call and ask when you were coming for a visit? How many times did you tell him you were too busy? He wanted to see you, Maggie.

He wanted to be around you, hug you, and spend time with you! Well, guess what? You won't have to worry about that one anymore. He's gone, Maggie!"

"*Shut-up Jake!!!* Maggie covered her ears with her hands and squeezed her eyes shut. "How do you know? You didn't hear our conversations. And besides, that is *none* of your business! So shut-up!"

"*None of my business?* You don't have a clue what goes on here when you are away living your big dream life. You have no idea how many times I've had dinner with your parents and the conversation always came back to you. How you were doing, where you were performing—and the big question, will you ever move home? That's what they always talked about. That and the fact they would love to have grandchildren, although that subject had stopped coming up. They missed you, Maggie!"

"I can't think about what goes on here! I'm busy with my career, but no one cares about that! Just because you love farming and you love living here doesn't mean I should!"

"So the truth comes out! You don't want to live here!

"No, I don't want to live here, at least not right now. Maybe someday, not now!"

"Are you happy, Maggie? Are you still running from God? Because if you are, the money you have and the money you will make will never satisfy you."

"I'm happy! I'm successful and I don't need God. I'm doing okay. I'm taking care of myself! Don't start preaching to me again!"

Jake didn't respond. He turned onto the next road, turned the car around and headed back toward Lake City. He was deflated and defeated. He'd lost the fight. He was giving up.

"What are you doing?" Maggie asked.

"We aren't going to dinner, Maggie. I'm taking you back to your mom's house. You need to make your reservations for your flight back to your life. Call Lizzie J. and see if she'll take you to the airport," Jake told her, never taking his eyes from the road. He didn't even want to look at her.

"Fine, if that's the way you want it," Maggie said angrily, crossing her arms and staring straight ahead.

It took ten minutes to get back to town, and not a word passed between them. Suddenly Maggie began to realize this argument was different. She could feel it, and she knew she'd pushed too hard.

"Jake...I'm sorry. Will you forgive me?"

"Maggie, leave it alone. I get your message. I've waited and waited. I'm done. Go back to the city, date other guys, and find yourself someone who loves New York as much as you do. Find you a money man. I don't care, find whatever it is you're looking for. I know it's not me."

"Jake, that's not true! It is you, it's always been you." Maggie was about to cry. This was different and she was afraid.

"Good-bye, Maggie. Go in and spend what little time you have left here with your mom. She needs you. I hope you have a happy life." Jake looked away from her and waited for her to get out of the car.

"Jake ... please," Maggie whispered, as she stared at him in disbelief. In all the years she'd known Jake, he'd never been so unforgiving. She looked away from him and they both sat looking straight ahead for what seemed an eternity.

Finally, he heard the door open and close. He never looked at her again as he drove away.

CHAPTER TWENTY-EIGHT

1972

ɪᴛ ᴡᴀs ᴛʜᴇ ᴇɴᴅ of February 1972, and Jake's melancholy attitude of the past few weeks began to lift as the days grew longer. Spring was only three short weeks away. As usual, the grapevine in Lake City had been abuzz with the news that Maggie Roberts had cancelled her trip home after Christmas, even though flights were leaving New York City well before the New Year. Jake's friends knew the subject of Maggie was off limits, but Jake wondered if it was his imagination or did everyone else want to talk about her the moment he entered the front door!

Caroline and her children had spent several weeks with Sal and Lillian. She'd found a job in Jonesboro, and her children had started school in Lake City. Now she was renting a house down the street from Lillian so her aunt would be available to help with the kids. Jake had offered to help her move in, but her furniture was being delivered from Tennessee and the movers would set everything up. So, instead, he offered to bring food for dinner. Jake had been at his dad's several weekends while Caroline was living in their house, and he admired how hard she worked and what a good mother to her children she seemed to be.

The movers worked fast, and soon every room in the small house was furnished. Caroline had marked her boxes, and each one sat in the room where it belonged, making it easier to find sheets, blankets and pillows. By nine o'clock both kids were tucked into bed and Sal and Lillian said goodbye. Jake stayed, and he seemed to be in no hurry to leave. He enjoyed being around Caroline—they were becoming friends. Being in her presence reminded him that he enjoyed female company and also how absent from his life Maggie had been for the past several years.

"How about coffee? Or would you rather have hot chocolate?" Caroline asked.

"Coffee sounds perfect. We didn't eat the cake I picked up on the way over—how about a piece of that with the coffee?" Jake asked her.

Caroline went into the kitchen and Jake could hear her rummaging in a box for the coffee maker. He sat down on the couch and looked around the room, noticing the different pieces of furniture that had been in the home she shared with Mike. Suddenly, Jake felt almost guilty sitting on the couch where he imagined Mike sat many times. While Caroline had been with his dad and her Aunt Lillian, he'd never given her situation a lot of thought. As he looked around at all the things from her previous life with her deceased husband, the reality of Caroline's situation hit him hard.

Mike died in the war in 1970, only two years before. That was about the same time Maggie's dad died and their relationship disintegrated completely. Was that prophetic, he wondered?

"Here, let me help you," Jake said as he jumped up and quickly took his cup of coffee from her.

"Thanks. I'll be right back—let me get the dessert," she replied sweetly.

Caroline returned, set the dessert on the coffee table in front of them, and eased back into the cushions. Dressed in a pair of old bell bottom jeans, she had pulled her hair up in a pony tail and didn't have a smidgen of makeup on. Jake noticed her brown eyes were almost as dark as his and seemed even darker without her auburn hair framing her face. Caroline had a natural beauty, and Jake knew now how inner beauty could make someone more beautiful on the outside.

"Ah, this coffee is good, thank you. You must be exhausted," Jake said softly.

"Thanks, and yes, I'm tired. I'm happy we have the beds set up so we can stay here tonight. Maybe this weekend I can unpack the rest of the boxes and get some pictures on the walls. Make it into a home."

"I don't have any plans this weekend. I might not be much help unpacking, but maybe I could entertain the kids for you."

"Thanks, Jake, that would be a big help and I know the kids would love it. Mike would always take them to the movies or out for ice cream when I needed to catch up on things at home," Caroline replied.

"It's hard being a single parent. Though I've never been one, I lived with a single parent from the time my mom died until I left for college. I'm guessing Lillian has filled you in on all the details about our family."

"Yes, she has. I've seen all the photos, the ones in the hallway upstairs. How long did it take for you to stop grieving?"

Jake didn't answer right away. He was trying to choose his words carefully, somewhat disconcerted by her question.

"I shouldn't have asked you that!" Caroline said quickly.

"No, it's okay, I was trying to find the words to tell you how it affected me, which might be completely different for Greg and Kristen. I was older and had more time with her. My mom was a teacher, so when I was home, so was she. I was with her a lot and we were extremely close."

"Mike was deployed much of the time. He'd been in Viet Nam six months when he was killed. Sometimes I think they have forgotten him except for looking at pictures. That makes me sad," Caroline said, tears quickly filled her eyes.

"Well, after all these years my memories have faded. Sometimes I panic when I try to remember her voice or her laugh, then I think God has a way of leaving us with the right amount of things He wants us to remember. And I have His promise that I will be reunited with her one day. That's what I hold to when I miss her terribly."

Neither said anything as they held their coffee cups, staring into space, each lost in their own grief called to the surface from conversation. It was a very intimate exchange and their friendship grew deeper that night. When Jake said goodnight, he pulled her close and hugged her. It had been a long time since either of them had experienced a hug from someone of the opposite sex, and they both enjoyed the physical contact. Jake wondered if they could be more than friends someday.

Jake came to Caroline's house early on Saturday morning and picked up Greg and Kristen. His plan was a day in Jonesboro, first shopping at the toy store, then lunch at McDonald's, then skating at the roller rink. He figured that would not only exhaust the kids but him as well.

Lake City was a small town, and Lizzie J. had heard Jake was spending a lot of time at his dad's on weekends. She knew he was a nice guy and figured he was trying to be helpful, until she saw him come into McDonald's that Saturday with Caroline's children in tow, all by himself. She was already seated with Trey and Maggie and had the advantage of watching him interact with Greg and Kristen before he saw her. There was a familiarity about the three of them that reminded Lizzie J. of Trey with her dad, Charlie, outside of church that Sunday so long ago.

Jake was carrying their tray of food to a table when he saw Lizzie J. She waved to him and asked them to sit with them. After everyone finished their food, the kids ran off to the playground, leaving Lizzie J. and Jake alone.

"Greg and Kristen seem like great kids," Lizzie J. said.

"They are. They aren't perfect, of course, but they mind their mom. I like being around them."

"What about their mom? Do you like being around her, too?"

"Sure, Caroline is nice. She's a hard worker. And a good mom," Jake replied, the sound of admiration coming through in his voice.

"I see her in church every Sunday. Is she a believer?"

"Yeah, she has a strong faith. I guess being a military wife and losing your husband in a war causes you to look beyond yourself to make sense of the world we live in," Jake said reflectively.

"She's very beautiful, in a natural sort of way," Lizzie J. said.

"Yeah, she's down to earth, for sure. I guess when you have so much responsibility you don't have a lot of time to focus on yourself," Jake said in a teasing voice.

"So what are you saying, Jake? That I need to take better care of myself?" Lizzie J. asked, and punched him on the arm playfully.

"Ouch, what'd you do that for? You know I think you're gorgeous!" Jake felt as though Lizzie J. was like a sister, and even though they didn't see each other often, they were very good friends.

"Sooo, do you like her?"

"Who?"

"You know I'm talking about Caroline! Do you like her?"

"I just told you I like her and I admire her."

"No, not like that. I mean like her, like her!"

"I don't know what like her, like her means. Be more specific — speak English."

"Oh, you! You know what I mean! Now tell me, do you like her?"

"You know, I really do. I feel very protective toward her and the kids. I enjoy helping her with things that are too difficult for her to do. She moved from Dad's to a rental this week, and I'm entertaining the kids while she unpacks boxes and puts things away," Jake explained, no longer teasing.

"Interesting. I know you've been lonely. Though I know I'm not supposed to bring a certain person into our conversation, I have to know. Do you think you could love Caroline as much as the other person I'm not supposed to mention?" Lizzie J. had been very good about not mentioning Maggie to Jake, but this situation seemed to be taking a very serious turn. She loved Jake as a friend, but Maggie was her best friend and she suddenly felt protective of her.

"Well, thank you for not bringing that up! I don't know. They are two very different people. I have a long history with the person you're not supposed to mention, and I'm just getting to know Caroline."

"I'm going to come out and say this, and I hope you won't

get mad at me. I love Maggie Roberts—she's been my best friend since kindergarten and I *know* she still loves you. And I think you still love her, too. Both of you are being ridiculous and one of you needs to give!"

The kids were busy in the playground and there weren't a lot of people around and suddenly their conversation became very serious.

"Lizzie J., you know, even though we were so young, I fell for Maggie the moment I saw her. I believed she would be the one I would marry. Of all the many instructions my mother gave me before she died, the one she believed was most important was to never marry an unbeliever."

"She was a very wise woman. So why have you waited for Maggie all these years? And what happened after her dad's funeral? I've asked Maggie and she won't talk about it."

"It seems silly now. There was a lot of frustration on my part that I couldn't keep stuffing down inside and I blew up at her. I became exhausted from being in competition with her career. I wanted her to put me first for a change."

"It must have been an ugly fight. You do realize the old saying *sticks and stones may break my bones, but words will never hurt me* is not true, right?" Lizzie J. had softened her voice and her demeanor. She realized Jake was opening up to her, and she prayed the kids or a worker would not interrupt them.

"It was ugly. I accused her of being selfish, not with only me but with her parents. They had just buried her dad and I was telling her how much he'd missed her and how she didn't care. I told her all she cared about was her precious career and someday she would lose her mother and lose me and she would have no one who cared about her. Thinking back on it, I realize how devastating those words and accusations were to her. It was cruel of me to say those things at a time like that. I did say them, and now she doesn't want to talk to me."

"How do you know she doesn't want to talk to you?"

"I called her apartment on Christmas Eve. She didn't answer."

"How does that mean she doesn't want to talk to you? She wouldn't have known it was you. Maybe she wasn't home," Lizzie J. suggested.

"Lizzie J., she was snowed in. Remember the big snowstorm, the one that cancelled all the flights? I figured she had company, probably the man I saw her with when I tried to surprise her. I was the one who was surprised." Jake's voice had changed. Suddenly he sounded angry.

"You don't know who he was or why they were together. I could've found out for you, if you hadn't sworn me to secrecy. She still doesn't know you were there."

"Honestly, it doesn't matter, anyway. I've moved on."

"How have you moved on?"

"I prayed for Maggie to come to know Christ for many years. It seemed she became more and more resistant. Then I started praying for God to change my feelings for her. Now, I pray that God will help me enjoy single life," Jake explained.

"You still love her though, don't you?" Lizzie J. asked.

"Maybe. I'm not sure. Since I've met Caroline I've started to see Maggie in a different way. I've been trying to change Maggie into the person I want her to be and that isn't fair. Caroline seems to be more suited to the lifestyle I want."

"Jake, you don't choose a mate based on your lifestyle. You have to love that person. Be very careful. Caroline has already been hurt. She is probably very vulnerable," Lizzie J. advised.

"Whoa, slow down. She's just a friend. Don't make it more than it is."

"I just remember how vulnerable I was after Andy died, and looking back I'm so happy I wasn't rushed into a relationship. It could have been devastating."

"Lizzie J., you're very blessed and I'm happy for you. Gosh, it's been great seeing you. Tell that husband of yours we need to get together. I need to get Greg and Kristen. We're going skating. Pray I don't fall and break something!"

"Thanks, Jake. Take care." Lizzie J. hugged him and watched through the window as he loaded the kids into his car and drove away. She sat for a while longer and her thoughts drifted back in time when she'd been a single mom and very, very vulnerable....

CHAPTER TWENTY-NINE

1965

ᴵN THE SUMMER of 1965 Lizzie J. was taking as many classes as she could manage. J.D. had carried such a heavy load every year, plus summer school, that he was graduating a year early.

Since the first day he came to her rescue, loaning her his car and babysitting Trey, they'd been inseparable. Even with his jam-packed schedule he somehow managed to find time to help her.

It had been almost two years since Andy's death. Trey was a constant reminder for Lizzie J., but not in a sad way. She felt blessed to know she would always have a part of Andy with her. Lizzie J.'s focus had shifted from her grief to the unbelievable, unimaginable love she felt for her son. Her love for Trey was a balm for her aching heart, and she knew it came from her core, her inner being of motherhood.

Lizzie J. had known since spring she was falling in love with J.D. It was a different kind of love…a mature love. They'd never actually dated. Their time together was spent at the apartment caring for Trey or studying or cooking dinner or folding laundry—mundane things.

Sometimes that kind of togetherness only happens after marriage, after the courtship is over and both people aren't always on their best behavior. Since Lizzie J. and J.D. had experienced together being happy, sad, tired, frustrated and sometimes angry, they felt they knew everything about each other. They'd seen the worst and enjoyed each other anyway. He'd never made any advances romantically, seemingly happy to just be friends. Lizzie J. *knew* he had patience. She'd seen desire in his eyes for her at the oddest times, but when she looked at him he looked away, breaking the mood. It was time, she thought, and she would need to be the one to say it first.

The next evening when J.D. came over, Lizzie J. was prepared. She'd asked her mom to keep Trey so she and J.D. could go out, alone. Lizzie J. smiled when she thought about how her mom squealed with delight like a little girl and said, "it's about time!"

Lizzie J. had lost the baby weight several months ago and looked like all the other college students. She chose the nicest outfit in her closet, took extra time with her beautiful hair, and used only a little mascara and lip gloss, deciding less is more. She still looked drop dead gorgeous. After all these months spent with J.D., she suddenly felt nervous. What if he rejected her? What if he didn't feel the same way? What was she doing? The doorbell rang, and Lizzie J. knew she was about to have the answers to all her questions.

"Hey, come in," she said to J.D. when she opened the door.

"Whoa, where are you going all dressed up? Do you have a date?" J.D. asked her, hoping she would say no.

"Yes, actually, I am going out on a date."

"Well, he's certainly a lucky guy. Do I know him?" J.D. felt sick, as though someone had punched him, and he was trying hard not to show it. Had he been such a good friend that she thought of him like a brother? Suddenly fear and dread filled his heart. J.D. had been trying to give her time to grieve the loss of Andy. How did he miss the signs that she was ready to move on with her life?

"He's here. You want to meet him?" Lizzie J. was nervous and it came through in her voice. J.D. thought she sure was excited about this date.

"Sure...I guess," J.D. said as he came in and closed the door behind him. He was thinking, no, I don't want to meet him, I don't care who he is. I can't believe this is happening.

"Come here." Lizzie J. took him by the arm, crossed to the other side of the room and stood him in front of a mirror.

"J.D., I would like to introduce you to my date tonight."

"Me?" J.D. asked, with disbelief and incredible relief.

"Yes, unless you have other plans, or you'd rather not," Lizzie J. answered, her heart in her throat.

"Ma'am, I'd be honored," J.D. said, looking into her eyes, a slow smile spreading across his face.

"Well, let's go then. Mom has Trey back in the bedroom. If he hears or sees you, we won't be able to get out the door."

"So where am I taking you on this date?"

"You'll see," Lizzie J. said as she grabbed a picnic basket on the table by the door. "Grab that blanket," she instructed.

"I'm guessing a picnic?"

"No, this is for later. It has dessert in it. Let's go to the car; then I'll tell you."

Lizzie J. put the basket in the back seat and J.D. threw the blanket back alongside of it, and they got in and sat down.

"Okay, little lady, where am I taking you?"

"How about eating at the little café out near Valley View that has such great steaks? My treat," she answered.

"I don't think so," J.D. replied.

"Do you want to go somewhere different?"

"No, I love that place, but this isn't your treat. I will not be remembered as a guy who went on a first date and let the lady pay. Not going to happen."

"Well, this was my idea and my first date. I should pay."

"Then you might want to start walking, because this car isn't going anywhere as long as you're thinking you're buying my dinner!"

"Oh, okay, start the car. I'm hungry."

J.D. smiled at her, started the car and backed out of the parking space. His mind was racing, trying to figure out what was going on and why the sudden date. He'd loved Lizzie J. from the first moment he'd seen her and had always suppressed his feelings. First, because he had respect for her relationship with Andy, then later out of respect for her grief. Throughout the past ten months they'd become friends, close friends. He loved her even more than he'd ever imagined he could. She was more beautiful on the inside than the outside. He knew her heart.

Lizzie J. smiled back at J.D., trying hard to control her excitement. She loved his red hair and ruddy complexion, and his eyes were as green as hers were blue. He'd also grown another inch in height since high school and stood six-three, changed from a skinny teenager to a muscular young man of twenty. He might not be Hollywood good-looking to a passerby on the street, but as she became friends with him over the past several months, the goodness of his heart turned him into the most handsome man she'd ever met. Lizzie J. had discovered the saying *beauty is in the eye of the beholder* to be very true.

They lingered at the dinner table and talked over another glass of sweet tea as they savored time away from their everyday life. The waitress brought their bill and Lizzie J. made a teasing attempt to take it from J.D. After he paid the bill they started to the car and J.D. asked her what was next.

"It's only seven. Why don't we drive to Craighead Forest and sit by the water and have the dessert I brought in the picnic basket. How does that sound?"

"Great—we should have about an hour or so before the mosquitoes come out to have us for their dinner," J.D. said and laughed.

"We can leave at the first bite!"

"Agreed!"

Fierce and fast moving summer storms had rolled through the area the day before and taken the heavy humidity out of the atmosphere. It was a pleasant evening. Lizzie J. had chosen the perfect day.

They walked side by side down the dirt path, through the grove of trees, toward the water. The tangled honeysuckle vines, growing on whatever they could cling to, supplied a sweet fragrance that created another dimension to their already heightened senses. The warm summer sun lay low in the sky, sinking lazily behind streaks of feathery white clouds, crafting beautiful hues of orange and red splashed across the horizon. Cicadas made their presence known, choreographing each melody as the males sang their invitation and the females fluttered their wings in reply. Mating sounds filled the summer air.

"This spot okay?" Lizzie J. asked.

"Sure, it's a good view of the water."

J.D. checked the area for rocks and sticks before spreading the blanket. Lizzie J. took off her shoes, wiggled her toes and sat down. J.D. stretched out on the blanket, put his hands behind his head and stared up at her. She gazed out at the water, trying to decide how to tell him what she wanted to say. Finally, Lizzie J. stretched out beside him and leaned over him so she could see into his eyes.

"Thank you for taking me out. I needed a break from books and diapers. It was also nice to eat out on a real plate and not food wrapped in paper!"

"Thank you for asking me out on a date. I'm usually the one to ask—this is a new thing for me. I think I like it!" he teased her.

"What do you want out of life, J.D.?"

"Whoa, that's one serious question! Or are you teasing me?"

Lizzie J. didn't answer right away. She stared into his eyes, and he could tell she wasn't teasing. Their conversation had turned to a serious topic. The future.

"I'm serious."

"Well...I want to finish college, go to law school and someday have my own law firm."

"That's all?"

"Is that all? That's at least another four years of school."

"What about your personal life? Do you want a family?"

"Sure I want a family. Why do you want to know?"

"We've spent a lot of time together over the last few months, and I've never heard you mention going out on a date or having a girlfriend."

"Maybe you haven't noticed that I've been busy the last few months. You see...I answered the phone one afternoon and offered to help this beautiful girl who needed a babysitter and a car...and we've become very good friends. She has a crazy, busy life, with a grueling schedule as a college student and a single mom. I've been spending all my free time with her."

Lizzie J. didn't respond right away, and for a few seconds J.D. thought she might think he was complaining. Then..."I love you," Lizzie J. whispered.

J.D. slowly turned to look directly at her. Her eyes were filled with tears and he thought she'd never been more beautiful.

"Marry me," J.D. whispered. Before she could answer he pulled her down and kissed her softly. A single tear fell from her lashes and J.D. knew she would be his.

"Marry you? Why do you want me to marry you?"

"Because I've loved you since the day you turned to look at me when we were introduced—the first weekend I visited Jake."

"How could you say you loved me that first day? You didn't even know me."

"Okay, I guess you're right. I thought you were gorgeous and I was so jealous of Andy. I liked him and I knew the two of you had plans for your future. I kept my feelings to myself and stayed away. I've never told anyone, not even Jake. I would've visited Jake a lot more often except I didn't want to see you and Andy together," J.D. explained as he stared out at the lake.

"It sure has taken a long time to tell me you felt that way."

"For some reason, when Andy died I stopped thinking about you. I began to feel guilty, even though I knew I had nothing to do with the accident. Guilty that Andy had died and I was still here and might someday have a shot at dating you. Somehow it didn't seem fair," J.D. replied.

"What changed?" Lizzie J. asked.

"After Trey was born and I saw you at church on Mothers'

Day, all the old feelings surfaced and I couldn't stop thinking about you again. You mentioned I never dated or had a girlfriend. I tried to date—I wasn't interested."

"Wow, all these months you've loved me and you never once said anything or indicated you cared about me other than being my friend. Why?"

"I liked getting to know you and becoming friends. I wanted you to get over your grief. I wanted you to love me for me, not as a replacement for Andy. So I waited."

"Thank you," Lizzie J. said softly.

"For what?"

"For waiting, for being patient and for being my friend first. You're a very wise man, J.D. I might have pushed you away if you hadn't given me time to fall in love with you."

"So will you?"

"Will I what?" Lizzie J. teased.

"Marry me?"

"Yes! Absolutely!"

THE CHRISTMAS AFTER the summer evening Lizzie J. told J.D. she loved him, he'd finally saved enough money to give her an engagement ring, and they planned the wedding for the summer of '66.

Jake was J.D.'s best man, and of course Maggie was Lizzie J.'s maid of honor. It was a small, intimate wedding with a reception at Nanny and Poppy's house.

It was a sweet ceremony, but tinged with a slight feeling of sadness. Andy's parents came to the wedding, and their presence was evidence they approved of Lizzie J.'s choice. After all, J.D. would be a father to their grandson. Lizzie J.s' love for Trey made her aware of how difficult it must be for them to see J.D., instead of Andy, standing beside her at the altar. They wanted to be there for her and Trey, and she would never forget their sacrifice.

Lizzie J. was given in marriage by her Poppy and Charlie, one on each side as she walked down the aisle. She still couldn't call Charlie dad, but he was okay with that and felt honored to be included.

Rita was happy for her daughter. She'd loved having the time with Lizzie J. and Trey and had tried to make each day count. Rita would be alone again, though, and that made her sad. Charlie had become a part of their lives, and he too was sad that his daughter and grandson were moving away. The whole family struggled with the knowledge that Lizzie J. and Trey would be moving with J.D. to Little Rock, where he would attend Law School.

Jake was somewhat depressed about all the changes too. Maggie was in school in New York, and now J.D. and Lizzie J. would be in Little Rock. Even though he wasn't happy with everyone moving away, Jake was content with where he was. He wouldn't graduate for another year because he'd not taken summer classes or carried a full schedule like J.D. He still worked for the Houstons and was happiest on the farm. He kept reminding himself that Maggie had only two years of school to complete in New York, and then she would be coming home.

After the wedding, Maggie and Jake helped J.D. and Lizzie J. move the few furnishings they owned into the apartment in Little Rock, where they would live for the next three years. On their drive back to Lake City that night, the same old conversation found its way into the darkness of the car.

"It's been a bittersweet week, hasn't it?" Maggie asked.

"Are you thinking about Andy?"

"Yeah, I'm so happy for J.D. and Lizzie J., but I never, ever thought I would see her marry anyone other than Andy. I guess it's a lesson in living for today, because we don't know what tomorrow will bring."

"You know, J.D. never told me he was attracted to her. To think he kept his feelings to himself all this time is amazing. I'm pretty sure his patience paid off. I loved hearing about how she was the first to say "I love you," Jake said and glanced in Maggie's direction.

"Lizzie J. is one of the most grounded women I've ever known. Not only in her common sense approach to life, but also in her faith. Not only do I love her because she is my best friend, but I admire her so much. She's such a role model for me, but I'll never be as good as she is," Maggie answered softly.

"Why do you say that? Lizzie J. isn't perfect. You do realize that?"

"Oh, I know, but she's so happy. Even after losing Andy, she never wavered in her faith. I was so angry and I don't understand why she wasn't too."

"I could give you the answer to that question, but I've tried before and you don't want to hear it, remember?"

"Yeah, I remember. Since we only have about three weeks of our summer vacation left, let's change the subject."

"Sure, we can change the subject. What did you think about the wedding?"

"I thought it was perfect. Everything about it was like

Lizzie J. Even though it was a small wedding, it was shared with the right people."

"So what kind of wedding do you want? Small, medium, large, inside or outside, formal or informal?" Jake asked her.

"Probably a little larger than Lizzie J.'s, but not huge. Very elegant and simple, and with only the people who are very important to us."

"To us? I don't think you've ever, ever said anything like that. Am I to assume you will marry me?" Jake asked excitedly.

"Now don't get too excited about us getting married anytime soon. I still have two more years in New York, and you have another year of college. But when I think about getting married, you are the guy!"

"We need to go to a wedding about once a month!" Jake teased.

"Oh, stop being so dramatic. You know I love you! I want to finish school, and by that time, you'll have already been out for a year and we can start our lives the right way."

"So what you're saying is that when you finish school, you are moving back to Arkansas?"

"Sure, I've always planned to move back. Why would I stay in New York City?"

"For the same reasons you wanted to go there in the first place," Jake replied.

"Well, when I finish school, there won't be a reason for me to stay. I'm coming home, Jake. I promise."

CHAPTER THIRTY

1972

A S MAGGIE REMEMBERED the promise she'd made to Jake almost six years ago, she wondered if he would ever again believe anything she told him. It was late April and the snow was finally gone, with a hint of spring in the air.

She'd had many arguments with God over the past four months. It was hard not to share her newfound faith with her family and friends, but she was obedient and it was paying off.

She was afraid if she talked with anyone from home she would be tempted to discuss the changes in her life, so as difficult as it was, she wouldn't answer her phone. When Maggie's mom called and couldn't get an answer, she would then call Maggie's agent to be sure her daughter was okay. As soon as Maggie knew her mom had called, she would send her a card through the mail assuring her she was just busy and would see her in June in Arkansas. Maggie also sent cards to Lizzie J. when she didn't answer her calls either.

In the middle of January, Maggie had listed her apartment for sale and flown to Memphis to look for a place to live. She was going home — maybe not to Lake City, but a little over an hour drive was a vast improvement over the distance from New York City.

But after spending a couple of days with a realtor in Memphis, Maggie realized she wanted to go *home*. An hour away seemed too far, so she rented a car and drove to Jonesboro, where she rented a house. She was tired of living in an apartment and wanted a yard and flower beds. She might have to hire someone to take care of them, but she could afford to do that.

Maggie spent two days in Jonesboro. She worried she'd see someone who knew her, so she tried to hide behind a disguise of sunglasses and a hat and swore the realtor to secrecy. Maggie wanted to drive to Lake City but resisted, wanting to have everything in place before she told everyone about the changes in her life.

Her schedule was already in place for the year and she felt obligated to fulfill it. It was hard to keep that pace along with playing at church on Sunday and attending the Bible study group she'd joined. But she was happy and content.

When she returned to New York, she met with her agent and had a difficult conversation trying to explain her need to change her successful lifestyle. She might as well have been speaking a foreign language; her agent just didn't get it. Their association would end when Maggie finished all her scheduled performances and no longer needed an agent.

When asked what she planned to do, Maggie told her she wasn't sure—God hadn't revealed that to her yet. Her agent left Maggie's apartment shaking her head, and Maggie prayed for her, hoping something she'd said might speak to her soul.

Things were falling into place. Whether her apartment sold or not, she was moving. She had promised everyone she would be home in June, but she was actually going in May. She planned to move into her house the week before Mother's Day and surprise her mom. That was only a few weeks away, and she could hardly contain her excitement.

Maggie had thought about calling Jake and telling him she was moving home, but decided that since they'd been estranged for so long, it might be better to tell him in person. She was also planning to ask him to marry her. It never occurred to her she might be too late!

LIZZIE J. AND J.D. had invited Jake and Caroline to their house a few times, and the four kids played well together. Lizzie J. felt disloyal to Maggie, but J.D. assured her she wasn't. Lizzie J. had prayed for Maggie for years and wouldn't stop now. She knew God was in the saving business and it was never too late. But still, she felt as though she was choosing Caroline over Maggie, and J.D. again explained to her that Jake was the one doing the choosing.

Jake and Caroline looked comfortable together. Lizzie J. didn't think they were in love, just comfortable. She worried that to Caroline, Jake had taken Mike's place, and to Jake, Caroline had taken Maggie's place. That was not good. She worried they both were settling, not on who they wanted but on who was available. A marriage like that was doomed from the beginning.

Lizzie J. was concerned because Maggie wouldn't answer her phone. She was getting cards or notes from her frequently in the mail, but that was odd, too. Finally, she left the kids with J.D. one afternoon and went to see Annie.

"Hi Lizzie J. How nice to see you," Annie said when she opened the door. "I hope everything is okay. This is an unexpected visit!"

"Awww, Annie, it's so good to see you." Lizzie J. stepped inside and memories came flooding back. "I love coming here. Even though it's a different house, all the furniture is the same and you're here. It's like coming home."

"You know you can visit anytime. I know those two children and that lawyer husband of yours keep you busy, though."

"They do, but that's not a good excuse. Do you have time to talk for a few minutes?"

"Sure. You want to sit in the swing on the back porch?"

"That would be great."

"How're your mom and dad? They haven't gotten married, have they?" Annie asked.

"No, but they should. They are together all the time. I keep asking them what they are waiting for, but they just answer something silly and ignore me. I tease Dad that he's afraid Mom will spend all of his money, then she says that's why she won't marry him, she hasn't made her own fortune yet."

"Well, it sounds like they're happy. I guess that's the main thing, and that you have them in your life. What a blessing for you."

"Yes, they are. How are you, Annie?"

"I'm fine. This year has been a little better. I'm finally getting used to living alone. It's still difficult though."

"I'm here for a reason. I guess you figured that. Have you spoken with Maggie since Christmas?"

"No. I've tried calling her, but she doesn't answer her phone. I've been getting a lot of cards through the mail though. In her last note, she did tell me that she has news to share with me when she comes home in June. Do you think she's met someone in New York and maybe she's getting married?"

"Oh, that never entered my mind! Jake went to see her about a year after Oliver died. He was parked across the street from her apartment and she came out with a man. Jake said they were arm-in-arm and looked as if they knew each other well. Jake left and Maggie never knew he'd been there. That's when he started saying he didn't want to know anything about her or even hear her name mentioned."

"Did she ever mention anyone to you?" Annie asked.

"No. I wanted to ask her about the man, but Jake didn't want her to know he'd been there. I'm worried about her. Things haven't seemed right since she changed her plans after Christmas and didn't come home for a visit," Lizzie J. replied.

"I know. I've missed her," Annie said softly.

"What do you think about Jake's friend Caroline?" Lizzie J. asked.

"I don't know much about her. I was introduced to her at church a few weeks ago and she seems pleasant. I heard her husband died in Viet Nam. Do you think she's more than a friend to Jake?" Annie asked.

"I know he likes her. J.D. and I have had them over for dinner a couple of times, but I tell you Annie, I feel as though I'm being deceitful to Maggie."

"You shouldn't feel that way. Maggie has made her choice, and I've begun to think she will never move back here, and maybe never marry. I remember when she was a teenager, before she started dating Jake. I always thought she would be married to her music, and sadly, it seems I might have been right," Annie said.

"I'm thinking about writing her a letter since she won't

answer her phone, and telling her Jake is seeing someone. I know they haven't been together in over two years, but Annie, I feel they are supposed to be. Do you think I should do that? J.D. told me to stay out of it," Lizzie J. said and smiled when she thought about his warning not to get involved in someone else's love triangle.

"I don't know, Lizzie J. If it will make you feel better, I guess it can't hurt. If she is truly over Jake and seeing someone else, she can toss your letter in the trash."

"Since the first day she left and moved to the city, I worried she would never return. I kept hoping. The entire time J.D. and I lived in Little Rock, we couldn't wait to move back home and be around the people we love. I miss her and I know you do, too," Maggie said wistfully.

"You know, Lizzie J., I've learned something very important over the years. You can change yourself, but you can't change others. I love my daughter and I'm very proud of what she's accomplished, but she has to live her own life."

"You're right, and very wise to realize that. I'm being selfish. Maggie does need to live her own life. Thank you for telling me that. Maybe I won't write that letter."

"Only you can decide if you should do that or not. Maggie loves you like a sister; she would understand."

"Thanks, Annie. I've got to get home before the kids have J.D. tied up in a chair," Lizzie J. said and laughed. She gave Annie a hug and promised she wouldn't wait so long to come and visit the next time.

JAKE AND HIS FARMHANDS were busy. They'd been in the fields preparing for planting time. It had been a wet spring, but it was the first of May and the ground had dried out. For some reason, Maggie seemed to invade his mind more when he worked the fields, probably because of all the times she came out to ride with him when she was home from school in the summer. He tried to push her image away and replace it with the image of Caroline, but today that trick wouldn't work.

He stopped the tractor near his truck to take a break, get a cold drink and walk around a bit. He'd been sitting on that seat for a long time and needed to stretch his legs. Maybe it would also clear his mind.

He and Caroline had been seeing each other since Christmas. He enjoyed her company, but he still felt as though she was a good friend like Lizzie J. He'd lain in bed many nights trying to figure out what his problem was. He hadn't seen Maggie in over two years, except when he'd seen her with that man in New York, nor had he heard her voice…nothing.

Caroline was a beautiful woman—intelligent, caring, compassionate and already a good mother. She was everything a man would want in a wife. Most important to Jake was her relationship with God, her deep faith. These attributes should be enough, but Jake realized the passion and desire he felt for Maggie was absent. God had never taken away Jake's desire for Maggie nor given him contentment living a single life.

And every night as he had this conversation with himself, his thoughts would inevitably turn to Maggie. She was the last person on his mind when he finally drifted off to sleep.

Then when he dreamed, it was always Maggie in his house, never Caroline. He would sleep fitfully and wake up the next morning to mull over the same dilemma.

Setting his drink on the tailgate of his truck, Jake suddenly realized that though he didn't want to remain single, his current situation was acceptable. His house and fifty acres had become home. When Jake purchased the property, he carved out another acre beyond the pecan orchard and left the rest to be planted in cotton. Picking the cotton in the fall was his favorite time. He loved the fullness of the white open bolls, and when he arrived home during the harvest, his heart was always full. He knew he was blessed.

When he remodeled the house, he also built a barn. He didn't have animals but decided a nice barn would complete the look he wanted. He was right. His property was so picturesque photographers often stopped to ask if they could take photos. Sometimes he wondered how many homes in Craighead County had family photos hanging on their walls with his barn or his house in the background.

The break was exactly what Jake needed. He decided not to think about marriage. As long as Caroline was happy with their situation, then so was he.

CHAPTER THIRTY-ONE

FORTUNATELY FOR MAGGIE, she'd signed a lease and paid her deposit on the house in Arkansas and could move in at any time. The buyer for her apartment in New York had bought it on the condition that possession could be within two weeks. She had already checked out moving companies, so when the sale finally happened, she knew who to call. The movers arrived early on May third, and by evening the apartment that she once thought she just had to have was as empty as it was the first time she saw it. When she walked through the bare rooms one last time, she didn't have any sentimental feelings but rather a feeling of freedom. She locked the door behind her, got into the new car she'd recently purchased, and drove to the hotel where she would spend one last night in New York City before heading south the next morning.

Studying her map the past few days, she decided Charleston, West Virginia was about halfway. She could make it home in two days of hard driving, or maybe three days at a more leisurely pace. Her furniture wouldn't be delivered until Monday, May 8th, so she would still spend at least one or two nights in a hotel in Jonesboro. Her plan was to get her house furnished and boxes unpacked before Mother's Day. She wanted to surprise her mom at church, and then take her to see she'd actually moved home. Every time she thought about the people she loved, Maggie's heart would almost burst with happiness.

The past couple of weeks her dreams had fluctuated between the dream in the cotton patch and the dream of Jake with another family. Maggie almost dreaded going to bed. Neither of her dreams ended the way she wanted, and it took half of the next day to make the images go away.

She did take three days to drive to her new home, and during those long hours on the road, Maggie had a lot of conversations with God. She'd learned that God never gives up on anyone. As long as you draw breath, He is available. On that snowy Christmas Eve she'd given her heart and life to Christ. Now she understood what it meant to be "born again." Maggie *knew* she was different.

Was her music still one of the loves of her life? Of course—it was a gift. She wasn't yet sure where she was supposed to use this gift, but she knew in time God would reveal His plan. Was Jake the other love of her life? Yes, she'd always loved him. But now her love for God came first. She would listen, she would follow, and let Him lead. Without God in her life she never had to choose between what she wanted and what God wanted for her. But now she needed to, and it wouldn't be easy.

Instead of staying in Jonesboro, Maggie decided to stay in Memphis. Sort of a mini-vacation. She went to the zoo, shopped at the famous Goldsmiths Department Store downtown, and ate southern fare every night to include cornbread muffins, cornbread sticks, and even fried cornbread. One might find a place in the city in the North that advertised cornbread, but it was a sham. Memphis cooking pleased her and she'd satisfied, for now, her cornbread craving!

Living in the South would certainly call for different décor than living in the North. So Maggie shopped at a few local stores that reflected the South and its people. She bought a treasure trove of so many things she began to worry they wouldn't fit into her car. They did fit, and with a packed car, she left on Monday morning and drove the seventy miles to Jonesboro. The movers were scheduled to arrive at noon, but when she pulled into her neighborhood around ten, they were there waiting.

At 6 p.m. on May 8, 1972, Maggie Roberts was again a resident of Arkansas. She said goodbye to the movers, locked her front door, and walked through her new home. All the furniture was in place and her bed put together, waiting on linens, but there was still so much to do to make this place a home.

One could get lost in New York City among a population of eight million, but Jonesboro was small, only twenty-seven thousand. It would be difficult to stay unnoticed for long. Maggie knew to stay as far away as possible from Indian Mall. Until the mall was built in 1968, everyone shopped downtown on Main Street, but the mall was the new place to shop, and now people from the surrounding area couldn't get enough of it.

For dinner the first night, she ate a burger and fries from McDonald's. She smiled as she ordered at the drive-thru, something she'd never done in the city. All these experiences felt new, but familiar. The next morning, Maggie drove twenty miles south to a town called Harrisburg to shop at a small grocery store. She only bought what she would need for the rest of the week.

Maggie didn't have another concert until July. She would have almost two months to visit and hopefully plan a wedding. Her plan to ask Jake to marry her after all these years was uppermost in her mind.

By Saturday night Maggie was so excited she doubted she could sleep. She'd bought her mom a beautiful corsage and planned to show up at church right before worship started.

When Maggie woke up the next morning, her bedroom was filled with early morning light, the rays of sun splayed across her bed and onto the wood floor, and she could hear the birds singing in the trees outside her window. It was going to be a beautiful spring day, perfect for starting the rest of her life, she thought. She would see Jake today....

Maggie could finally stop hiding out in her new home. She checked in the mirror one last time before leaving to be sure she'd chosen the right clothes. As she looked at her reflection, a feeling of déjà vu came over her. Suddenly the image in the mirror looked like her sixteen-year-old self that Sunday afternoon she was trying to decide what to wear on her first date with Jake. She wasn't a teenager any longer and ten years had passed, but a feeling of uncertainty washed over her. She chastised herself, grabbed the corsage and her purse, and went to her car. Maggie was on her way.

Only fifteen miles separated Jonesboro from Lake City, and before she knew it she was turning off Highway 18. Around the corner she could see the water tower and Carters Gin. Another right turn and there was the church.

She parked her car, took a deep breath and headed for the door. Sunday School had ended and people were going to the sanctuary. Maggie tried to avoid eye contact because she didn't want to be delayed before she found her mom. As she went up the stairs and into the sanctuary, she scanned the pew that her mom and dad had claimed as their own. She was there!

No one was seated in the pew behind her mom, so Maggie slid in, put her hand on her mom's shoulder, leaned down close and said, "Happy Mother's Day." Annie Roberts thought she'd heard her daughter but figured it was her imagination until she turned and saw her. Maggie quickly went around and entered her pew. Annie stood up to embrace her.

Maggie was surprised at her emotions. She'd never been so glad to see her mom and couldn't imagine how she'd stayed away so long. Finally she pinned the corsage on her mother's dress and answered a few questions without giving away her other surprise about moving to Jonesboro.

More and more people were coming in and realizing she was there. Then she saw Jake enter the sanctuary and excused herself with an "I'll be right back."

Her legs were weak and her hands shaking. Age was being very kind to Jake—he was more handsome than ever. As Maggie walked toward him, she could see in his face the moment he recognized her. Maggie had to compose herself to keep from running to him.

"Jake…how are you?" Maggie asked him haltingly.

Jake didn't answer immediately. He knew it was her, but it was such a shock he couldn't find words to reply. Everything felt surreal. Before he could answer her, Caroline came up beside him and looped her arm through his.

"There you are. I've been looking for you. The kids are waiting in our pew. You ready?" Caroline asked.

Maggie and Jake continued to stare at one another, and finally realization dawned on Caroline when she looked at Maggie. Caroline had seen enough pictures to immediately recognize her, but honestly if she'd never seen her, but only heard about her, she would have known her by the almost visible energy passing between them. Jake finally found his voice.

"Hello Maggie. I'm fine. Caroline, this is Maggie. Maggie, Caroline." It was an awkward few seconds, but they were all mature adults. Maggie was the first to speak.

"Hello, Caroline. It's nice to meet you. Please don't let me detain you. Church will be starting at any moment. Jake, it was good to see you," Maggie said, hoping her voice didn't sound as shaky as it felt. She turned and went back to her mom before Caroline could reply.

Maggie was trembling so much that her mom could feel it. Annie leaned over and asked, "Are you okay? Do you want to leave?"

"Oh Mom, goodness no. I'm perfectly fine."

As church started, Maggie sat in a state of shock. She couldn't figure out why no one had told her Jake had a girl-friend. Or was he married?!?! She did hear the word kids. She was a beautiful woman who obviously knew Jake well. And they had their own pew?

Maggie tried hard to still her heartbeat and slow her breathing. Where were Lizzie J. and J.D.? It was Mother's Day—they should be here. She wondered what else had changed since her last time home. Was moving here a mistake? A huge mistake? Should she have answered her ringing phone?

Somehow Maggie was able to remain calm through church, smile at people who looked her way and act as though every-thing was as it should be. When church was over and people stood to leave, she tried not to look around. She did not want to see Jake.

But as she was shaking hands with people who came to see her, and turning from person to person, she inevitably saw him. He was across the sanctuary, holding a little girl in his arms, as his lady friend talked with someone else. Jake was watching Maggie. Their eyes locked for only seconds, then Maggie looked away.

"Mom, is it okay with you if I meet you at your house since we both drove here, then go out for lunch?" Maggie asked.

"Sure, you go on. I'll be there in a few minutes," Annie said.

Maggie was able to get through the people with only a couple of short conversations. She got to her car and couldn't leave fast enough. What had happened was worse than either of her bad dreams.

As Maggie drove to her mom's house she began to pray. By the time she pulled into the driveway, she'd calmed down and decided she needed to get answers before she jumped to conclusions. She wanted to find out exactly what had been going on the past two-and-a-half years. Her anger at Jake—and closing herself off from the people she loved—could have caused consequences beyond repair.

As Caroline and Jake left the church to walk to their cars, the kids skipped on ahead.

"Are you okay, Jake? Did you know Maggie would be here today?" Caroline asked softly. She knew Maggie's presence had affected his demeanor. During the church service she was aware his mind was on the other side of the sanctuary, but she also knew he never looked Maggie's way.

"Yes, I'm fine, and no, I didn't know she would be here. I haven't seen her or talked to her in over two years. I will admit it was quite a shock," Jake said, trying to sound as though it made no difference to him.

"Do you still want to come over for dinner tonight?" Caroline asked.

"Of course. Hey, I'm fine. Maggie being in town doesn't change anything. See you about six?" Jake asked, and tried to smile at Caroline the way he would have before he saw Maggie, who suddenly had managed to turn his world upside down.

"Okay, see you this evening. Come on kids. Let's go. Tell Jake goodbye!"

Driving home, Jake couldn't stop himself from looking down the street where Maggie's mom lived. Sure enough, there was a strange car in the driveway. He felt his stomach churn.

MAGGIE WAS WAITING in her car when her mom arrived.

"Do you want to unpack before we go out to eat lunch?"

"No, not now. But I do have a big, big surprise and I think you'll like it."

"Sounds mysterious. Where is this big, big surprise?" Annie asked and laughed.

"Come on, get in and I'll drive. We're eating in Jonesboro, and that's where my surprise is."

"Is this your car or a rental?" Annie asked as she looked at the expensive new car Maggie was driving.

"It's mine. I bought it last week."

"You haven't owned a car since you moved to the city. Why did you decide to own one now?"

"You'll understand once you see my surprise."

They rode in silence for a few minutes. Annie wanted to ask questions about Jake but was hesitant to bring the subject up. But she didn't have to.

"So I'm guessing Jake has a girlfriend?" Maggie asked, trying hard to sound as if it meant nothing to her.

"I guess she's a girlfriend. They've been seeing each other since right after Christmas."

"I don't understand why you or Lizzie J. didn't tell me."

"Maggie, you haven't talked to me since Christmas Eve morning when I called and you told me you were snowed in. And Lizzie J. came to see me because you haven't talked to her either, and she was getting concerned. And you told me you were coming home in June and you show up today. What's going on?"

"I guess now is not the time for all of this. We're almost there. We can ask questions and get the answers we both need after I show you my surprise."

Maggie had never seen Jake with another woman, and had never known what it felt like to be jealous, to feel as though someone else had the one who belonged only to her. She was shocked at how scorned and somewhat violated she felt. But the realization slowly dawned on her that Jake didn't belong to her. Maybe since their separation, he'd stopped loving her. Just because she loved him didn't make him hers....

"Where are you taking me?" Annie asked as they left the business area and started into the residential streets.

"Patience, Mom. We're almost there."

Maggie turned onto her street and pulled up in front of the house she'd rented.

"Let's get out. I want to show you something," Maggie instructed.

Annie didn't ask any more questions but dutifully followed her daughter, not having any idea about what she was soon to find out.

Maggie put her key in the lock, turned it and pushed the door open.

"Mom, I want you to be the first to see my new home!"

Annie walked into the house. She was dumbfounded. She recognized Maggie's furniture and other personal items she'd seen in the apartment in the city, but she still couldn't grasp what this meant.

"I don't understand," was all Annie could say.

"Mom, I've moved home," Maggie said, and put her arms around her mom.

Annie began to cry. She could count on both hands the number of times she'd seen her daughter since the day Maggie graduated and began her career. Annie had grieved the loss of her husband Oliver all alone, and these past two-and-a-half years had been very hard.

"Oh, Mom, I'm sorry for the way I've been all these years. Please sit down. I have other news I've been waiting since Christmas to share with you."

When Maggie finished sharing her heart and all that had happened since Christmas, they were both drying tears.

"So it's true? You've come home?"

"Yes I have. Finding out I have an eternal home led me back to my earthly home. I still don't know what God wants me to do with the rest of my life, but He'll lead me if I dare to follow," Maggie said.

"Maggie, I know Lizzie J. and Jake have both prayed for you over the years. Do they know?"

"No, I wanted you to be the first to hear what has happened the last few months, and to explain why I wouldn't talk to anyone. I had to be sure the decisions I was making weren't coming from anyone other than God."

"How long has it been since you spoke to Jake?" Annie asked her daughter softly.

"I haven't talked to Jake since Dad's funeral. It's sad to think how selfish I was. When Jake tried to talk to me about it, I didn't want to hear it because deep down I knew it was true. We said some ugly things to each other. I owe him an apology, even if he has someone new in his life."

"I wish your dad was here today to hear your good news. He would be so happy," Annie said wistfully.

"I'll see him again one day. Dad is happier where he is right now than he could ever be on earth. And he wouldn't want to come back. I know that now. But it doesn't keep us from missing him!"

"Maggie, you do realize your daddy was proud of you and all your accomplishments. He would always say, 'My Maggie goes after what she wants and she's a hard worker too,' and he loved you so much."

"Thank you for telling me that. I always felt loved by both of you. I'm so sorry Daddy never knew how much I loved him," Maggie replied sadly.

"Don't think for one minute that he didn't know you loved him! We both knew!"

They grew quiet, Maggie thankful that she still had her

mom, and her mom thankful that her daughter had come home.

"Mom, are you hungry?" Maggie asked.

"Starving!"

"Let's go have lunch, then we'll drive back to Lake City and I'll drop by and surprise Lizzie J."

"I don't know if it will be a surprise. I'm sure by now someone in town has called her and given her the news that you were at church this morning!"

As they drove back to Lake City, Maggie tried not to glance down the road at Jake's house, but she did. She knew the property, but she knew it as old and run-down. She could see from the highway that it definitely didn't look the same. She could see the barn too.

"I hear his house is charming," Annie said to her daughter.

"I was so shocked when I heard he bought that old place, but then I guess in a way it fits Jake."

"Instead of going to Lizzie J.'s first, why don't you stop and see Jake?" Annie suggested.

"Mom, he has a girlfriend. I'm obviously too late. Running after him is something I'm not going to do," Maggie said adamantly.

"Maggie, do you still love Jake? Did you come home for him?"

"It doesn't matter. I wanted to come home. Yes, I'd planned to ask Jake to marry me; he'd asked me enough times through the years. I figured it was my turn. Maybe God has other plans for me and for Jake. I don't have the right to interfere in his life. We aren't teenagers ... somehow we grew up," Maggie replied quietly.

"I'm sorry," Annie said.

"Mom, please don't tell anyone what I told you. I would be embarrassed."

"Of course. I won't tell anyone."

"I'm not coming in the house right now, but I'll be back after I visit with Lizzie J., okay?"

"Sure. Have a nice visit. You sure you're okay?" Annie asked.

"Yes, I'm fine, but thank you for asking. I love you, Mom."

"I love you too, Margaret Mae Roberts."

Annie closed the car door and watched as her daughter backed down the driveway. She waved as she drove away. Annie was happy her daughter had moved home, something she thought would never happen. But she knew Maggie was hurt and a little humiliated, and as a mom she wanted to fix it, to make the hurt go away, like all the band-aids she'd applied to skinned knees so long ago. A broken heart can't be bandaged, though, at least not by a mom. Maggie would have to work this out on her own.

Maggie drove through town before she went to Lizzie J.'s., a routine she started her first visit home from college — driving up and down streets, checking to see who had painted their house a different color, added a front porch or installed a new screen door. She always drove by the school where she'd spent thirteen years of her life. She loved hearing the kids on the playground and the flag whipping in the wind flying high on the pole, but today was Sunday and the playground was empty, as well as the flagpole. But she could still say hello to all the places she'd missed and longed to see. Maggie also wanted to see Jake's property, and she knew a few back roads that would get her close enough to see the house without driving past.

Maggie stopped at an angle on a dirt road that gave her a

good view of the house. At first sight her breath caught. It was charming and picture perfect, nestled in the center of the land with the new barn slightly back and to the left. Shoots of green could be seen here and there in the surrounding fields as the cotton, recently planted, began to emerge. Pecan trees planted years ago, now a mature orchard, lent their own enhancement. A wide expansive front porch held up by thickset posts graced the front of the home, and the empty porch swing looked blissfully inviting. Maggie sat spellbound, staying longer than she'd intended. Reluctantly, she did a u-turn and went back the way she'd come.

As she drove to Lizzie J.'s, Maggie realized she could have already been married to Jake. She wondered how she'd missed the mark so badly. And how could the change in her soul so completely change the desires of her heart? She knew....

Lizzie J. and J.D.'s house came into view. Maggie could feel her emotions spiraling out of control as she got out of her car and stepped onto the porch. She wanted to surprise Lizzie J. and was hoping no one had told them she was home. She knocked on the front door and stood slightly to the side. J.D. opened the door, and before he could say anything, Maggie put her finger to her lips to shush him.

"Where's Lizzie J.?" Maggie asked quietly.

"Stay right here and I'll tell her someone is here to see her," he whispered and winked.

Maggie could hear him calling to Lizzie J., and her asking who it was. Then she was there.

"Surprise!" Maggie said as she jumped from the side to right in front of her friend.

Lizzie J. didn't reply with words. She squealed like a little girl and grabbed Maggie, and the two women hugged and jumped up and down as they'd done so many times through the years.

"Is it really Maggie Roberts?" Lizzie J. pulled back, holding Maggie's hands and looking her up and down dramatically.

"It's really me," Maggie said, and suddenly she began to cry.

"Hey, what's wrong? Come on in," Lizzie J. said, and pulled Maggie inside and shut the door.

"I'm sorry, I'm such a mess," Maggie replied. She looked around the room and thought how good it felt to be here. A slight breeze came through the open windows and scattered the Sunday newspaper lying on the floor by the couch. A glass of sweet tea sat on the side table. A dog barked outside as kids rode their bikes up and down the street. Maggie could see the beautiful backyard through the open door to the screened porch. It was an oasis.

"It's okay to cry. It's been a long time since you've been home. When did you get here? Why didn't you tell me? I can't believe I'm standing in my house with Maggie Roberts!"

"It's a long story," Maggie replied as she regained control of her tears. "Where are the kids?"

"Maggie is taking a nap and Trey is at a friend's house. Can you stay awhile? Does your mom know you are here?"

"Yes, I can stay and yes, Mom knows, and I'm never leaving again," Maggie said with such conviction that Lizzie J. knew immediately she was about to hear something very important.

"You want a glass of tea?"

"Yeah, only if it's sweet," Maggie replied as she lowered her body into a comfy-looking recliner.

"Are there other kinds of tea?" Lizzie J. teased as she left the room.

J.D. had watched their exchange out on the porch. He heard them talking as they came in the house, so he came out of the bedroom to say a proper hello to Maggie. After giving her a hug, he excused himself to give the women the privacy he could tell was needed.

Lizzie J. came back with the tea and set it on the table beside Maggie. Lizzie J. had her own glass, and after placing it on the table beside the couch, she tucked one leg up under the other one, sat down and looked at Maggie.

"Okay, spill it! What's going on?"

"Lizzie J., it's so complicated that I don't even know where to start."

"Well, up until your dad's funeral and your big blowout with Jake, I pretty much know your whole life. So a couple of years shouldn't take too long," Lizzie J. replied, and smiled to encourage Maggie to start there.

"Two years went by fast. In one way it seems like yesterday, but when I think how long it's been since I've talked to my dad or Jake, it seems a lifetime ago," Maggie said wistfully.

"So what did you mean when you said you were never leaving again?"

"Okay, the real changes have happened since Christmas Eve."

"Why? What happened on Christmas Eve?" Lizzie J. asked.

"I went to church," Maggie replied simply.

"By choice?"

"Yes, but it started a few months before that when I went to a bookstore and wound up buying a Bible and a book on finding my purpose in life," Maggie told her softly.

"You bought a Bible?" Lizzie J. asked quietly. Surprise was evident in her question.

"It changed my life. The Bible, I mean. I began to study and search the scriptures to find what everyone I'd grown up with had, except me. So on Christmas Eve, in knee-deep snow, I walked to a church a few blocks from my apartment."

"I'm speechless," was Lizzie J.'s only reply.

"It was a beautiful church, rising up majestically amidst all the other buildings. The scene in the city that night was breathtaking, as if the whole city was waiting on the arrival of the Savior of the world. I played the piano for them that night."

"Wait, I'm confused. You played the piano at the church? How? Why?"

"Before the service started, there were people going up and down the aisles asking if any of the worshippers could play the piano because their pianist was sick. Before I knew what happened, I told them I could."

"Well, yeah, I guess you could! What did they think about having a famous person playing for their service?"

"They didn't know who I was until the service was over. As people were leaving I began to play The Hallelujah Chorus. Everyone stopped and sat back down. Then a few people recognized me and word circulated all through the church. But Lizzie J., I wasn't playing for those people. I gave my life to Christ that day and I was playing for Him," Maggie explained quietly as tears slipped down her face. Maggie had been telling her story while gazing out the open window, as if seeing the scene she was describing. Finally, she looked over to Lizzie J. who had not said a word.

"Oh Maggie, I'm so happy for you. I've prayed for you for years and years. Now we are truly sisters! But why wouldn't you answer your phone? Why wouldn't you talk to me or your mom? Especially with this kind of news!"

"I'd planned to, but then I decided I needed to let God lead me for the first time in my life without outside influences. I know you and Mom love me, but I had to learn to hear from Him."

"I hear what you're saying, but I feel like I should pinch myself to be sure I'm not dreaming this conversation. So what did God tell you?" Lizzie J. asked and smiled, tears gathering in her eyes.

"I sold my apartment in New York. I'm living in Jonesboro," Maggie said, a sly smile on her face. Lizzie J. didn't respond right away, trying to comprehend her words.

"I'm confused."

"I rented a house and moved from New York last week. I live in Jonesboro. I promise, it's true!"

"You've been here for a week?"

"I wanted to surprise everyone, but especially Mom since today was Mother's Day. I showed up at church this morning with a corsage and surprised her. Then I took her to lunch and showed her my new home. She cried."

"I'm stunned. What about your career?"

"I'll finish out the year and the schedule that is already in place, and then we'll see what God has for me. I honestly don't know what He wants me to do, but I have faith that He will show me."

"You've come home?"

"I've come home. We can go to lunch, I can babysit, we can meet for coffee, we can talk, we can laugh...what else would you like to do?"

"I'm still speechless. Until I see your house, I'm not sure I can believe everything you're telling me," Lizzie J. said.

"Anytime, my door is always open and it only takes about fifteen minutes to get there. Can you believe it?"

"I have to ask this question. Was Jake at church?"

"Yes…and I met Caroline. I think that was her name. That was quite a shock. I asked Mom why no one told me he was dating, but she explained how that was my fault since I haven't talked to anyone since Christmas. Do you know her?" Maggie asked.

"Yes, a little. I hope you aren't mad at me, but they've been here for dinner with us," Lizzie J. said apologetically.

"Lizzie J., I could never be mad at you for that. J.D. is Jake's best friend. So what is she like? Who is she and does she live here?" Maggie was trying her best not to cry again, and Lizzie J. was aware of her struggle.

"Her husband died in Viet Nam about two years ago. She's Lillian's niece who came to visit at Christmas and decided to move here with her two children. She's a nice person. She works for a law firm in Jonesboro. Not with J.D.'s firm though," Lizzie J. added.

"She sounds like what Jake has been wanting since we graduated from high school. Does he love her?" Maggie had to ask.

"He's told me he likes her, but he's never mentioned love. When they're together they seem more like friends. She knows about you, and I think she is reluctant to have any other kind of relationship with Jake. And it's only been two years since her husband died—she could still be grieving."

"That is so sad," Maggie said.

"Maggie, Jake went to New York to see you."

"When?"

"About a year after your dad's funeral and the big fight."

"I didn't see him. What did he do there?"

"He was in his car across the street from your apartment when you came out with a man. Jake said the two of you were arm-in-arm and laughing and talking like you knew each other well. Were you dating someone?"

Maggie was deep in thought about who had been with her ... Miguel.

"No, I wasn't dating anyone. It must have been Miguel. He's from Spain, another pianist who came here for two years on the concert tour. I went to dinner with him a few times, but when he wanted to be more than friends I stopped seeing him. I can't believe Jake saw that and thought we were dating. He could have asked me."

"He was angry. I think, after giving in and going all the way up there to make things right, he felt betrayed to find you in your apartment with another man. That was the final straw. When he came back, he wouldn't mention you and didn't want to hear about you."

"That is so unlike Jake," Maggie said.

"He's waited a long time, Maggie. He wants to get married and have a family. Trey and Maggie love him so much, and he is so good with them. He should be a dad," Lizzie J. said softly. She was torn between her best friend and Jake. Through the years she had watched Jake, alone, waiting.... As much as she loved Maggie, she could also see that Maggie had taken for granted Jake would always be waiting.

"I told my mom this, but I want you to promise you won't tell anyone, not even J.D. Promise?"

"Sure, I won't mention it if you don't want me to. What?"

"I was naïve enough to think Jake would be glad to see me. Lizzie J., I'd planned to ask Jake to marry me. Isn't that crazy? What was I thinking? We aren't in high school; this is real life. I'm embarrassed."

"So you still love him."

"I do. I've always loved him, but I was selfish. I thought it would be so great to be a success, and quite honestly, I thought it would be great to be wealthy. It's been a lonely life. Once my eyes were opened, I knew I had to move back home. To be around the people who love me."

"Are you going to tell Jake how you feel?"

"Oh, goodness no! But I do plan to apologize to him for the way I acted. I won't interfere in his new life. I love Jake—I want him to be happy."

"What if Jake can't be happy without you?"

CHAPTER THIRTY-TWO

*J*AKE HAD KEPT his plans to have dinner with Caroline Sunday evening. He tried to be in the present and enjoy her company, but the vision of Maggie from the morning's church service kept distracting him.

"Jake, did you hear me? Do you want a piece of pie?" Caroline asked for the second time.

"Oh, sure, sounds good," Jake replied and smiled at her.

"I don't want to pry into your life, but I feel Maggie's presence today has really affected you. Do you want to talk about it?"

"Seeing her was so unexpected, and yes it has affected me, no use denying it."

"Do you still love her?" Caroline asked softly.

"You know, Caroline, I'm not sure I even know what love is at this point in my life. I thought I did. Now I'm not sure," Jake said sadly.

"I've told you a lot about Mike and how we met, and about our marriage, but you've never spoken about Maggie. I've tried not to bring the subject up, but tonight it feels like the elephant in the room."

"Sorry, I probably should have cancelled and stayed home instead of bringing you down with me."

"Oh, I'm okay, just concerned about you. Whether you think you know what love is or not, you're not over Maggie Roberts," Caroline told him.

"Well, you do know how I feel about marrying someone who's not a believer. I remember telling you about my mom and all the things she told me. So the way I see it, it doesn't much matter how I feel about Maggie—it matters whether she's right for me. And besides, she has obviously moved on with her life."

"She was at church this morning. Maybe she's changed in the last two years," Caroline suggested.

"Nah, she was only there because it was Mother's Day. She turned her back on God when Andy died and became angrier and angrier. We only had one great conversation about my faith in the whole time we dated. After that she didn't want to hear about it. I kept praying for her and so did Lizzie J., but her heart is hard toward the spiritual aspect of life."

"Maybe you were trying to save her."

"What do you mean?"

"Sometimes we need to share our faith and then get out of the way. You do know God can draw people to himself without your help. Just because she hasn't been around you or Lizzie J. in the last two years doesn't mean her heart can't change."

"That's true, but I guess I've waited so many long years, I'm skeptical that will ever happen," Jake replied.

"That's not giving God much credit," Caroline said and smiled at him.

"Well, she sure has never listened to me. She probably won't stay long anyway. She will want to get back to her big city life," Jake said sarcastically.

"Sounds like someone needs to be praying for you. I hear bitterness in your voice. That will eat you alive, Jake. You have to forgive her or you'll never be able to move on with your life."

"I know that's true, and I also know it's hard to do. I think I'll call it a night. Thank you so much for the dinner and letting me vent. Sorry you had to hear all of this."

"Not a problem. Plenty of people have listened to me in the last two years since Mike died. We all have to talk things through."

"See you in a few days. Don't work too hard this week," Jake said.

"Take care and don't you work too hard either. I know you'll be in the fields early and will stay late. It's that time of year," Caroline said. She closed the door as Jake went out to his car.

On his way home, Jake took a detour and drove past Annie's house. He was surprised to find no unfamiliar car in the driveway. It was late and he wondered why Maggie wouldn't be at her mom's. Maybe she was at Lizzie J.'s, he thought. So he turned back the way he'd come and drove past Lizzie J. and J.D.'s house, but the house was dark and only their vehicles were in their driveway.

Jake drove home slowly, deep in thought about how he actually felt about Maggie. Time had changed them both. He didn't know if he even knew her any longer. She'd lived in the North for the past eight years and they'd seen very little of each other since she had begun her career. His heart was here in Arkansas, in the very soil, the good earth, the simple life, far removed from the cosmopolitan life people lived in large cities. Was he in love with a dream? Someone who didn't exist except in his mind and his dreams? All Jake knew for sure was that she was in his mind, a lot. That Sunday night she was in his dreams again....

AFTER VISITING WITH Lizzie J. on Sunday afternoon, Maggie went back to her mom's house and had dinner. She didn't stay late, though. She was exhausted, physically from the move and emotionally from the discoveries about Jake. The day had turned out so differently than planned.

On Monday morning, Maggie spent time reading her Bible and looking for direction. Now what, she thought. But after thinking through everything that had happened the day before, she realized she was still happy to be home. She felt almost giddy realizing she could see her mom or Lizzie J. anytime she wanted.

A week had gone by since she'd moved into her house. She loved it. When house hunting in January, she'd almost given up. Her realtor had shown her newer homes, one-level brick structures with no character at all. Maggie kept trying to see something in each house that could make her feel at home, but nothing spoke to her heart. She'd always loved older two-story homes, some even built many years before WWII.

That evening, Maggie drove around town alone. A few blocks away from downtown she saw a sign advertising a property for rent. Maggie had owned her apartment in New York and had never thought about renting, but she was open to the idea. So she decided to check it out.

Maggie's heart was in her throat as she pulled up in front of a lovely old two-story, sitting high up off the street with steps leading to the sidewalk, leading to more steps inviting you to the front porch. This was it...her new home.

It was the next day before Maggie could see the inside, but during the night she'd dreamt of what it should look like. If the interior needed work, that was even better. She had the money to make her dream come true. She was pleasantly surprised. The house had been updated. The only changes she planned were painting and having the wood floors refinished.

Her realtor negotiated the rental agreement with the changes Maggie wanted to do at her own expense. The house was vacant and Maggie could start the process of changing the interior to reflect her style. She was excited!

Maggie had worked hard to make it look like home before she brought her mom to see it. This morning she walked through each room, carrying her cup of coffee and making a mental note of items she wanted to buy to go with all the other things she'd bought in Memphis.

When she first saw the inside of the house, she was amazed there was room for everything she owned, even her piano. In her apartment in the city, she'd tried not to play late in the evenings, concerned she would disturb her neighbors. Now she had the freedom to play anytime of the night or day, and as loudly as she wanted. She was home....

However, living in Jonesboro and knowing she was only a few miles away from Jake made it difficult to ban him from her thoughts. Was Jake thinking of her this morning? Had anyone in town told him she'd moved home? Could close proximity to someone ignite or rekindle a love you'd previously shared? Would it matter, or was he in love with the beauty who had looped her arm through his in such a possessive manner yesterday?

Thinking about Jake, her tears started and she couldn't stop. What if he no longer loved her? Her love for Jake had been a consideration in every drastic change she'd recently made. But, she thought, she had sought God in all her decisions too, searching diligently through the scriptures for the direction He wanted for her life. Could the rest of her life not include Jake? She couldn't fathom that.

Maggie finally decided she needed to seek out Jake and ask his forgiveness for the awful things she'd said to him after her daddy's funeral. And she felt convicted about the way she'd always manipulated Jake to have things her way throughout their relationship. She now knew that was wrong, and she wanted Jake to know that she knew it was wrong.

It was almost noon, and most days Jake dropped by Walt and Erma's grocery store for sandwiches made in the meat department. A couple of sandwiches, some potato chips, Hostess Twinkies and a couple of Cokes were always on the menu. Or Jake might go to the Root Beer Stand out on the highway for burgers and fries. Either way, Maggie felt confident she could find him.

She pulled her hair up in a pony tail, threw on some shorts and flip-flops and left the house. As she backed out of her garage and down the driveway, she caught a glimpse of her face in the mirror. Smiling, she thought how different life was here. In the city, she never went out without make-up and nice clothes. Her attire today had been reserved for vacations at the seashore, not running errands. It was another way she felt free from the shackles of the life she'd lived the past few years, always worrying about how she looked to the public. Now she no longer cared.

Maggie felt as though she'd left her house only moments

before when she came to the parking lot of the grocery store. She didn't know what kind of truck Jake drove, but there were none here, so she waited. She had on sunglasses and hoped nobody would recognize her. Since few people knew she was here, she felt confident she could avoid being seen.

People came and went. Some she knew, some she didn't. She finally decided to drive out to the highway — maybe it was a burger and fries kind of day. There were no seats inside, so customers ordered food at the window and either ate in their vehicles or sat at the picnic table. Maggie drove slowly past, looking into each truck. No Jake.

Just as she approached the grocery store parking lot again, a black truck, dusty and dirty, pulled in ahead of her. Her breath caught as she recognized him, and she suddenly felt terrified. She had to do this now or she would never have any peace.

He'd already exited his truck, and right before he rounded the corner of the store she yelled his name.

"Jake!"

Jake whirled around, completely surprised. He knew it was her voice but couldn't figure out where she'd come from. She was getting out of a beautiful new car and walking toward him. He felt trapped. But having nowhere to go, and not wanting a scene, he walked toward her.

"Maggie," was all he said. Then he looked at her and waited. But while he was waiting, his heart was about to beat out of his chest and his hands were shaking. God, why did you make her so beautiful?

"I need to talk to you. Can we go somewhere for a few minutes? I promise not to take too much time," she said.

"I can't right now. The workers in the field are waiting for their lunch. What's up?" Jake asked, trying to sound nonchalant and hide his true feelings that her mere presence had evoked in a matter of seconds.

"This isn't very private, but I need to tell you what's on my mind," Maggie said, searching his face for some sign he still cared what she thought. She saw nothing.

"Sorry, it's the best I can do right now. What's on your mind?" His words were short and curt.

"Jake, I want to ask you to forgive me for the things I said to you after Daddy's funeral. That's one thing. The other is to ask you to forgive me for all the times when we were dating that I manipulated the situation to keep from telling you the truth. That was wrong. Can you forgive me?" Maggie asked earnestly, trying hard not to cry.

Jake could see she was being honest and truly meant what she was saying. He could see a change in her. No...he felt a change in her. What was different? Maturity? No, he thought, it's deeper.

"Well, I owe you an apology too. The timing was so wrong. What terrible things I said to you when you had just lost one of the two most important people in your life."

"Forgive me?" Maggie asked again as she watched a change in his eyes, the hardness she'd first seen falling away and softness taking over in those gorgeous brown eyes she loved so much.

"Yes, Maggie, I forgive you. Will you forgive me?"

"Of course. It was a very trying time and we both said things we shouldn't have said. Thank you, I feel much better. I know you're in a hurry so I won't keep you."

"I do need to feed those hungry guys in the field. When do you leave to go back to New York?"

Maggie searched his face and realized he truly had not

heard she'd moved home. She figured Lizzie J. would have called him last night, or at least first thing this morning. All the little old ladies who passed on information in this small town must have slept in this morning, she thought, and she had to stifle a chuckle. Something else she would have to get used to again.

"So you haven't heard?"

"I guess I haven't. Heard what?" Jake asked.

"I don't live in New York City. I moved home a week ago."

Maggie could see the shock in his face. He actually took a step back, almost as if he didn't want to stand so close to her.

"Moved home as in here, this home?"

"Well, close. I rented a house in Jonesboro and moved in the week before Mother's Day. I wanted to surprise Mom and I knew unless I could show her she wouldn't believe me."

"Are you serious?"

"Yes, Jake, of course I'm serious.

"What did your mom say?"

"She cried."

"Have you seen Lizzie J. and J.D? Do they know?"

"Yeah, I surprised her yesterday afternoon and spent some time with her. It feels good to be back."

"I bet it does.... So you live in Jonesboro...crazy. Hey, I must take the food out to the field." Jake's voice sort of trailed off as he backed up a few steps.

"Okay, Jake, thanks for listening. See you around," Maggie said, opening her car door and watching him walk around the corner. Her hands shook as she started her car and pulled out of the lot and onto the street. So Jake had his guard up. Protecting himself. From her....

JAKE WASN'T SURE if he had all the lunch orders right or not. The guys would have to eat whatever he brought back. Being confronted by Maggie so unexpectedly was worse than running into her at church. At church, people were watching and Caroline was with him. In the grocery store parking lot, he had nowhere to go and nobody who could take him by the arm and pull him away.

His heart still raced out of control and he felt everyone could see his distress. They'd been apart for two years and he still wanted Maggie Roberts. What was wrong with him? He was twenty-seven and she was twenty-six, and in the ten years since he'd fallen so head-over-heels in love with her, they'd never made love. He'd been the strong one with the commitment to wait until marriage; Maggie had been willing and had at times pushed him to his limits. Jake had always heard that if you have a sexual relationship while dating and you break up, it feels as though you've gone through an actual divorce. Well, he had news for everyone — it feels that way regardless!

On the way back to the field, Jake stopped by Lizzie J.'s and made plans to visit with her and J.D. that evening. Neither one of them acknowledged why Jake wanted to come by. They both knew.

Jake worked the rest of the afternoon with eyes to the skies. Dark clouds had slowly been developing and he knew a storm was brewing. When the first drops of rain started, the workers headed to the end of the field before they got stuck in the mud. Work was over for the day.

Jake got home before dark. Standing in the shower, hoping

he wouldn't get struck by lightning as the storm raged outside, he tried to make sense of the past couple of days. Two years ago he'd missed Maggie so badly that he had bought an airline ticket, flown to New York City, rented a car and drove to her apartment, where he'd gotten the shock of his life when she emerged with another man. Then after not wanting to even hear her name mentioned for the following year, he succumbed to the spell she seemed to have over him when he called her apartment this past Christmas Eve.

Since meeting Caroline, Jake had tried to erase Maggie from not only his life but his memory. He'd failed miserably. Turning off the water and saying a quick thank you to God for keeping him safe during the lightning, he got dressed, went into the kitchen to find something to eat, and then decided his appetite had disappeared since the conversation with Maggie earlier.

Jake drove to Lizzie J. and J.D.'s house, taking the long way around. He needed time to think. Now that he wanted answers, he was a little embarrassed about demanding Maggie's name never be mentioned in his company. He suddenly realized how immature he'd been.

As he exited his truck and started up onto the front porch, Jake wondered what he was about to hear.

"Hey Jake, come in," Lizzie J. said as she opened the door wide.

"Hey, how are you?" Jake asked and gave her a hug.

"Uncle Jake, Uncle Jake, you're here!" Trey yelled and threw his arms around Jake's legs.

"Hey Trey, how's it going little man?"

"Great. Hey, can we play ball before it gets dark?"

"Trey, remember, I told you we have to talk to Uncle Jake

and you would have to watch TV or read a book. Remember, that's why Maggie went to spend the night with Nanny and Poppy," Lizzie J. reminded him.

"It's been raining and too wet anyway. If the skies are clear tomorrow, but the fields are still too wet for me to work, I'll come back after dinner and we'll play, if that's okay with your mom," Jake said.

"Yeah, sure," Trey said with disappointment clearly in his voice.

"Come have a seat, Jake. Can I get you something to drink?"

"Yeah, a glass of sweet tea sounds good. Got any?" Jake asked.

"Am I breathing?" Lizzie J. asked him with a smirk.

"Sorry, I forgot. You do drink sweet tea for breakfast, lunch and dinner. Where's J.D.?" Jake asked.

"He took Maggie to Nanny and Poppy's. She's spending the night with them. She wasn't told you were coming and you know why," Lizzie J. said and rolled her eyes.

"Hey, I can't help it if she loves her Uncle Jake!"

"Here's your favorite glass. I'm going to run upstairs and get Trey settled with something. Be right back."

The storms had rolled through the area quickly and brought with them a cool breeze. The windows were open and the door to the screened porch as well, beckoning to Jake. He took his glass of tea and walked out onto the porch, staring into the back yard. Dusk was descending and the skies had cleared, revealing the twinkling stars one by one. In the flat farmlands of northeast Arkansas, the sky loomed large and majestic over the earth. For a few minutes Jake was aware of God's presence. He loved these God moments and needed one tonight.

"Hey, there you are," Lizzie J. said when she found him.

"It's nice out here. Do you mind if we talk here?"

"Of course not. Do you want to wait on J.D.?" Lizzie J. asked as she sat down.

"It's not that I don't want him to hear what I have to say. I simply need information."

"What's going on, Jake? I can tell something is wrong. We've known each other a long time," Lizzie J. said softly and leaned toward him in her chair. She knew what was coming and she wanted to help without telling him things that Maggie should be telling.

"I saw Maggie today. She was waiting for me in the parking lot of the store and yelled to me when I started in to pick up lunches."

"I knew she was home. She came to see us yesterday afternoon."

"Did you know she's moved to Jonesboro?"

"I didn't know before yesterday. Jake, I hadn't spoken to Maggie since Christmas Eve when she called to tell me she was snowed in. I called several times over the last four months and she never answered her phone. Then I started getting cards from her in the mail, which she'd never done before. Not long ago I went to see Annie to see if she knew what was going on."

"Did she?"

"No, Annie was as surprised as you and me when she found out yesterday that Maggie had moved back."

"What's she doing? What is this all about?" Jake asked.

"Maybe you need to be asking Maggie these questions. What did she say to you today?"

"It was so strange. She was driving a new car. She had on shorts, flip-flops, no make-up and her hair was up in a pony tail. I swear she looked about eighteen. I was defensive. She makes me that way, so my side of the conversation at first was a little abrupt. She wanted me to forgive her," Jake said softly.

"For what?"

"For her part in the yelling match we had after Oliver's funeral. That I could sort of understand, but then she wanted me to forgive her for how she manipulated the truth about certain things when we were dating. It was so uncharacteristic."

"What did you say?"

"I told her of course I forgave her, and I asked her to forgive me. We'd said some ugly things. I learned you can forgive the things said to you, but it's hard to forget them."

"Is that all?"

"I was in a hurry, but I asked her when she was returning to New York and that's when she told me she'd moved to Jonesboro. I was so shocked, I stuttered something and left."

"Isn't this what you've always wanted?"

"It was, but with no contact in the last two-and-a-half years, I'm beginning to question a lot of things. Lizzie J., I feel as though she is someone I don't even know."

"So are you telling me you don't love Maggie?"

"I don't know. Is she the same Maggie? If she is, then I don't want to go through that again. I waited years for her. I don't know what she's been doing the last couple of years, but it sure didn't have anything to do with me. Maybe that guy broke her heart and she decided to come back here. I was always here waiting for her — maybe she decided I would still be here."

"Jake, she wasn't dating anyone. I asked her yesterday if she'd been dating. The guy you saw her with was a man from Spain who is also a pianist. He was nothing to her, just someone who was also on tour."

"Did you tell her I went there and saw her? Please tell me you didn't," Jake pleaded.

"I did tell her. I'm sorry, but she was upset about seeing you with Caroline yesterday at church. Now see, I promised myself I was not getting in the middle of this and now I am. Jake, you need to go see Maggie and get your answers from her!"

"It's okay, and you're right I should be talking to her. What else did you and Maggie talk about yesterday? What did you tell her about Caroline?"

"That you had told me you liked her. She asked me if you loved her and I told her I didn't know. She said she wouldn't interfere with your life. That she didn't have a right and she wasn't surprised you were dating someone."

"Well, I'm not sure you could call it dating," Jake replied.

"Do you think Caroline loves you?" Lizzie J. asked, much to Jake's surprise.

"No, not in the way you mean. Caroline is still grieving over Mike. I don't think she is even aware of it, but I see it. And yesterday she told me I wasn't over Maggie Roberts. We are a sad couple, are we not?" Jake said quietly.

"Jake, go see Maggie. Go talk to her, find out why she's back and what her plans are. I could tell you more than I'm telling, but I won't — this should be between you and Maggie," Lizzie J. encouraged.

"Do you know why I came here to ask you the questions I needed answers to?" Jake asked her.

"Maybe," Lizzie J. said with compassion.

"I'm afraid of her. I'm afraid of the power she has over me. I want to get married, start a family and fill my house with people who love me and will be there when I come home at night. I don't think Maggie Roberts can be what I need, but I still want her. That scares me," Jake explained.

"Maggie's back, Jake. She's come home. She has reasons, and you may be surprised about what those reasons are and what caused her desire to move back. But you have to ask her."

But he didn't....

CHAPTER THIRTY-THREE

THE HIGH CEILINGS in her house, and the old oak trees with their wide canopy of cover shielding the hot summer sun, allowed Maggie to use her ceiling fans and attic fan to keep cool on most mornings. She'd purchased two window air conditioner units that hummed on and off from about noon until bedtime. Even though Maggie had lived in Arkansas most of her life, the past eight years had spoiled her with New York's lower humidity, and she needed to adapt.

Maggie had lived in her house six weeks and it had become home, a place of peace and serenity...her refuge. She worked hard to become part of Jonesboro, distancing herself from Lake City. Her mom and Lizzie J. visited here when they wanted to see her. Maggie didn't feel she could constantly see Jake and Caroline at church together. Actually, she didn't even want to see Jake alone. It was too painful.

Checking out several churches in the small city of Jonesboro, she finally decided on Central Baptist, a large church that allowed her to be somewhat invisible. That didn't last long, though. People knew her and knew she was famous. But after several Sundays of Maggie sitting in the same pew, everyone accepted her as part of their church family. She was just...Maggie.

Jake continued seeing Caroline. Maggie knew this because every time Lizzie J. came to see her, Trey and little Maggie constantly talked about Uncle Jake, Caroline and Greg and Kristen. Lizzie J. would look over them to Maggie apologetically and try to change the subject. Maggie would shake her head at Lizzie J. that it was okay and engage them both in conversation. She didn't know they talked about her when Uncle Jake and Caroline came over to their house and brought Greg and Kristen to play. The four children were all completely unaware of the tension in the room when those conversations came up.

Annie came to see Maggie a couple of times a week. They would have lunch together and sometimes go to a movie in the afternoon. Even though Annie's life would always be in Lake City, she was still overjoyed to have Maggie here, and their mother-daughter relationship blossomed. Annie was very thankful.

The financial investments Maggie had made were good ones, and allowed her to have this time to listen for God's direction in her life. Opportunities had been presented to Maggie for four major concerts in the coming year. Once she'd announced she might not be in concert in the future, the value of her performances skyrocketed. Every time something happened in Maggie's life that she knew was a God thing, she wondered how many of these moments she'd missed in the first twenty-six years of her life.

The one thing she didn't have peace about was Jake. She loved him, and deep down she believed he loved her. However, she wouldn't interfere in whatever kind of relationship he had with Caroline. Maggie was a believer, she'd come home, she'd rented a house and was a permanent resident of the state of Arkansas and always would be. If none of this mattered to Jake, it was up to Maggie to come to terms with her loss.

Maggie was interviewed by the local TV station. The city was excited to have a celebrity among them. The newspaper also did a couple of pieces, one on the front page. In one of the articles, Maggie gave a short testimony of her salvation experience this past Christmas Eve in Manhattan. She also shared how happy she was to be home in Arkansas.

Jake ignored the articles and didn't watch the interview. The people around him, including Caroline, didn't mention anything to Jake about what Maggie had said.

Caroline was struggling, though. She was still grieving the death of her husband, Mike. They'd been high school sweethearts and enjoyed a great marriage. He'd been a wonderful husband and father and her best friend. She did like Jake but didn't feel their relationship, whatever kind it might be, was right for her and the children. But she was lonely, so she continued seeing him.

And this was the state of affairs between Jake and Maggie since Mother's Day. Nothing had changed. Sometimes Maggie felt she might as well be living in New York, and only some of the time could Jake forget she was only fifteen miles away.

JAKE ASKED CAROLINE out to dinner without the kids. He felt she could use a grown-up night, and frankly he needed one too. After a quiet dinner in the nicest restaurant in Jonesboro, they got into the car heading back to Lake City.

Jake made a suggestion. "It's a nice evening. Why don't we go to the park and take a walk?"

"Sure, sounds good. Greg and Kristen were excited to spend the night with Lizzie J. and J.D., so the evening is mine, which is an unusual treat," Caroline replied.

After arriving at the park, they walked along the path leisurely and finally sat down on a bench in a secluded area. They sat together quietly for a few minutes. Jake had always thought she was a beautiful woman and he did care about her, but he couldn't love her the way he should and knew it was time for a serious discussion about their relationship, or the lack of one.

"Can I ask you a personal question?"

"Sure, what do you want to ask me?" Caroline asked innocently.

"Do you want to get married again? Do you think you can love another man like you loved Mike?"

Caroline was quiet and reflective and didn't answer right away.

"I'm young, Jake, and my children are young and need a dad. So yes, I would like to get married again. But after the wonderful marriage I shared with Mike, it will have to be the right person and I will have to love him a lot. What about you? Maggie has been back for several weeks and you haven't pursued her. Why not?"

Jake looked away from Caroline and was quiet for several seconds.

"I'm in a sad situation. Marrying Maggie would be in direct opposition to what God would have me to do," Jake finally said.

"I don't understand. What do you mean?"

"Caroline, I've told you before. Maggie doesn't want anything to do with God. She won't even go inside a church."

"Jake, have you seen Maggie or talked to her since Mother's Day?"

"No, well yes, but briefly. She approached me in the parking lot of the grocery store on the Monday after Mother's Day. She apologized for the things she said during the fight after her dad's funeral. But the weirdest thing was her apology for the way she always tried to get her way when we were dating."

"Was that the whole conversation?"

"No, I asked her when she was returning to New York and that's when she told me she'd moved back. I was so shocked. I mumbled something about being in a hurry and rushed off."

"Did you read the newspaper articles about her or watch her interview on TV?"

"No, I didn't want to see her or read about her. Why would you think I would do that anyway?"

"Oh, I don't know, maybe because you've loved her since you were seventeen, and you might be a little curious?"

"I've been guarding my heart. I don't trust her. I've asked her to marry me more times than I can remember and her answer was always the same. Maggie is married to her music and her career. She doesn't have time for me and a family. I have to accept that, no matter how much I might want the situation to be different."

"Let's go back to my house—there's something I want to show you," Caroline said suddenly, taking his arm and pulling him up.

"What is it?" Jake asked.

"I can't explain; it's something you will need to see for yourself."

They were quiet on the drive back to Lake City. Arriving

at Caroline's, she unlocked the door and told Jake to sit down while she found what she wanted to show him.

"Here, read these. They might open up a whole new world for you," Caroline said and smiled.

Jake opened the clasp on the manila envelope, wondering what was inside.

"Why did you save these?" Jake asked as he looked at both newspaper articles about Maggie.

"Maybe because I know you a little better than you think I do. I knew you probably wouldn't read them since no one can mention her name. Women have what they call intuition. I know you've tried to hide your feelings, but sometimes they appear on your face or in your moods. Those times weren't lost on me. It was grief, maybe from a different source than my grief, but grief is still grief."

"But why should I read them?"

"Do you consider me your friend? Do you trust me?"

"Yes, but…."

"Just read," Caroline insisted.

Caroline leaned back onto the couch and was quiet as Jake began to read the article. She waited for him to reach the part she wanted him to know. And she knew when that happened.

Jake stopped reading, letting the paper fall to his lap. Caroline saw the tension go out of him and his shoulders relax. But she wasn't prepared for his tears. Answer to prayer was all Jake could think as he cried unashamedly. Caroline handed Jake some tissues but remained quiet as he tried to comprehend the news he'd just read—news he'd prayed for over the past ten years and could have known about weeks earlier.

"Do you believe this?" Jake asked.

"Why would she lie about it? From what I've been told, she was never embarrassed for people to know how she felt."

"I guess you're right. Why wouldn't she tell me?"

"Jake, how did you feel when you were in New York and she came out of her apartment with another man? Did you ask her, or did you assume the worst? The first Sunday she was home, she saw you with me. What did you think she would think?"

"But why didn't she tell me the day she waited for me at the grocery store when she apologized?"

"You told me that when she told you she'd moved home, you stuttered and walked away. That wouldn't have been an indication to me that you were still interested."

"I was so shocked. And I'm confused. I honestly thought you came here for me. Egotistical of me, I know, and I'm sorry. You'd lost Mike and I'd lost Maggie, and I figured God had a plan."

"Maybe God did have a plan for me to come here and get to know you. Jake, you know God places people in our lives for a purpose. Maybe my purpose was to keep you from marrying someone and making a huge mistake. Another woman who had not experienced true love and a Godly marriage might have talked you into a relationship that could have been disastrous, right?"

"Yes, you're right, that could have been a disaster. And I said those very words to Maggie a long time ago."

"So, are you going to go see her?"

"I don't know what to do. I had no idea. When I didn't see her at church I assumed she'd never changed. I'm so surprised she is going to church in Jonesboro. Lizzie J. never said a word," Jake said.

"Jake, she rented a house! She didn't move in with her mom—she put down roots. You didn't read the rest of the article or the other one. She's also stopped the concert tour. The article said she was only doing four concerts next year. I think her change is real, Jake, and I think she came home for you."

"I know you think I'm crazy, but I'm skeptical."

"Nope, I don't think you're crazy. It has been so long in coming you're finding it hard to be true, and that's another reason you need to go see her," Caroline encouraged.

"Some man, some day is going to be so blessed when you fall in love with him," Jake said softly and hugged her.

"I know," Caroline teased.

When Jake left Caroline's house, the first stars were making an appearance in the summer sky. It was early evening, and needing to find out where Maggie lived, he decided to stop by and see Lizzie J. and J.D.

After giving Jake the information he'd come for, Lizzie J. and J.D. stood on their porch holding hands as they watched him drive away. They sat down on the porch swing and talked about love and how it happens. Everyone has a story and everyone loves their own, at least when it turns out right!

CHAPTER THIRTY-FOUR

AKE HAD SOMEONE ELSE to talk to before going to see Maggie, so the next morning he went to see Annie. Since she'd moved to her new house after Oliver died, and Jake and Maggie had been estranged since then, he'd never been inside.

"Well, hello Jake, come in," Annie said when she opened the door, unable to hide her surprise.

"Thanks, Annie. If you have a few minutes I really need to talk to you."

"Sure, have a seat. Do you want something to drink?"

"No, thank you, I'm fine. I'm sure you're wondering why I'm here," Jake said and smiled at her.

"I'm wondering, but I'm sure it has something to do with my daughter."

"Yes, it does. I read the newspaper articles last night at Caroline's. She's been a good friend to me and she's very wise. I had no idea about Maggie's salvation experience on Christmas Eve. Did you know?"

"I didn't know until Maggie moved home. You didn't read the articles until last night? Why not?" Annie asked.

"Because I was still angry and I refused to read the articles, and I didn't watch the interview on TV either. Did you know she was moving back home?"

"Not until Mother's Day. When she showed up I was as surprised as you were. She took me to see her house and then she told me why she'd moved back."

"What did she say?"

"She realized Arkansas was her home, was tired of living in the city and wanted to be back around the people she loved."

"Is that all?" Jake asked.

"No, but it's all I can tell you. If you want to know more, you need to ask Maggie," Annie said gently.

"Caroline says Maggie came back for me. Is that true?"

"If you want to know more, Jake, you need to ask her."

"I'd like to ask your permission to ask Maggie to marry me. I know we're older and she doesn't live under your roof any longer, but I would still like to have your permission," Jake said earnestly.

"Of course, Jake. You know Oliver and I have loved you for years like the son we never had. I would love to see you and Maggie get married. Go ask her," Annie encouraged.

"What if she says no?"

"Go ask her Jake, go," Annie said and gave him a playful push toward the door.

"Thanks, Annie," Jake said and gave her a quick hug.

Jake wanted to surprise Maggie. He wasn't sure what she did with her days since she wasn't out of town on the concert tour. All the way to Jonesboro he prayed she would be there. He also prayed that everyone who was encouraging him knew Maggie's heart and her real reason for this move. Please, God, don't let her turn me down again.

It seemed only minutes had passed before Jake parked in front of the house Maggie had rented. He loved it, and it reminded him of his own house. He sat in his truck for a few minutes, calming his racing heart and trying to still his shaking hands.

Maggie's only plan for the day was to work outside. The house had a lovely backyard with many borders and flower beds. She had discovered a love for digging in the dirt. She slept in until eight, had coffee on her patio while there was still morning shade, read her daily devotional and got dressed to work outside. She always tried to do her gardening before noon or after dinner. She loved these days of no make-up, comfortable clothes and her hair pulled back with a headband or up in a ponytail. Sometimes she smiled when she realized how much she'd changed in only a few weeks. She glanced at the clock and hurried to get outside; it was already nine-thirty and the glaring summer sun would be unbearable before too long.

Her work shoes sat by the back door along with her gloves, and she would grab them both before going outside. But as she started to the back of the house, the doorbell rang. She hesitated. Maggie wasn't expecting anyone, but finally decided to see who it was. Her front door had windows on either side, which gave her an advantage. She could usually see who was there, and if it was someone she didn't know or a salesman, she would ignore them.

She tip-toed through her house and looked out. The doorbell rang again. Maggie couldn't see anyone but thought she would answer the door anyway.

"Coming," Maggie yelled.

She opened her door.

"Jake?"

"Hi Maggie," Jake said softly.

"What are you doing here? How did you know where I lived?"

"Can I come in?" Jake asked.

"I'm sorry—sure, come in," Maggie said, opening the door wide. She was so shocked. He was the last person she'd expected to see.

"You look pretty much like I must have looked when I saw you at church on Mother's Day."

"You mean complete surprise?" Maggie asked.

"Yeah, I was surprised. How are you?"

"I'm good. I was about to go out to the backyard and work in my flower beds," Maggie explained as she looked down at her clothes and bare feet.

"This feels surreal, you living in Jonesboro and working in flower beds," Jake said as he looked around. He could see her piano in the adjoining room.

"It did to me too, at first. But not now. I love living here and being close to my mom and Lizzie J. It's been fun spending time with Trey and Maggie, too," Maggie said while wondering what he was doing here and why he was being so nice.

"You're still beautiful," Jake said, surprised to hear himself say that. She still had her freckles, all visible without makeup. He had so missed her, almost as if part of him had been absent. Being so close to her was almost too much as he felt desire for her rising within him. He wanted to touch her, to kiss her and hold her.

"Thank you," she replied. Then as she searched his expression she asked, "Jake, why are you here?" They still stood right inside the door, Maggie still holding onto the doorknob.

"Can we talk?" Jake asked her, his eyes reflecting his feelings as they always had. Maggie noticed and thought about how she'd always felt he had an old soul. Her heart squeezed with love, and she prayed he wasn't coming here to tell her he was marrying Caroline.

"Sure, come on in," Maggie said and closed the door and led him into her living room. "Take a seat."

"Thanks," Jake said as he sat on the edge of her wingback and she sat down on the couch across from him.

"So what did you want to talk to me about?" Maggie asked after a few seconds of silence.

"Why did you move back home, Maggie? What changed?"

"Why do you want to know? You have someone new in your life, so why could you possibly care why I moved home?"

"Caroline is a friend, nothing more. I could possibly care because I love you," Jake said, his eyes full of emotion.

"She's just a friend?"

"Just a friend," Jake said quietly. "Honestly, in the beginning I wanted it to be more, but my heart was somewhere else and Caroline knew that. She's a very wise woman."

Maggie didn't respond. Her heart raced and she was afraid she would hyperventilate. She stared at him trying to comprehend the things he was saying.

"I see you have a Bible," Jake said and nodded toward the side table.

"Yes, I bought it almost a year ago. Everything explaining how and why I bought a Bible was in the article in the newspaper. It's no secret," Maggie said, thinking he'd known about her salvation experience since she'd first moved back and given the interview.

This time Jake didn't reply. He couldn't stop looking at the Bible on the table.

"If Caroline is only a friend, why have you waited all these weeks to tell me this?" Maggie finally asked.

"I didn't know," Jake whispered as he moved his eyes from the Bible to meet hers.

"Didn't know what, Jake?"

"I didn't know about Christmas Eve in New York. I didn't know about the months you spent all alone searching for God's direction. Not until last night. I'm so sorry," Jake said.

"You didn't read the newspaper article? Lizzie J. didn't tell you? How did you find out last night?"

"Caroline had saved them and insisted I read them. Now can you tell me why you moved back?" Jake pleaded.

"After I surrendered my life to Christ, I began to seek God's plan for my life. Without a doubt I began to know in my soul I was supposed to move home. And ask you to marry me," Maggie answered. She felt her heart literally skip a beat as she held his gaze.

Jake stood up and reached for her. She took his hand and he pulled her into his arms. For several seconds they held each other, letting go of all the past hurts, misunderstandings and fears. They'd started falling in love as teenagers, but they were adults now. Jake noticed how different she felt, her breasts against his chest, her body supple and womanly. Maggie noticed the change in him too. Muscular, his body hard from the farm work, his whiskers darker, even though he'd shaved not long ago. They were no longer boy and girl but man and woman. Their desires for each other were magnified by the separation and the joy of discovering they were finally on the same page. Jake kissed her.

Still holding her in his arms, Jake said, "I've loved you from the first day I saw you. I've prayed for you and I've waited. But

I don't want to wait any longer. So don't you have a question to ask me?"

"Jake, will you marry me? Now? I've waited for you too and I want all of you."

Jake hesitated for a moment, which caught Maggie by complete surprise. But then he replied, "If we get married, can we live on the farm?"

"Yes," replied Maggie, "we can live on the farm."

"And can we have kids?" Jake asked.

"Yes, replied Maggie. "I really, really want to have your babies! As many as you want, within reason."

"What's within reason?" Jake asked as he smiled. Then before she could think how to answer that question, he continued, "Yes, Maggie Roberts, I'll marry you," and he kissed her again with a passion he'd controlled for far too many years. Maggie kissed him back, and her fingers automatically became entwined in the curls above his shirt collar. Their kiss finally stopped, but they held each other tightly, both of them wanting confirmation that the other was real and not another dream.

"I love you, Maggie Roberts. Don't ever leave me again," Jake whispered.

"I'm never leaving you, Jake Martin. I'll love you forever," Maggie whispered back. "Now can we go see my future home?"

"Right now?"

"Sure, why not? I've only seen your house from a short distance on a side road. But it's lovely, Jake—you did a great job restoring that old place."

"I bought it for you. I'd planned to tear the house down and build a new one for you. But when you didn't move back, I decided I liked the house. It was nestled so nicely on the land. I hope you'll like the inside."

"Let me get some shoes on and then let's go. I'm so excited, and we can go by my mom's and tell her you agreed to marry me," Maggie teased.

"Yeah, like she'll believe I was the one causing the four-year delay," Jake shot back with a grin.

Maggie locked the doors, the plan for yard work a distant memory, and had to get control of her excitement to keep from skipping like a little girl down the sidewalk to Jake's truck.

They held hands on the short drive, reluctant to let go, as if the other one might disappear. When they turned off the highway onto Jake's road, Maggie's excitement was almost a fever pitch. The past few weeks had been tinged with sadness for Maggie. Now, as they stopped in the driveway of Jake's house, she realized what she'd come home for was finally becoming a reality.

"Well, what do you think? Do you think you can live here?" Jake asked her, his beautiful brown eyes almost black with emotion.

"I love it! But first we have to have a wedding."

"Come on in, I want to show you something."

Jake opened the front door, and when Maggie stepped across the threshold, she was as captivated with the inside as she was with the outside. The old house had nine-foot ceilings and large windows. Jake had refinished the original wood floors and added lots of molding and trim along with transoms over all the doors. He had built a staircase to the large attic and finished it for second floor space. The kitchen and bathrooms had all been gutted and rebuilt too. For Jake, the work had been both a labor of love and a way to take out all of his frustrations. Maggie could tell Jake had put his heart into this place and she was in love again…with this house.

Jake gave Maggie the tour and ended on the back screened porch overlooking the cotton fields that surrounded the house on three sides. The fertile fields were full of cotton stalks, their green leaves rustling in the gentle summer breeze. Maggie had never enjoyed picking cotton, but she loved the farmland and the scene before her had appeared in her dreams on many lonely nights in the city. She felt she should pinch herself to be sure she wasn't still dreaming.

But then Jake came up behind her and wrapped his arms around her. "What do you think?"

"It's beautiful, Jake. God's country, don't you think?"

"Hey, sit here for a minute. I'll be right back."

Maggie sat down in one of the comfy chairs and thought to herself this would be her morning coffee spot every day when the weather was warm enough. Jake had walked back to the doorway and was watching her. He thought his heart would burst with the love he had for her.

She turned and looked at him, and he smiled.

"Maggie, I know you asked me to marry you, but I'm a traditional guy, so I have something to ask you." He took a couple of steps, then got on one knee in front of her. "Margaret Mae Roberts will you marry me?"

Jake opened his hand and in it he held a dazzling, brilliant cut, one-carat diamond, set in a fourteen-carat white gold ring. Maggie was speechless. She simply stared at the ring and finally her eyes met Jake's.

"Where did you get this?"

"At a jewelry story."

"When?"

"Shortly before you graduated and told me you were staying in New York City," Jake replied softly.

"You kept it these last four years?"

"It was yours and it gave me hope, every time I could bear to look at it. Today is why I kept it. Do you want to wear it?"

Maggie held out her hand and Jake slipped the ring onto her finger.

CHAPTER THIRTY-FIVE

N THE FALL of 1972 the cotton crop gave an excellent yield. As far as Maggie could see, the white fluffy bolls spilling out of the hulls gave the fields surrounding their house a scene reminiscent of the snowstorm in the city last Christmas Eve. In the warm October sun, the white tent gave shade to their guests who would witness her and Jake exchange their wedding vows. She could hear the violinist playing the music she'd chosen, the strains mixing with the sounds of their guests talking as they crossed the lawn to the tent.

She could see the caterers carrying the food into the barn for the reception. She and Jake had worked hard decorating the interior. White lights had been strung around the rafters and would be the only lighting along with the glow from the candles on each table. Hurricane globes set over pillar candles were encircled with cotton wreaths picked fresh from the field. They could have paid someone for all the work, but to them it was a labor of love. The planning had been an easy time of mixing her love of classical music for the wedding and Jake's love of current music for the reception.

Just as Maggie had said to Jake so long ago, they were very

selective about the guest list. There were two people missing from that list; her daddy and Jake's mom. She wouldn't have her daddy to walk her down the aisle and Jake wouldn't have a mother-son dance at the reception. But Maggie did believe what she'd read in her Bible. We are each given a certain number of days, and her daddy had lived his and Jake's mom had lived hers. They missed them both every day.

"Maggie, stop staring out that window. You've got a wedding to go to!" Lizzie J. said. She was Maggie's matron of honor and was trying hard to keep her bride in line and on time.

"Sorry, I was just admiring the scene from here. I'm so happy we decided to get married here on the farm. What a gorgeous day," Maggie said and held her arms straight up as Lizzie J. slipped her wedding gown over her head.

"My sweet Maggie, you are so beautiful. I'm so happy for you and Jake. Now I want grandchildren! You do know that don't you?" Annie said sternly.

"Mother!" Maggie admonished, "give me time!"

"MAGGIE, WAKE UP!"

Maggie was so tired. She heard Jake calling her name and she tried to fight through the fog to answer him, but she wanted to sink further down in the bed and pull the covers over her. But then she heard it! A baby's cry. Her baby's cry! She'd been in a deep sleep and dreaming about their beautiful wedding. It had been a year ago, and October had come again with a gift…a gift of life.

Maggie opened her eyes and saw Jake standing beside the bed with their new baby daughter. He laid the baby in Maggie's arms so she could nurse her. She had a hearty appetite, but refused a bottle, so all Jake could do was assist. He went around to the other side of the bed and scooted in close beside them.

"Our little October girl, Sadie Ann Martin. It was such a sweet idea to name her after both of our mothers. My mom would be as proud as Annie if she knew she had a namesake," Jake said to Maggie. Their eyes met, and then they looked down to the life between them that their love had conceived.

And October had again brought the cotton fields to life as well. Out on the porch later that morning, as Maggie rocked Sadie Ann, she breathed in the scent of the surrounding fields as she listened to the sound of Jake's cotton picker. As she saw the dew glistening on the open bolls of cotton, it dawned on her how blessed she was that she'd finally come home. She'd experienced the success and fame of the bright lights of the city, but realized God had guided her home to Jake and their life in the country. Maggie Roberts Martin smiled as she thought about saying she would *never* pick cotton again. One should never say never, because in the end, she'd picked cotton....

Also by Linda Dunlap Hulen:
Her Final Gift